The

Stepsister

JENNY O'BRIEN

LARGE PRINT EDITION

DEDICATION

To Jo Robertson.

ALSO BY JENNY O'BRIEN

THE IRISH SERIES:
IDEAL GIRL
GIRL DESCENDING
UNHAPPY EVER AFTER GIRL

THE ENGLISH SERIES:
ENGLISHMAN IN BLACKPOOL
ENGLISHWOMAN IN PARIS
ENGLISHWOMAN IN SCOTLAND
ENGLISHWOMAN IN MANHATTAN
ENGLISHWOMAN AT CHRISTMAS

HISTORICAL:
RESCUING ROBERT DUNKIRK

FOR CHLDREN:
BOY BRAINY

ACKNOWLEDGMENTS

As a reader I used to always skip over this section, as a writer I appreciate just how important it is.

Firstly, thanks must go to the family of Paula McDaid who donated a handsome sum to *Ernie's Angels, to have her name included within this book. I hope you like my Paula, I did my best. Thanks too to Marie Banton, for arranging the raffle.

This was a very different book before book blogger and friend, Jo Robertson, agreed to critique an early copy. Jo, without your input I doubt I'd ever have managed to publish. This book is dedicated to you with my thanks.

As a nurse I know a little about pharmacology but *not a lot*. Thank you, Ana Marquis, pharmacist extraordinaire, for your help.

I know even less about law. Thanks to Matt Himsworth, Director at Himsworth Scott for your assistance.

And as for my knowledge of both telescopes and Dutch Genealogy... Thank you, Dr Ray Butler, Director of BSc in Physics with Astrophysics at NUI Galway and Yvette Hoitink, Dutch Genealogy.nl.

I've found that writers are the most amazing bunch of people around. A very special thanks to Valerie Keogh, who writes thrillers for Bookouture and Suzie Tullett, who writes Romances for Bombshell (Bloodhound).

Vanessa Marsh, I love tagging along at the very back of your swimming escapades but someone has to be last. That swim in October on Cobo was amazing - It's an honour to include you in my scribbles.

Finally, thanks as always to my family. There'll be buns for tea…

Jenny

PROLOGUE

I died yesterday, or so I've been told.

Yesterday is the day my life changed but how or why is still a mystery. There are things I know and there are things they've told me but I can't seem to trust any of it.

I know I'm a woman but I don't know my age. I know how to hold a cup in the same way I know it's rude to stick the end of a knife in my mouth. So, somewhere along the way, someone cared enough to drill manners into me. Those are the things I know, the things I can trust but as for the rest...

They tell me I'm in Holland but can I believe them? I don't remember if I'm Dutch but I also don't remember if I'm not. I can't speak Dutch. I've been trying all morning but can one lose a language overnight? I seem to have lost everything else. Who knows? Maybe I took the wrong train or something and just rolled up in the wrong city. That would make sense, except that it's not just my sense of place that's missing. It's my sense of everything. I have no name, no age and no identity. Yesterday I died and today I'm still here.

They've left me alone now while they puzzle out what to do. In the meantime I'm going to try to remember stuff. I don't know how long they'll leave me alone but I need to take this opportunity to come up with some answers to all the questions they've been throwing at me like who the hell I am?

Slipping out of bed, I recoil as bare feet meets cold tiles, but that's not going to stop me. Pulling the back of the hospital gown closed in an effort to retain some degree of dignity, I shuffle over to the bathroom and then the mirror only to stare into the face of a stranger.

It doesn't matter what I look like or that I'm suffering from the worst case of bed-head known to man. It doesn't matter that my eyes are green or that my hair is that shade of nondescript mouse that keeps colourists in business. The only thing that matters is my reflection, which holds no clues to my identity.

I'm a stranger to them. I'm a stranger to me.

My body holds a clue though - just one.

I push up my sleeve again to stare at the tattoo on my arm. The tattoo puzzles me. It's not me, or part of me or who I think I am and yet it's there, a large indelible letter V.

I have no idea what it stands for. Oh, I'm not stupid or anything or, at least, I don't think I am. I can't quote which exams I've passed or if indeed I've ever attended school but I do know V stands for victory. But what does it mean to me? Am I victorious? Am I making a statement about something? It must be important because it's the only tattoo I have. It's also the only clue.

I'm tired now. My eyelids collapse over my eyes and I remember the cocktail the nurse told me to swallow like a good girl. I want everything to go away. I want to hide under the blankets and forget. I've already forgotten...

Part One
Chapter One
Past

'Why on earth would someone leave us a house, Vee?'

'I don't know and more to the point, I don't care.'

I push the letter across the table with a frown. The frown isn't for the letter or the fact that my stepsister has deigned to visit. The frown is for the tip of my nail-bitten finger which should be long and red instead of short and stubby. But the state of my nails is the least of my worries. My eyes drift back to the pile of brown envelopes that will need some sort of action on my part - I'll get around to them but not yet.

'That's even more bizarre given your background,' her eyes shifting to glance down at the letter. 'After all, it's not as if you have any relatives or even any next-of-kin.'

'I had thought that you were—?'

'Get real. You know what I mean,' she says, fingering the small bunch of keys that accompanied the letter. 'There must be some mistake. Why did they leave it to you as well when you're a...?'

'A what? An orphan? A foundling? A charity case?'

'Don't get all smart with me, Vee. Everyone around here knows all about your history so there's no need to rub it in.'

Everyone except me, but I let that old argument rest. If I start dragging up memories I'll never be rid of her. Instead, I decide to go on the offensive if only to make her go away.

'Look, Nessie. I have no idea why anyone would leave us both a house. Well, maybe you with all your rich clients,' I say with a smile. 'But me? I've no idea why anyone would leave me anything and, quite frankly, I don't care. I have no interest in travelling to the Netherlands for what is most likely a case of mistaken identity.'

'I agree.'

'You agree?'

I pick up my mug for something to do. Ness agreeing with me is a first. But as a lawyer she obviously knows about such things.

'Phew, that makes things easy then, doesn't it?' I throw her a smile, reaching for the letter. 'We'll bang this solicitor an email about mistaken identity and that'll be the end of it.'

'You'll do no such thing. Just how stupid are you? We've been left a Canal House in the centre of Holland with no strings and you just want to give it away. Not only that,' she adds, tapping the letter. 'He has a cash offer, including all the contents.

What if there's something of value, like a haul of diamonds?'

'But it's a mistake. It has to be.'

'Mistake, my arse,' she interrupts, rolling her eyes. 'I'll just bet you haven't even thought about the children.'

'But I don't have any.'

'Not yours. Mine.'

'Ha. You don't have any either, or is there something you're not telling me?' I raise my eyebrows.

'Now you're being flippant. I have every intention of having kids one day and this is just the boost I'll need.'

'Er, you seem to have forgotten that this house has been left to the two of us and not just you.'

'But, you've just said you don't want it?'

'Look Nessie, you're the lawyer here. There is no way some stranger has left us something like a house. It's the stuff of dreams and I, for one, don't want to be arrested down the line for fraud or misappropriation of funds. I have a business to run.'

'Oh, do listen. I've given up my Zumba class at *Beau Sejour* to come here and you can't even be bothered to offer me a biscuit let alone an ear.' she says, flicking back her hair. 'Robert has left you and good riddance, if you ask me. It's not as if you were married or anything. In fact, it's a blessing he ran off with the office temp before the wedding. Now he won't be legally entitled to a penny. The sooner you drag yourself out of the doldrums the better for all of us. You need to pull yourself together and get with the programme. There's a lot of money at stake and moping around with your heart on your sleeve isn't doing anyone any favours, least of all me,' she snaps, pulling out a crumpled packet of cigarettes.

Here we go. The old head versus the heart debate – give me a break.

'There's nothing wrong with the way I live my life.'

'There's nothing right. No wonder Robert…'

'Just hold on a minute. I don't interfere with your love life and I expect the same level of curtesy in return.'

'Love life, is it? Your love life is as extinct as your sex one,' she says, pulling a smirk. 'Just when was the last time you got—'

'Just because I happen to think there's more to a relationship than what goes on below the waist.'

'Well, you should know. You need to take a good long look in the mirror, Vee. You know I love you but moping about like something furry the cat's dragged in isn't helping anyone. Just look at you,' she says, sucking in a lungful of nicotine before blowing it in my direction. 'When was the last time you washed your hair, let alone had your nails done?

Even a shower would be good,' her nose wrinkling up in disgust. 'And I'm not even going to start on the flat because pigs live in better.'

'I'll get around to it.'

'Yes, you will, and now's as good a time as any. Off you go and have a good old scrub. I'll load the dishwasher and search for something to eat.'

I don't respond. What would be the point? Scraping my chair back I shuffle into the bedroom, my grungy slippers flapping against the laminate flooring.

Stripping off my clothes in the direction of the overflowing wash basket I head into the tiny shower cubicle, one part of me, the previously fastidious part, agreeing with everything she's just said. But the other part, the larger part, couldn't give a damn. There's no one to see; no one to smell and no one to suffer the silence.

I'm holed up, twenty-four hours a day, with only four walls, interrupted by the odd window and door for company. There's the TV but, trawling through all the Netflix series Robert and I used to watch is another form of agony and as for the iPad... Every song holds a memory, a secret code hidden between the notes; our first dance, our first kiss, our first Christmas. Ten years of togetherness means there are ten years of memories to eradicate. Not so easy when even the simple act of taking a shower brings a whole new set of images along with the first jet of spray. Huddled now on the bottom of the shower tray it doesn't matter that the water raining down on my skin has turned ice-cold.

Nothing matters anymore. I allow myself the luxury of grief wallowing. It's something I'm becoming an expert in but, with the sound of the front door banging, I have all the time in the world for such self-indulgences.

I stare at the water, swirling round and round in concentric circles down the plughole and I wish that I was brave enough to join it. It wouldn't take much, just one slash from the blade even now winking at me from the shelf by the sink. With one slash I wouldn't have to worry about Robert and his russet-haired floosy or where the next bill was coming from. With one sweep it would all be washed away in a stream of red and there wouldn't be anyone to regret the loss.

I have no family, very few friends and nothing to live for. Ness might miss me but she'd soon move on and she'd have the profits from the Dutch house to console her.

I don't know what stops me except perhaps cowardice. I don't have anything to live for but, funnily enough, I also don't want to die. Dying would be the easy way out. No, I'll find a way back to some sort of equilibrium and if it kills me along the way then so be it.

She's left but not without leaving the stale smell of cigarettes behind and her lipstick-smeared mug. But she's also taken something. She's taken the letter, not that I mind. The letter is the least of my problems. I have no intention of travelling to Holland to see some barge house or other. I have no intention of doing anything except what I'm already doing, which is trying to get my life back on some kind of track. She's right about one thing. I don't mind about the house and I certainly don't mind about the money. She can have the lot and, when the cops come to hear about it, she can be the one *banged-up abroad* and good riddance.

Drifting back into the kitchen I must admit that she's done a good job at cleaning up. Of course, everything will be in the wrong place but it's a start. I reach for the kettle and my favourite mug only to slam it back down on the counter. Even the mugs have memories. I stare at the image of the *Eiffel Tower* etched into the pottery. We were on a mini-break in Paris when he dropped a diamond ring into the bottom of my expresso cup, the cup I insisted on smuggling out from under the watchful eye of the waiter.

It's funny how one thought, one memory is one too many. I root around the cupboard under the sink for a roll of bin bags. Ness, for all her bossy overbearing ways, has actually done me a huge favour as I start stripping out everything and anything with even a hint of Robert. The pile, started by that poor stolen mug, grows steadily. I layer the kitchen table with anything we'd bought together. The plates we bought in Rome. The salad bowl his mother gave us last Christmas. The steak knives we won in that raffle.

With the cupboards and drawers empty I head for the bedroom and the wardrobe; the wardrobe we chose together. But, as I'm not prepared to lug it down three flights of stairs, it's going to have to stay. Pulling the doors back I stare at the empty space where his Armani suits and Oxford shirts used to hang but he's even taken the hangers. What's left lingers in the bottom of the ironing pile and I feel the first giggle burst forth at the thought of his dress shirt. He'd bought it in Paris and, when he comes looking for it, I'll happily direct him to the *Mont Cuet* rubbish dump.

I hesitate over my wardrobe. As an artist I live in jeans and t-shirts but I do have a few nice pieces that he's either bought or persuaded me to buy. But now is not the time for the faint-hearted. I pluck the peach ball gown off the hanger and start searching for the matching shoes. I won't wear it again. I won't wear any of it again and so the pile grows.

I end up with nine bin sacks and a streamlined flat. If it's any more streamlined, I'll be eating with my fingers. I take a sip from the only mug that's left. Placing it down on the counter, with all the gentleness it deserves, I spread butter on my toast and eat it standing over the sink while I add side-plates to the short list of non-Robert essentials. It has to be a short list because, without the extra money from his lawyer's job, I'm going to struggle to live, let alone eat. My mind flicks back to the shower and my thoughts of earlier. Then I wanted to die. Now I want to make a success of life, if only to show Robert I can.

Chapter Two

I first notice him in *Dix Neuf* over the top of my *latte*. I probably wouldn't have looked up from my notebook except for the sensation of being watched. One second I'm trying to think of a way to reduce the cost of the flat and the next I'm conscious of the hairs on the back of my neck standing to attention.

Lifting my head, I scan the packed café. It's only a quick glance but I notice him straight away. He's the only one sitting alone and the only one that appears to be studiously avoiding everything as he scowls into his cup. It must be him and yet how can it? Surely there's nothing about me that could possibly be of interest to someone like him? He's large in every way possible; large but not fat. Broad shoulders, wide back, long legs and hammer-throwing hands curled into fists. I focus on his hands and the white-tipped knuckles before veering my attention back to the figures scattered across the page.

Those hands worry me. He worries me and yet I have no reason to feel threatened by some angry stranger in the busy arcade *brasserie*. This isn't London or New York. This is little *ole* Guernsey where the closest we come to crime is who stole the cabbages off *Muriel's* veg stall. But that doesn't change the fact I know he was staring. It wouldn't be so bad if he'd raised his head and thrown me a smile from those brown, green, blue eyes of his. It wouldn't be so bad if he'd started a rambling conversation about this and that. It wouldn't be so bad. I'm a twenty-nine-year-old woman and, even though it's been a while, I do still remember what it's like to be chatted up.

I settle my cup back against the saucer with an abnormally steady hand. Artists must have steady hands. They must have the ability to shut out all distractions while concentrating on their current masterpiece or, in this case, the disparity between my list of incomings and outgoings. I shouldn't be sitting in a café frittering away both time and money. I should be squirreled away in my attic with distant views over Castle Cornet while I work on thumbnail sketches for my current storyboard. But I'm not in the mood. I don't know what I'm in the mood for but work isn't it.

Flicking over the page I close my eyes briefly before picking up my pencil. With fingers flying across the paper, in no time I have a pretty decent image of the man, even down to his black leather shoes and the way his brown hair rests on the collar of his jacket.

I stare at the image just as, moments before, I'm positive he was staring at me. I still have no idea what colour his eyes are and I'm not sure if I've captured the shape of his jaw but, when I glance up to check, he's already disappeared into the crowd of Christmas shoppers thronging the pavement outside.

Grabbing my bag and, with arms only half in the sleeves of my coat, I follow in his footsteps but there's no trace. My head twists this way and that but it's useless to see through the crowds of last minute shoppers as the clock ticks its relentless countdown to Christmas. It's as if he's never been and all that remains of the episode is my sketch.

'Alright love, did your friend catch up with you earlier?'

My hand grips the homemade sliced loaf, pressing the soft white flesh between suddenly anxious hands. I know it's him just as surely as if he's followed me into the shop and tapped me on the shoulder. But who is he? What is he? And more importantly, what does he want with me?

'Yes love, earlier today or was it yesterday?' Paula shoves her glasses up her nose with print-stained fingers. 'He tried the flat but—'

'He tried the flat?'

'Yes.' She frowns. 'He knows where you live.'

It's funny how soft the bread is under my fingers, squidgy even - so much softer than brown or even wholemeal. Comfort food, slapped with half a pound of butter dripping off the side. Sounds muffle. Mrs McDaid disappears and all that's left is the bread mangling under my hands and the thought that he's following me. Not that she needs to tell me. I knew after that first time. Something tingles. Some shadow, from the long distant past, shifts like a curtain to reveal a hidden memory from my childhood. I know he's following me because I've been followed before.

A bell peals. A door is pushed. Sounds invade and I'm standing by the counter with a squashed loaf and her words still ringing in my ears.

He knows where you live.

Back at the studio it doesn't take long to transfer the drawing onto canvas and, with a few quick slashes from my brush, I create my first work of any quality since the door slammed on the last of Robert's *Louis Vuitton* cases. By necessity, I've had to leave his eyes partially concealed under hooded lids - I can only guess at the colour. By inclination I've lacerated paint, quick and dirty, onto the surface and created something dark and slightly sinister.

Stepping back and surveying my work there's nothing *slightly* about it. This man is sinister and, as my gaze roams over his features, I wonder whatever possessed me to put paint to canvas? I don't want this picture even though it's good, very good. I want nothing to do with it. I've captured his essence, his heart although I doubt if that organ resides inside his chest. I've created something and, just like the man, I don't want anything to do with either it or him. And yet…my eyes run over the lines and grooves. There's something here, some depth that I can't begin to guess at.

I turn my head to the window and the view of the castle, where it stands proud of the breakwater heralding the entrance to St Peter Port harbour. This is my muse, my soul even. When things aren't going well, when all sense has left my world, I find solace in the swirl of the sea as it edges the rock in white mist. But there's no solace to be had as I feel his eyes follow my thoughts. I stamp my feet like a five-year-old denied a treat and, in a flash, I've relegated him to a prison of white as I drape a sheet over my easel.

There. Done. Finished.

I'm suddenly restless but not for work. I must work if only to stave off the stream of brown invading my letterbox like a virus. I've been tardy of late and work has changed from a flood to a trickle. But I still have a couple of loyal writers that are willing to wait for the next illustration by Victoria Marsh.

Despite the pressure and lingering sense of worry, I take a couple of minutes to check my phone just in case Ness has texted me about her travel plans. There are two messages. I pull a grimace at the first.

Just back. I need my dress shirt for tonight. Robert x

If he hadn't left the kiss I might have relented but there's nothing I hate more than a hypocrite. He couldn't wait to dump me as soon as he realised who the new office temp was. The teenage daughter of his boss, with legs up to her armpits and hair, teeth and tits to match, was eminently preferable to scruffy old me without a relative to my name. But I don't mean to be uncharitable. It's not his fault he's a yellow-bellied wimp with the courage of a gnat and a taste for the ridiculous, like his frilly French shirt, which is the bitch of all bitches to iron and the reason it lives on the bottom of the ironing pi… My smile broadens to a grin.

Robert doesn't know one end of an ironing board from the other and I'm pretty sure ironing isn't amongst the skills of his bimbo, living as she does in the lap of luxury along Fort George. I even remember which bag I've put it in. I rip the seam and hurl the fragile silk into the tumble drier on an extra-long, extra-hot cycle before shoving the *ruined beyond redemption* shirt into a carrier bag and texting him back that it's on the doorstep.

The second message doesn't tell me anything I don't already know. It's from Ness.

Darling - picked up my tickets for Holland. I leave on the 'red eye' tomorrow, if you could give me a lift to the airport and I'll hand over Nigel at the same time. You know how he detests kennels. He'll be company for you. Hugs, Nessie xxx

I throw the phone on the table next to the tube of cerulean blue I'd chosen to rule the painting. Allowing her to take the lead in this is one thing. But to be dumped with Nigel at the same time is something else entirely. I'd already told her I didn't care about the canal house and I don't. I couldn't give a toss about something so nebulous and indistinct as a house in Holland. It's not as if it's somewhere I'd ever dream of living and that's not even taking into account there's no way someone has just upped and willed me a half-share in a property, whatever the location.

I have no recollection of the events that led to my abandonment on the steps of Victor Hugo's former Guernsey residence but, that's not surprising being as I was only hours old when they found me. I'm forever that abandoned baby, wrapped in the arms of the person that loved me the most, until she left me alone on that top step. I had no name, until social services issued me one in a flux of panic. Abandoned children might well be something that happens in other parts of the world but in Guernsey it was a novelty that sent everyone into a tailspin.

My mother is long gone. For reasons, only known to her, she abandoned me to my fate and my future without a family. Oh, I have a family of sorts, if you can ever call a stepsister, who's always viewed me a nuisance, family. Ness was only a bump when her parents happened upon a little discarded bundle, of what they thought rags, on their way home one night. It was only when they saw the rags move did they think they had either a cat or a rat on their hands.

The pealing of the doorbell pulls me out of the past and back into my studio where the shadows have lengthened, and the temperatures fallen. I peer out of the window only to dash back at the sight of Robert's car blocking the narrow lane beside the house. Days ago, even weeks, I'd have taken him back into my life and my bed. I wouldn't have asked for anything other than to have things revert back to their previous footing. But, now with my heart exploding in my chest and my pulse drumming in my head, I know it's too late. We're too late. If we'd married earlier…if we'd let the expected course of our relationship follow the predicted pattern of wedding and kids, we'd probably now be tripping over the nappy bin. But, the clock can't be turned back on our relationship. That clock has ticked on.

Now that I've had a taste of independence, I'm not going to give it up any time soon.

The ringing turns to thumping. I listen with closed eyes until a car door slams and an engine throbs to life. Part of me wishes that I'd found the courage to fling the shirt in his face, instead of cowering behind the door. But, I've always been the family doormat and, with Nigel about to descend, it looks as if that's not going to change anytime soon

'Thanks for picking me up. You know what taxis are like this time of the morning.' Ness wrenches open the door of the back seat and I'm suddenly arrested by the smell of wet dog. 'Be a good boy for Aunty Vee, poppet,' she croons, settling into the passenger seat and cramming her leather holdall between her knees.

'You're not taking much?' I say, throwing a swift glance at her bag before pulling out into Queens Road.

'Yes, well,' her smile blinding. 'It's a good opportunity to buy a new wardrobe now that we're about to come into some real money. Have you heard any more from Robert, by the way? I don't know why you let him slip through your fingers. You're never going to find someone like him again.'

'What? Someone who's going to drop me like a rock cake as soon as a sexy Danish pastry comes on the scene? No, thank you very much. I've had my fill of all the Roberts I can take.'

I'm certainly not proud of my behaviour yesterday. But I didn't expect him to react in quite the way he did, my attention now on my phone resting on the dashboard and the increasingly abusive texts that spell out, in more than one language, what an absolute bitch I am. But being ashamed of my behaviour is no reason to discuss it with my stepsister. After all, she never discusses her love life with me.

'How long are you intending on being away?' I finally manage, the lights from the airport runway glowing in the distance.

'Oh, not long, although I do have an open ticket. I thought I'd see what the men in Holland are like, for a change,' she says on a laugh before turning in her seat. 'You wouldn't mind checking on Ma for me, would you? I usually visit on Saturdays and she'll be expecting someone.'

I knew it was coming but I still find it a surprise - Ness, the dutiful daughter, who takes her responsibilities to her mother seriously. I crunch the gears. Perhaps Robert is right, my gaze flicking to my phone. Perhaps I am a bitch of the lowest order. Perhaps, instead of criticizing Ness's pity visits, where a bunch of crappy flowers is meant to make up for all of her previous failings in the daughter department, I should just be glad she visits at all.

Has she forgotten that I already visit her mother once a week? But, for all of my stepmother's mothering instincts and nursing background, she only ever had room in her heart for one child and that wasn't me.

When they found me on that doorstep the best thing for all concerned would have been if she'd persuaded him to drop me off at the nearest children's home. I wonder to this day what madness made her decide to take on a baby she had little time for and certainly little patience. It ruined her relationship with Ness's father. It ruined her and it certainly didn't do me any favours.

As children went I wasn't the worst. Being abandoned does tend to alter one's perceptions about what's important. If behaving could earn me even a glimmer of a smile from the stony-faced woman who'd decided to adopt me, on some whim or false sense of duty, then I'd have been the best-behaved child in Guernsey. But it was never enough. Whatever I said was wrong. Whatever I did, I could always have done better. But Ness, for all her precocious ways, could do no wrong in her mother's eyes. She was the golden child, fated to be adored and, in being adored, spoilt. Not that her mother could ever see it. I was made to feel like some Cinderella type except that there was never a chance of me going to the ball. There was no chance of escape until I was old enough. I moved out on the morning of my sixteenth birthday.

'She probably won't even realise I'm not there,' Ness says, unclicking her seatbelt.

That's true. However, despite the dementia, she always knows when it's me. It's there in the tilt of her head and the way she never seems to look me in the eye. She recognises me or, at least, something in me that she remembers she doesn't like. I still don't know why I bother to trek halfway across the island once a week and yet every Tuesday evening, despite the weather or any plans I might have to the contrary, I'm pressing the buzzer on the intercom of the dementia care unit.

A little nod is the only response I'm prepared to give as I follow her out of the car. I run my eyes over her retreating back, taking my time to examine the smart boots and fake-fur coat, a sharp contrast to my paint-splattered denims and scruffy leather jacket. I should hate her, the girl that had everything I craved when I was growing up; the love and affection of a mother, a history, a past and a secure future. I should hate her but, funnily enough, I can't. We're the same; her and me, the same but different. I lost my history, my past, my parents when I was abandoned but Ness…Ness lost her father when he decided that two babies were two babies too many.

If it hadn't been for Ness, wanting to pop into the shop for her favourite magazine, it's unlikely I'd have spotted him.

For once I'm not in a hurry. I have no Robert to rush home to. No meal to cook and, whilst I love my current job of painting London buses, it could never be labelled artistically inspiring, however magical the words accompanying the drawings will be. So, wasting five minutes fingering boxes of Guernsey fudge that I don't really need, isn't going to do any harm to anything except my figure. I grab two boxes and head for the till only to come to a complete stop.

He's right in front of me, head averted, eyes averted, hand brushing over the rack of newspapers standing in the doorway.

I know nothing about him; nothing apart from his face. The way he stands. The curve of his shoulders thrust back, hands loose by his side. I know he'll have a slow, deliberate walk even though I've never seen him move. I know his fingers will be long and strong, my gaze now on his hand, a hand I recognise. But, instead of being curled around a cup, he's clenching onto a boarding pass.

So, he's in transit, is he? He's going to disappear out of my life without revealing his interest. His eyes, I still can't see his eyes; the colour, the expression, the direction. But I know, as if it's heralded from a loudspeaker that just seconds before he was staring at me.

I drag my hair from my face, the strands greasy and uncombed, not that it matters. When was the last time you heard of stalkers complaining about unwashed hair? It's not as if they give a damn whether their quarry is salon ready or scruffy as hell. I'd laugh at the thought but it's far from funny and I tuck my hand in the pocket of my jacket, fumbling for my keys. Keys are my road to freedom; the keys to my car, the keys to my flat - he knows where I live…

I feel the breath squeeze past my lips, my attention interrupted by Ness, her arms full of trashy magazines.

'The queues! I thought I'd never get to the till,' she moans. 'I'll send you a text when I land. Oh, this is for you,' she adds, handing me a key. 'I got another one cut just in case you change your mind. We could spend a few days in Amsterdam. Think about it.' She gives me a swift kiss on the cheek before walking beside me to passport control.

She suddenly stumbles to a halt, staring in front of her. The one thing Ness never does is stumble, unless there's a man involved. The airport is heaving and I can't begin to imagine which man has taken her fancy. She has an eclectic taste in the male species and I rarely see her with the same man on her arm twice. He's bound to be tall, good-looking and wealthy. All her men are tall, good-looking and wealthy. In fact, I wonder why she didn't have a go at Robert; after all, they work together. The thought gets pushed aside by another. I wonder if she can possibly mean my man, not that he's mine.

My gaze follows hers and I see what she sees: him.

What does she see? A threat? An omen? A warning or just a man?

He turns and follows and now I wonder if I was wrong. Just who's following whom? My hand clenches inside my pocket, my nails digging deep into my palm. That day in the café I'd sat lingering over my coffee and my sums while Ness had rushed on to some meeting or other. What if he hadn't been following me? What if he'd been following her? I'd only assumed the man in the corner shop had been looking for me but what if he'd been looking for my stepsister? As a solicitor, with a high-profile and often controversial career in matrimonial law, she guarded her privacy above all else. The only weak link in her armoury was her continued efforts to help me. She was ex-directory and lived in an apartment with more security than Fort Knox. Had I led him to her? Had he been following me in an effort to get to her? And even now was he about to board the same plane to Gatwick and then Holland in the hope of causing her harm? It seems a very long way just to make a date.

I pull her to a stop, ignoring the heavy flush on her cheeks or the way her eyes are still staring at his back.

'Look, do you really need to go all the way to Delft? We can easily contact the solicitor and…'

But she unhooks my hand from her arm before dragging me into a brief hug. 'Let me be the lawyer here, Vee. After the couple of months I've had on that last case, I could do with sorting out something simple like a house transaction. Don't forget to visit Ma and give Nigel a hug from me. I'll be back before you know it.'

He's gone. He's boarded the plane, the same plane as Ness. I know because I watched from the viewing gallery with a coffee going cold. Is it my imagination or does he pause on the top step, his shoulders squared, his head tilted as if he wants to turn, to raise a hand in silent salute? No, my imagination is running away again. I settle my untouched mug back on the table. He wasn't following me. He's no stalker except in the imagination of a neurotic, recently-dumped woman. To stalk me, he'd have to be desperate. He doesn't look desperate. He's gone. Ness has gone. I'm still here with a phone full of abusive texts and a man to avoid—another one.

Chapter Three

She's small, bird-like, shrunken. Has she always been like that or is she fading before my eyes? I stare over the top of her threadbare scalp to the bare walls and speculate, for the thousandth time, why she'd never tried to at least make this, her home, feel homely before it was too late. The other rooms at *La Maison de Memoire*, rooms I walk past each week, are crammed with other people's mementoes from the past. Photos, cushions and books all paraded in a cacophony of colours, styles and tastes. For them, this is home. This is their sanctuary, their safe place to live out the rest of their days in comfort with their memories all round them. I can't begin to comment on what it means to her.

There is no peace to be had in this place, her place. No sense of calm tranquillity. There is a restlessness, a transience as if she never expected to stay and yet stay she must. She couldn't escape even if she wanted to. Her mind, always the sharpest of blades, has blunted to a weak parody. I should take pleasure in her inability to wound but, with the inability to wound comes the inability to rectify. She never wanted to make peace. Now, as her eyes cloud, she'll never be able to change the past; a past I can't begin to comprehend.

Today is a bad day, one of her worst. Porridge has been thrown and the tell-tale stain lingers down the front of her pale blue jumper. The strands of hair are just that. The skin shrivelled against bone, the lines fractured across her cheeks in a myriad of strokes. I drop the flowers on the bedside table, fingering the tall, proud lilies with their creamy leaves and dark centres. Such beautiful flowers; flowers I hate above all others simply because they remind me of her. Just like the flowers, there's always been a darkness where I'm concerned. She's never forgotten and, glancing down at her pale blue eyes, I know I'm still hated under the mantle of confusion that shrouds the person she once was.

'Hello, Marilyn. I have your daughter to see you today.' The auxiliary throws me a sympathy-laden smile, before darting through the door with the flowers in her hand. I wish I could follow. I'm not her daughter. I have no rights in this room and I have no need to stay apart from a deeply-rooted need to know just why she's always hated me.

I take the seat opposite, the cold plastic biting into the back of my legs a reminder that I'm not to stay long. I stare at her, at the room and I wonder, as I wonder each time I visit, why I've come. I don't want to be here and she doesn't want me. Today I'm here because of Ness but I swear a solemn promise that this will be the very last...

'It's about time.'

My head jerks at the scratch of sound, my eyes riveted to her paper-thin lips screwed into a tight ball. It's about time for what? Tea? Bed? To leave even though I've only just arrived?

'I've been busy at work,' the sentence ending abruptly for lack of a substitute word for mum.

I don't call her mother. I've never been able to get even the first syllable past my lips, despite her badgering.

'After all I've ever done for you and you humiliate me in front of the other parents?'

I can almost hear her screams. I don't care; I care deeply. She's no mother to me. I don't call her anything. I'm certainly not on first name terms with this woman so the silence lingers. She never speaks more than a couple of sentences and, over recent months, not even that. It's as if her mind has closed that final door, something I've become resigned to. After all, it's harder for her daughter. I'll visit for a few minutes before sneaking out of the door like a thief.

But, just like this has been a different week with the house and the man, now she is different, chatty even. Beneath the dull blue of her iris, a spark ignites. A claw stretches and grips, her rounded nails biting deep into my flesh.

'You're just like her.'

I stare back. I wasn't expecting her to speak, not now. Just who does she think I look like? My fingers reach up to my hair, which I've worn loose for once instead of pulling it back into a tight ponytail. If I had my way, I'd have one of those pixie cuts but Robert liked my hair long. I make a mental note to book an appointment with the hairdressers at the earliest opportunity.

'That tart of a mother of yours.' She pulls her lips back, saliva pooling in the cracked corners.

My mother, a tart? I feel my mouth open but I'm too shocked to do anything other than just let it hang. She must be confusing me with someone else. But who? There's no one. She has no friends, no acquaintances and no family apart from her daughter and me, and I certainly don't count her as family. More like a burden, a burden of responsibility when the last thing I should feel is responsible. She's brought all this on herself. She was a druggie and a drunk. No one towards the end wanted anything to do with her, least of all me. Her mind, usually the sharpest of instruments, started failing in my teens. As the eldest it was my duty to drop across the road to the petrol station with her purse clutched in my palm. Half a litre of whiskey and two pot noodles on a good day. On a bad one there wasn't enough for the noodles. And she wonders at my hatred. But a mother? Surely she wouldn't have hidden that from me? I've seen the press releases. Oh yes, finding a baby in Guernsey even made it onto the front of both the Mail and the Sun not to mention a brief spot on Channel Television. Where is she? Who is she? Who the hell abandons a baby in the midst of winter? Not any mother I'd want. But I still have a right to know.

I examine her face for any signs of recognition but the spark dulls and only the shell remains. My hand is released and she resumes her usual rhythmic occupation of pleating her fingers through her skirt, over and over and over again. She won't answer me now, I'm lucky I got what I did. No, lucky isn't a word I'd choose. I was an orphan when I walked into the room and I'm still an orphan.

I decide to stay a while but all I get for my efforts is a weak coffee and a sore bum. There's no further conversation. There's nothing except an empty woman in an empty room. I pick up my bag, determined to ask Ness next time I see her if she knows what her mother means. Marilyn had no friends that I remember and visitors to the house were few and far between. Perhaps there are photographs but, glancing round the room, I know there won't be. There's nothing here for me from this woman. I don't know what she means by her words or if indeed they're just random. But it doesn't matter. She's not really telling me anything I can do anything about. They searched long and hard for my mother at the time. The trail will be ice-cold by now.

The auxiliary is back to clear the cups, her sing-song voice rambling on about the weather.

'It looks like rain later and its late-night Christmas shopping in town too.'

'That's a shame. Tell me, does she ever get any visitors apart from my stepsister?'

'No, no one at all apart from the odd psychiatrist.' She pauses at the door, juggling the tray on her hip. 'We haven't seen your stepsister for a while. Is she away?'

'Something like that.'

I take one last look at the room. The empty shelves…the empty woman. There's nothing for me here.

Guernsey seems lonely all of a sudden. There's no Robert, no Ness and no need, or inclination to trek out to the dementia care unit. Even my phone has decided to ignore me. I check the blank screen for what seems like the hundredth time. Robert has obviously given up abusing me about his shirt and good riddance. Of Ness there's not a peep. She promised me she'd text when she arrived. Her promises are meaningless.

It's funny how much I miss the contact, welcome or otherwise. I've always been a solitary soul with no friends to speak of. Before Robert there was Ness and no one else. I'd learnt, from an early age, that people were fascinated about my orphan status.

It was something they couldn't get past. The questions in school were as numerous as they were repetitive.

No, I don't know who abandoned me. No, I've never bothered to find out and finally no, I don't give a monkey about being an unwanted cast-off - lies of course. I'd love to be able to draw a line through the past but there is no place to start on my quest. No one had come forward at the time and, outside of that, there is little else I can do. The one time I asked Ness's mum she'd clammed up and refused to discuss it further. I'd got more information from an old edition of the Guernsey Press than I had from her.

The only interaction now is with Nigel, a relationship born out of necessity and tolerance. Nigel, like his owner, is spoilt rotten and even though it's against everything I stand for, I'm looking after him as if he's a king, in case he decides to abandon me too.

I'm working. I'm eating, after a fashion and taking the pampered poodle for long walks down to Havelet Bay and up onto the cliff path towards Fermain. After three weeks I'm feeling fitter than I've felt in years and, if I still can't sleep it's more to do with Nigel lying horizontally across the bed with his nose pressed into my ear, than due to any feelings of loneliness.

Saturday arrives with a flash of rain and a dog determined to drag me out, despite the wet

Frowning and cajoling doesn't work, nothing works. Before I know it, I'm squelching up the steps towards St Martin's Point, the hazy backdrop of Herm in the distance and I remember all the reasons why I've never been tempted to get a dog.

As soon as that git of a stepsister of mine gets in touch, I'm going to post you, recorded delivery and see how you like it.

I glare down at Nigel but all I get is a brown-eyed unblinking glare in return. He's obviously never studied the subtle nuances of human behaviour or he'd have turned back for home with a waggy tail and apologetic bark instead of dragging on his lead in completely the wrong direction. It's lucky for him that my phone buzzes through a text in time to interrupt my darkening mood.

My first thought is it's not Robert and I don't know what to think about that. I'd be lying if I still didn't hope that he'd dump the bimbo and come crawling back to oust Nigel from his side of the mattress. But it's not Robert - it's Ness.

Hello Darling, sorry I haven't been in touch but I'm having a whale of a time over here. I've met the most amazing Dutchman, Manus van der Hooke. Such a hunk. I really do think this is it. Don't phone me. I'll phone you x

I stare from the phone to the dog and back, with a frown. She hasn't bothered to tell me what's happening with the house, a house I legally own half of. The fact that I don't want any part of it has nothing to do with it. I'd at least expected her to come back with an estimate from the estate agent and not some drivel about some random Dutch bloke. That was the whole point of the exercise or so I'd thought.

I bend down and run my hand across Nigel's back; Nigel, the self-professed love of her life and she hasn't even bothered to ask about him. She hasn't even bothered to ask about her mother, not that I can tell her much. And this Manus, what about him? Is he the man on the plane, the man I thought was following me? It's all a little quick, even for her.

'Come on, Nigel. Let's get you home and after, I'm going to send your owner the text from hell.' I heave him up and haul him back down the hill for a bath.

My life is unravelling. Ness is loved up, somewhere in Holland, while I'm left to look after both her dog and her mother. Oh yeah. I've been back to see Marilyn a couple of times but only after the home phoned to find out when Ness would be returning. There's some issue with fees but I'm not getting involved with that little package of problems.

No sooner than the door closes behind us than the phone rings but it's not Ness. It's her boss wanting to visit her apartment to pick up some papers.

After she's taken what she wants I show her out the door, pushing against the handle just to check that the lock has caught.

'I really can't say when she'll be back. She's dealing with a property we've inherited and...'

Mrs Duquemin's attention shifts from her phone to my scruffy ensemble of faded jeans and jacket. I blush.

'Well, Miss, er, if you could tell your stepsister that if she doesn't get in touch pretty quickly I'll have to reconsider her position in the firm.'

And just how do you expect me to do that? She's not answering any of my calls or texts.

But my lips remain closed. I no more know how to get in touch with her than I do a stranger in the street, a stranger like that man at the airport; a man I can't seem to get out of my mind. Despite her text, despite the ridiculousness of it all, I know he was following me.

I stand on the pavement and watch as she pulls open the door of her Audi before screaming out into the traffic. If I can't get in touch with Ness, pretty quickly, the world is going to collapse down on her head just like it's collapsing down on mine. I'm holding onto my flat by the skin of my teeth but, after the last lot of drawings, the orders seem to have dried up. There are bills to pay and no handsome hunk to share them with.

I'm still on the pavement. Her boss has long gone, heading towards the roundabout and up St Julian's Avenue. I have no need to stay welded to the spot. I have food to buy and a dog to walk, not to mention a book agent to harangue in the unlikely event that someone wants to commission some drawings by the extremely talented Victoria Marsh. But still I stand, statue-like, my gaze riveted on the couple walking towards me, their bodies entwined by hand and by hip. I have to move, to twist away but I can't. It's as if an invisible force-field has pinned me to the spot, an invisible force-field called regret. This is what we had and despite everything, this is what I still crave.

He never loved me. I know that now and I know it still hurts. It hurts like a bitch. I was convenient. I was easy and I was expendable when something better came along. My eyes travel from her long russet locks to her spray-on jeans before finally halting at a diamond the size of a brick. He'd proposed to me too, I remember; just the once, but never with a rock like that as an image of my tiny speck of a diamond comes to mind. The size of the stone hadn't mattered at the time. Now all that matters is the finality of his ring on someone else's finger.

She's dragged him to a halt, her electric blue eyes determined. Her chin thrust out. Crystal has won the prize. Now she's going to gloat.

'I'd like you to be the first to congratulate us. Robert and me.'

'Robert and I, my love,' he interrupts, a small frown punctuating his brow.

'Whatever! We're engaged. Look,' she adds, waving the boulder under my nose with a smirk.

'How lovely.' Is my voice strong enough or will she guess that it's not just my heart that's splintering at her feet? How is one meant to behave in such situations? It's not as if anyone's bothered to write the rulebook on social etiquette following a breakup.

'It is, isn't it,' she croons, talon-red fingers clawing at his favourite Armani. He won't like that and I see his frown deepening. There's a lot she'll need to learn about Robert and groping in the street is part of the first lesson in keeping Robert happy. 'Daddy and Mummy are looking at St James for the wedding, although I'd quite like Vegas. I have a thing about Elvis.'

Is she for real? My eyes focus on Robert and that frown. He might have snagged the biggest prize of all but I suddenly find room inside my own pouch of misery to feel sorry for her. Robert likes perfection. Something that's always puzzled me because perfect is the one thing I'm not. But, on a good day when my mood is veering on the right side of confident, I have to admit that somewhere along the line I've been lucky. My genetic makeup, whatever that may be, has blessed me with clear skin and thick wavy hair even if the predominant colour is mouse. My eyes, when I bother to look at them, are more feline than human and framed with the longest lashes. My body, the thing that has caused me the greatest angst over the years, is medium tall and medium thin. Funnily enough it's also the part of me that has improved drastically over the last few weeks. But then there's nothing like a bad break-up to suppress one's appetite. I don't want to eat and when I do, I can't afford to.

Robert can't look me in the eye and for that I'm sorry. He was always more of a friend than a lover - now he's nothing. I was abandoned on the steps of that house; I've been alone ever since. Now Ness has abandoned me too.

Something breaks inside, something irretrievable, something essential. Something I don't feel I'm going to be able to fix anytime soon.

Chapter Four

'You say your sister has been missing for over a month now, Miss?'

'Actually she's my stepsister. She's been missing since the 8th of December to be exact.'

I should have thought about it weeks ago but, with Robert and then her texts, I'd sort of let it slide. Yes, my stepsister is missing but not really. She's loved up abroad with some Dutch bloke. I'm far from her keeper. In fact, it's probably the reverse. We can often go for months without any contact so this lull in our relationship didn't resonate as anything out of the ordinary. It was the second text that had me thinking; the second text that forced me out of my feelings of inertia and prompted me to drag my footsteps up Smith Street and towards the police station.

His voice continues. 'And you decided to wait until now to report it?' he looks up from the form he's filling out and I don't have to be a mind-reader to read his thoughts.

'Yes, well. I wasn't sure until yesterday that she was actually missing.'

'Yes?'

'Yes.' I pause, trying to pick my words carefully. 'I received a text a few days after she arrived.'

He stops writing, replacing the cap on his pen before laying it across the form and staring directly at me. 'And what did this text say, exactly?'

I struggle to avoid the directness of his gaze, his unsmiling face, the stillness of his hand as he rests it next to the pen. I've been judged and, in being judged, found wanting. And somehow now, in the privacy of the small windowless office he's taken me to, it's me on trial. I should have reported her missing weeks ago. I should have done more to find her when the care home contacted me for the umpteenth time that they still hadn't heard from her. But I'd had no one to turn to, no one to advise me as to what I should do. Something I'm now going to have to live with.

I root in the bottom of my bag before handing him my phone.

His gaze flicks from the screen, to me and back, his pen again uncapped and flying across the page.

'If you scroll down she sent another one last night.'

Manus and I have decided to get married and I'd like you to be by my side. It's in two weeks so not much time. Text me your flight number and we'll meet you xxx

'And that's worrying you because? I'd think you'd be delighted to have a wedding to go to. If it was my wife she'd be out trawling through the hats in Creasey's.'

'It's not that. Of course, I'd be delighted but where's the rest of it?'

'The rest of what?' his look sharp.

'I'm looking after her mother and her dog and not even a *'how are they doing'* or *'give them a hug from me'*. She has a job, a flat, a life over here and yet she's just dropped off the face of the planet without a thought for anyone else in her life. I don't think so.'

'I still think you're worrying unnecessarily. Technically she's still in touch and therefore not missing but I'll make some tentative enquiries and see what I come up with.'

'What happens now?' I say, the silence oppressive; the only sound the scratch of his pen and the beat of my heart.

'Well, I can't really file her as missing yet. But, what I will do is check the facts you've already provided.'

'The facts?'

He places the pen back on the document, carefully lining it up with the edge of the paper before lifting his head.

'That she was actually on the flight to Gatwick and then on to Schiphol or, like you have intimated, that she has gone off somewhere with this Manus. When we've verified these facts, we'll check with all the hospitals and the local police force about any unidentified women over the last month to see if they fit the description you've provided.' The pen shifts, the cap in place and he pushes back from the table.

'And this Manus van der Hooke?'

'Ah yes,' He lifts his head. 'We'll perform some preliminary enquiries to check if he's a person of interest.' He throws me a smile. 'There is another option for you, of course.'

'And that is?'

'Travelling over to Holland to see if they meet you off the plane.'

Part Two
Chapter Five

Arriving in Holland with a fractious dog that's been penned up in a cage for the last hour isn't the best of ways to arrive in a new country. Pet passports might be a great idea but currently I wish I'd never heard of them. After clearing Customs, I have no time to take in the strange sights. I'm dragged out of the airport, my rucksack slung across my shoulder, Nigel pulling me towards the nearest tree.

If it wasn't for a kindly passer-by bribing him with a slice of chicken from his sandwich I might still be there trying to coax him back into his basket instead of climbing aboard the next train to Delft.

I don't know all that much about the country outside of a couple of school projects. In fact, I'm ashamed to admit that my knowledge of Holland can be summed up in three words. Bicycles, tulips and windmills. But arriving in the beautiful, flower-festooned Delft, I quickly have to add a whole host of adjectives to my limited knowledge like stunning, breath-taking, quaint and unexpected. Everywhere the tall, narrow buildings are dripping with flowers from an assortment of window-boxes. There are even flowers emblazoning the railings that mark the canal edges. And bicycles. So many bicycles. There are bicycles everywhere and with an assortment of riders.

Nigel mutters to himself but I ignore the grumbles. I'm captivated by the old buildings casting their shadows across the still waterways. I'd never thought to come to Holland. Now I'm annoyed at what I've been missing out on all this time.

The taxi negotiates a bridge before finally pulling up outside a tall, narrow house and any preconceived notions of what to expect are stripped back by the first sight of our inheritance.

The house is in a stream of other similar structures; all tall, narrow and bordering the canal. But our house, the middle one, holds a hint of neglect under its red brick exterior. Is it the lack of flowers in its derelict window boxes? Or the faded-to-grey paintwork edging the windows? Or is it the fact that all the other properties have the appearance of well-kept and well-loved homes and this one just seems a little tired?

My eyes flash from the taxi meter and back to the house. I can do this, I've done a lot worse. It's only a house, a house that I'm going to put on the market. I shove my fears back where they belong and concentrate on trying to count out the unfamiliar currency while the cab driver unloads my rucksack and dog basket onto the pavement next to Nigel.

The taxi has long gone and still I stand on the top step, the cold metal of the key pressing into my skin. There's nobody about and yet I feel the eyes of the world upon me in this strange land. There's nothing to be afraid of and yet there's everything... Ness still isn't answering her phone despite the odd text filtering through and the truth of it is I have no idea where she is. She didn't meet me off the plane as promised. I arrived hours ago and, following a frantic airport search and numerous announcements over the tannoy system, I finally realised that she wasn't coming.

It's been over a week now since her last text, and no one seems to be interested apart from her employer and her mother's care home. The local police, once they realised that a man was probably at the heart of her disappearance, didn't want to know. She's not the first woman to drop everything for a man and she won't be the last.

So, here I am in Holland on a wild goose chase as I try to follow in my stepsister's footsteps. I've left it as long as I dare. She's been gone six weeks. Some would say six weeks isn't long enough. After all, she's a grown woman in charge of her own destiny. Some would say six weeks is far too long.

The crunch came when she didn't show up for Marilyn's birthday, a birthday she's never missed. I attended, a bunch of flowers in one hand and a crappy card in the other, one of those anonymous ones that say nothing inside except Happy Birthday, which is all the sentiment I'm prepared to commit to.

I'd expected her to show. Oh, there wouldn't have been an apology or even a smile on her lips. There'd have been nothing except a show of affection for the woman she hadn't bothered with since she'd hopped on the plane. It was only when she failed to appear or even send an excuse that I began to worry in earnest. Whilst Ness isn't known for being the most considerate of individuals, she'd never willingly miss her mother's birthday.

There's probably nothing much I can do. After all, I have very little to go on. I know the date and time her plane was due to land at Schiphol Airport but, after that, there's no trace. The only thing I have of any substance is a name, the name of a man. The name of a man I don't want to meet for fear of it being him. And yet what have I got to fear? So what if he's having an affair with my stepsister? They're both consenting adults and, even if he has a wife and a nursery stuffed to bursting, it's still none of my business.

I twist the key in my hand before inserting it into the lock. I have no idea who this Aldert de Wees was or what he was doing leaving us a house; it seems so ridiculous. But, after I've found Ness and her paramour, I'm going to spend the rest of my impromptu holiday sifting through what clues there are before placing it on the market.

I might even go abroad for a spell when it's sold. I'll certainly have enough money to do what I want. What wouldn't I give for some man to whisk me away like that; some man who loved me despite the paint splatters and uninspiring ponytail hairstyle. I shake my head and the dream disappears. Instead of palm trees and hunks I'm faced with a plain wooden door in desperate need of a coat of paint.

How can one fall in love with a house? Houses are inert objects. They're something to store stuff in; a place to pull the drawbridge up and lock out the rest of the world. And yet, standing here with my feet on the doormat that's exactly what I do. I fall in love with this house.

As an artist I've always relished space; a light bright environment in which to breathe, think and imagine. That's what first attracted me to my top floor flat along Hauteville; that and the fact it's where I started out. It seemed like fate when I finally decided to strike out on my own that a flat came onto the market within a *stone's throw* of Victor Hugo's former Guernsey residence.

But this house…this is a work of art. There's an absence of light in the long narrow hall and in its place dim shadows and dark corners. There's too much to see at one glance, which is probably why I drop my bag by my feet and head for one of the mahogany barley-twist chairs flanking the matching hall table. My attention strays to the chequer-board flooring, its surface polished to a mirror finish. The wood panelling lining the walls is interrupted by shaded wall sconces, which at the flick of a switch cast a dull yellow glow across every surface. It's true that everything has dimmed and mellowed with age. This is an old man's house resplendent with treasures from the past but nothing can distract from the beauty inside. The outside might be unkempt, untidy even, but the inside has been cared for by a loving hand.

I feel a cold shiver race up my back and turning, realise that I've left the door open, not that I suppose it matters. The house is tucked between a couple of similar, tall, narrow houses; tall, narrow houses that border the canal. But even so I hurry towards the door and slam it shut before returning to the chair, my hands clutching at the arms. The door is shut but the fear remains and reality hits. I'm in a strange country and a strange house, a house that we've been left for some unknown reason.

Everything is different as the truth of my situation colours my thoughts. Moments before I was enthralled by the house and everything in it; the perfect house, with its seventeenth-century façade and authentic period features. But I wouldn't be here if Ness hadn't disappeared into thin air. Just where the hell is she?

The house can wait as I leap to my feet, an unexpected but welcome spurt of energy coming out of nowhere. There is one lead; a name. I'd tried Googling him before I left but it was useless. For such an unusual name Holland is full of Van der Hooke's. But a Dutch house is bound to have the one thing a Guernsey flat doesn't; a Dutch telephone directory. First though, I'm in need of caffeine.

The kitchen is a throwback from the dark ages with nothing modern except a kettle, a kettle that's seen better days. I rinse it out thoroughly before filling and I repeat the process all over again with a beautiful gossamer-thin porcelain cup. I'm more of a mug person, and a chipped one at that, my mind veering towards the mug resting upside down on my draining board back in Guernsey. As it's now the only one I own there's little point in tidying it away.

You can tell a lot about a person from their house. All I'd known about Aldert de Wees was his name, but I can add good taste and a love of the finer things to this short list. Whilst everything is old it's also more suited to an upmarket antique shop than an old man's home. I don't know the first thing about furniture, outside of an Ikea catalogue. But the house has the feel of the homes featured in the dog-eared copies of Country Life that litter the rack in my King's Mills dentist's waiting room.

There's nothing to eat in the bare cupboards and I can't be bothered to fathom out the sinister looking coffee machine that takes up most of one worktop. I should have picked up something when I'd stopped for dog food but I hadn't given it a thought.

The coffee is instant and that's all I'm interested in. It doesn't matter that it's a little gloopy around the edges. It will do until I can get to the shops. The lack of food is irrelevant. I'm not hungry. I haven't felt hunger since Robert left. Funnily enough my attitude to food is probably the biggest change in my life since we separated. St Peter Port is a gourmet's delight and we took great pleasure in sampling its menus from Italian, Chinese, Indian, English and, of course, French. But that's all gone. I now eat when I'm hungry and as I'm rarely hungry, I rarely feel the need to eat. If it wasn't for the need to keep Nigel in doggy treats I'd have given up shopping altogether.

Talking of Nigel, I hurry back to the hall and where I've left him flopped across the rug in the centre of the floor. I never thought I'd have to fly over the North Sea with a poodle boasting the worst haircut imaginable tucked under my seat but then again, I never thought I'd be visiting the Netherlands. It's not that I have anything against the place and tulips are one of my favourite flowers. It's just that it's never featured on any of our travel itineraries. In addition to Paris there was a delightful weekend in Rome for my birthday and a trip to New York one Christmas but that's as far as we'd travelled. We didn't get the chance to visit Holland. Now I wonder if he'll take the bimbo? Then I stop worrying as I bend my knees to stroke Nigel's back. If it's bad for me what must it be like for him? Ness was his world and I'm a very poor, second-best substitute.

'Come on, boy. Let's see what you think of Dutch doggy food.' I lead him into the kitchen before picking the cheapest looking plate to spoon jellied chicken lumps onto the centre. It doesn't look that hot but what do I know. After one investigative sniff worthy of a chief wine taster, he promptly wolfs down the lot before flopping beside the stone-cold radiator, his nose resting on his paws.

'How to make me feel guilty, little man,' I grumble, although I do agree with him about the temperature. It's so cold I haven't been brave enough to take off my hat and gloves not to mention my coat - Switching on the central heating moves to the top of the list of things to do after I've made a cursory effort to find this Manus person. I owe it to Ness.

The telephone is in the lounge, resting on a table beside the largest of chairs. Aldert must have been a giant amongst men. I eye the green velour seat with a frown before sweeping my gaze around the rest of the room. Everything is clean and tidy; too clean and tidy. There's no indication that anyone's used the room recently and that's a worry. I'd at least hoped for a trace of Ness in an old magazine or perhaps a discarded coat or scarf littering the sofa. But there's nothing.

It doesn't take me more than two phone calls, the most embarrassing calls I've ever had the misfortune to make, to realise just what a stupid idea it was. I finally slam the receiver back into the cradle before slamming myself into the chair. I've never felt more stupid or useless than just now and that's taking into account my patchwork history. I thought everyone in Holland was meant to be fluent in English but obviously not as I remember the snarling mix of vowels and consonants that I couldn't begin to unravel.

It wasn't even the first call that was the problem. The woman had been polite, in a hurry but polite and had swiftly switched to English in that curious unaccented speech of the well-educated. She knew of a *Meneer* Manus van der Hooke and had swiftly rattled off a lengthy telephone number. It was the second call that flummoxed me. But, being greeted by a string of Dutch from an answer phone with no glimmer of understanding was always going to be a nightmare. It's just a shame I hadn't taken the time to consult the phrase book I'd picked up at the airport; another mistake in a growing catalogue of errors.

I wonder what else I've got wrong. I wrap my arms round me, tears gathering to overflowing but I don't bother to brush them away. There's no one to see and no one to care. I thought it would be so easy to find her. After all, she's not missing, not really. She's just shacked up with some Dutch bloke. I thought all it would take would be a flying visit to Delft. But there's nothing, not a trace.

Something shifts in the corner, a grunt, a snuffle and I remember poor old Nigel still waiting patiently for me to sort out the heating while I mess about on the phone. I struggle to my feet and make my way to him. I'm no more in the mood for walking round the block, with a bad-tempered dog dragging on his lead, than I am jumping in the canal. But I'm even less in the mood for cleaning up doggy puddles or worse.

It's dark outside, dark and cold; colder than Guernsey by a good few degrees. There's no one about as I follow Nigel snuffling along the edge of the canal, his nose almost glued to the pavement.

It's pretty here, my gaze drawn to the street lights bouncing across the water. Guernsey is pretty but pretty in a different way with its raw beauty encapsulated by wild and rugged beaches coated with white sand. But here in Holland it's no less beautiful, just different. The water's gloomy, gloomy and with barely a ripple across its smooth surface. It looks murky with a thin film of green - It's certainly not water I'd like to swim in. I swim in Guernsey all the time. In truth, if it wasn't for my daily dip in the Bathing Pools I'd probably have gone out of my mind by now. But there's nothing like a dose of freezing cold water to turn one's body back to the basics of warmth and nourishment.

'Come on, Nigel.' I pull on his lead and direct him back to the house and the glimmer of light just visible through the shutters; shutters I'd secured before leaving. It's not that I'm overly security conscious but I'm alone in a foreign country with a guard dog that's pretty useless for anything other than walking, sleeping and eating.

On entering the hall I'm quickly reminded of my promise to sort out the heating as a stream of cool air follows. I bend down to pat Nigel's fur before removing his lead, again shoving central heating to the top of my list of priorities, closely followed by a bottle of wine. I'm not a great drinker; having a step-parent who's a drunk put a stop to that. But, just recently I've found myself reaching for a bottle of red with an increasing regularity. On the rare evenings I deny myself the pleasure of a glass I find I'm unable to sleep more than a couple of hours and 2 a.m. is the worst time to lie awake with only the muffled sounds of Nigel's snores to keep my fears company.

Oh, yes, I have fears just like any normal person although I'm probably far from normal. What's this 'normal' anyway? If it's sitting watching Netflix with a Chinese every evening then I'm as far from normal as normal can be. My fears are probably the most normal thing about me. I fear that I'll never find love again and that I'll spend the rest of my days alone and lonely, leading a half-life existence without either a partner or a child to break the cycle. There was no man before Robert and no man since. It's funny that men only seemed interested after Robert had decided to take me on. It was as if I wasn't a viable dating opportunity with my history and my hang-ups. Men didn't see me as a woman; somebody to take out before letting in. But when I lost Robert I lost much more than a friend and a lover, I lost faith.

This standing about shivering while I talk to Nigel isn't getting me any warmer as the stone cold of the tiles seeps through denim and skin before finally embracing bone. And poor old Nigel has four paws in which to feel the cold. I heave him up with a careful hand and place him in the centre of the chair before dragging the throw from the back and wrapping his paws in wool, getting a lick for my efforts.

I have no idea where the central heating controls might be, certainly not upstairs. The kitchen comes up a negative on all counts as I combine the search for heating controls with the search for wine. Either he's run out or he keeps his wine hidden, my eyes flickering to the only door on the whole ground floor that I haven't investigated.

I know there's a basement, not because the house demands it but, with its *stately home* façade and fancy gables, it would be a shame if there wasn't. I'm just hoping that it's common sense and not wishful thinking that leads me to think the only place for a control panel in a house like this is in a cellar and, with a bit of luck, it's also full to the rafters with cases of lovely wine.

The door creaks when I pull it back on its hinges, which probably should have warned me. It certainly makes me pause on the top step while I search for a light switch. I finally find the smooth edges of the socket and, with a quick flick of my wrist the world changes from black to pale grey.

I stand, poised on the top step, staring down into the small, dark space with more shadows than I'm happy with. The place is obviously a defunct space and completely empty apart from some wine racks leaning against the far wall. There's also a board of switches, which look suspiciously like fuses and, hopefully, a control panel for heating. With a bit of luck, there'll be hot water too. The idea of a glass of wine and a long soak in the bath starts to beckon. But, first I have to descend the steep staircase, something I'm increasingly reluctant to do, my gaze returning to the bright light streaming in from the kitchen.

Of all the stupid women - What's there to be frightened of? I mutter, even though, with Nigel still curled up in the lounge, I can now officially add talking to myself to the ever-growing litany of mad quirks.

My hand grips the rail, the wood firm and unyielding under my fingers. I'm eager to get this over with. Surely it can't be that difficult? All I have to do is flick a couple of switches before heading back upstairs to wine, bath and bed…

I should have looked down before launching myself but, oh no, I'm too engrossed in images of wine and water to bother about something as essential as where my foot is actually going. Where there should have been a step there's a ruddy great hole and I find I'm scrabbling in mid-air for a foothold that doesn't exist. Arms stretch, muscles extend to breaking and finally I lose grip on wood, on space, on time, on reality as I let go and drop to the floor of the cellar below.

It's the sound of whining that wakes me, although I haven't been asleep. The world might be trying its damnedest to get me but lying in the middle of the floor for a quick snooze has never been my style. Give me a feather bed and cosy quilt over rock-hard concrete any day.

Is that my voice calling out to Nigel to stay put? Surely not? But, if it's not mine then I really am in trouble, if lying injured in the middle of the basement with no obvious means of exit isn't trouble enough.

Oh, yes, I'm injured. There's pain, lots of pain – everywhere. There's blood too, black and sticky between my fingers as if it's been a while since the fall. But time makes no sense down here. It could still be today, or tomorrow for all I know. I remember the watch that Robert gave me, the watch that I'd sold to fund the flight. I'd have sold my engagement ring too if I hadn't flung it back at him in a fit of pique. But I don't mourn either; time and diamonds can't help me now. The only thing that can help is my mobile; my mobile that I've left in the bottom of my handbag. The one thing I thought I wouldn't need on my trip to the cellar was my handbag – big mistake.

I need to move when moving is the last thing I want to do. Everywhere hurts. Although, apart from my head, I don't think anything is damaged beyond repair.

Nigel's grunts have turned into barks, loud enough to wake the dead. But I know I'm not dead because I can hear the sound screaming through my brain like a siren. The migraine of all migraines descends and thoughts of death are a welcome alternative. I'm not prone to headaches, of any sort, so when they do hit they're a big surprise and one I have no coping strategies for, apart from a darkened room and silence. Down here all I have is a light I can't switch off and a blasted barking dog.

I still haven't done anything about moving and I must if only to prove to Nigel that I'm actually alive. The very last thing I need is for him to jump down and join me. I roll from my back to my front, feeling muscles, tissue and skin for any sign of injury. But, apart from sprains and strains, everything is working pretty much as usual. The world is dizzy when I draw my knees up in preparation to go from lying to sitting so, instead of moving, I just stay as I am while I try to puzzle my way out of the fix I'm in.

No one knows I'm here apart from Aldert's solicitor and the likelihood of him checking up on me on a Friday night is less than zilch. There's an open door that I can see no way of reaching unless I'm an Olympic pole-vaulter and oh yeah, I don't have a pole. If I was a chippy and had some tools I could, of course, try to rebuild the staircase because there is lots of wood and the remnants of the hand rail. But, I've never been any good at home improvements. Changing a light bulb and threading wire through a plug is the sum total of my skills in the DIY department.

So, I'm left with shifting my sorry ass and seeing if there's anything in any of the dark corners that will help in what's turning out to be a disaster of an evening. In fact, just like my life, one ruddy great disaster. Ness's parents should have left me where they found me. It would have been best for everyone.

There's nothing. Well, that's not quite true. There's wine and lots of it. I'm no expert on wine. I'm not really drinking it for any other reason than to help me to get to sleep. Do they even make wine in Holland? I have no idea and, at this juncture, I don't really care. But, if I end up dying down here, at least it won't be due to dehydration.

The floor is hard but I'm past caring. Nigel has disappeared again. I have no idea what he's up to but the muffled barks continue so he's obviously found something to interest him. I regret Nigel. I regret dragging him all this way. I only hope that someone finds him before it's too late; I've already resigned myself to my fate as I continue banging on the copper pipes that scale the wall, reverberating the sound up towards the ceiling. My only hope, my only idea is that the house next door is occupied and that someone gets annoyed enough to come and investigate.

A phone rings; once, twice, three times. It continues ringing, on and on, but there's no one to pick up. Maybe the person on the other end will get fed up and decide to visit in person. Maybe not…

I know it's late, or should that be early? Time steals through me like a thief and suddenly the effort is too much and my shoe falls through my fingers. I see the wine. But, now it's too much of an effort as my head splits open and I allow the pain back in.

Chapter Six

Mijn God!

I hear the words; words that don't need translating. But it's too much of an effort to respond. Just as I've lost all sense of time, I've also lost all sense of feeling, apart from the pneumatic drill, pile-driving a hole from the back of my head and through to the front - it's succeeding.

'You're hurt. What happened?'

I open my mouth to speak only to close it again. Something's wrong, something I can't put my finger on and my mind is too woolly to puzzle it out. There are questions or there should be questions, if I can be bothered to form some words worthy of that esteemed punctuation mark. Questions like, who is he and how did he get in? The one thing I do remember is locking the front door. I should be relieved that the ordeal is over. But is it? Is it over or has it only just begun?

I run the tip of my tongue over parched lips, feeling the cracks and tasting blood. I'm obviously covered in the stuff, which probably isn't a bad thing. What man is going to either hit on or actually hit an injured woman? Hopefully not the one now standing in front of me. I crank open an eye and find I'm staring at his legs. They're clothed in denim, like half of the world's population. I notice his hands, his fingers curled around his knees, large hands but without the long, slender, artistic fingers I'm used to. I frown. These are sturdy, strong hands used to doing a hard day's work with no nonsense fingernails, cut short. This isn't a man to worry about himself or indeed take himself too seriously.

Robert's hands were a thing of beauty, hands I'd always intended to sketch before executing in pastels or perhaps oils. I'd even considered moulding them in clay when sculpting really isn't my thing. But, then again, Robert took up more room in the bathroom than I did, with his creams and lotions. This man wouldn't know what a cuticle remover was and as for going for a manicure…Robert was always fussing and picking at his nails. My attention drifts to my own grimy hands, splattered with blood and heaven-only-knows what else and I wonder suddenly what my two-timing fiancé ever saw in me.

I want to know more about this man, so unlike Robert. I want to see the face that belongs to those hands. But now I'm scared, scared and incredibly vulnerable. I'm injured. I'm alone. I'm frightened and the need to remain motionless pushes out all other thought. If I don't move perhaps he'll think I'm already dead.

But something must have given me away. Either that or he's a mind-reader. Whatever the reason, suddenly a head appears across my line of vision as he crouches down and meets my gaze. And there he is in front of me; the man from the café, the man from the airport. The man I'm most afraid of. Words slip out before I can restrain them; mad, random words that only make sense to me.

'Burnt Umber with a hint of Vandyke brown, I should have guessed.'

'You should have guessed?' The voice is whisper soft before it fades into the distance. I don't want to leave but struggling doesn't make any sense. He'll do what he wants, with or without my permission. His face wavers into a frown before dissolving under my lids and a welcome black obliterates all colour, light and sound.

'You're back. Good. Drink this.'

I've been back a while. How long a while is difficult to gauge as the watch situation has yet to be resolved. It doesn't matter how long I've been back; seconds, minutes but probably not hours. I'm not sure I'm a good enough actress to play possum for hours.

It's fascinating just how much information can be garnered with one's eyes closed. I know, for instance that I'm not in the Dutch house; my Dutch house. I can't begin to guess where I am or how I got here. But when I left the lounge there wasn't a fire burning in the grate, the flames leaping up across the back of my lids to the gentle sound of spitting wood. The room is so warm after that stone cold floor and the sofa is so soft. I know it's a sofa. I've spent many an hour in the very same position, my head at that funny no-man's-land angle and my legs just that little bit too long to fit neatly over the seats. It's not my sofa and it's not Aldert's. His was a *sit up and beg* version in matching green pushed into the window recess and not in front of the fireplace. What else? I know I'm not alone. I don't know who's with me but they're close by, no doubt with their eyes trained in my direction; a creaking chair, the crinkle of a paper, a long sigh. All sounds I'd usually dismiss but now they take on a sense of importance, entirely out of sync with their homely nature.

I try to heave a calming breath without moving a muscle. If he was going to harm me, surely he'd have done it by now? So I try to dismiss the fear. It's warm and comfortable on the sofa. I've never been more afraid of anything in my life as I am of this man.

He's moved now and, with one hand behind my head, seems intent on forcing some strange smelling liquid down my throat.

'I don't want...'

'It's all right. I'm not going to hurt you. It's only something for that headache.'

I stare up at him. I don't trust this stranger but, what can I do? I can fight. I can argue. I can refuse.

'I never said I had a headache.'

'You didn't need to,' he laughs, placing the medicine cup on the floor before hovering his hand over mine. 'May I?' He doesn't wait for an answer before lifting my hand up to my forehead. 'You're lucky it's only mild concussion. You have an egg on your head that would do a goose proud. It will be sore for a couple of days, no more.'

His words don't make sense. The last thing I remember is tripping down the stairs and landing on that harder than hard floor. How the hell did I end up here and with him of all people? Oh, I remember him. How could I ever forget? The café...the airport and here he is again in Holland. Coincidences like that just don't happen. But anger soon pushes away any other emotion and where before I was petrified now a red-heat fills every pore.

I can't be here, not with him. I'm alone and vulnerable but I still have my wits, for what they're worth. I have one chance to get away and it's now when he still thinks I'm injured and incapacitated. I lift my head.

'Hey, where are you going?'

But I ignore his words. Grabbing the corner of the settee between clenched fists I propel myself from lying to sitting, if you can call it that. The room spins, my head explodes and a wave of nausea struggles up my throat to join the party. My colour must have faded into oblivion because now, instead of the fire crackling, there's the sound of running feet and the feel of a cold metallic bowl against my fingers while a gentle hand brushes my hair off my face.

'It's all right, *liefje*. Just concentrate on your breathing. In through your nose and out through your mouth. You can't rush these things, you know,' and his hand continues to stroke my head as if I'm a little girl. 'You're safe here now. No one is going to hurt you.'

If only I could believe him, but I can't. I can't believe a word that comes out of his mouth. Oh, I don't disagree that at the moment he appears to be the epitome of helpfulness with his medical DIY and reassuring words. But how do I know that he's not the cause of my current misfortunes? I wouldn't be here if it wasn't for Ness going missing and I just know he's tied up in it somehow.

The nausea wavers but the bone-cracking explosion in my head continues and I allow him to give me the medicine. It will either kill or cure and, just at the moment, I don't give a damn.

I'm suddenly resting back on the sofa with a cool flannel against my forehead and blessed darkness as the light dims - all that's left is the glittering flames, hovering somewhere against my lids. He doesn't speak and apart from the feel of something warm and woolly against my skin and something cold and wet against my hand, senses dull and sleep finally claims me. My last thought is of Nigel and his reassuring head under my fingers. I'm glad he's brought him here, wherever here is. Nigel is far from a guard dog with his short legs and waggy tail but he's familiar in a world that has suddenly become increasingly confused.

Chapter Seven

Something is different, if there haven't been more than enough changes to contend with already. It's still dark and warm but now, instead of a woolly blanket, I'm wrapped in duvet and dog, as Nigel shifts to snort in my ear.

Just like before, I examine my surroundings without moving a muscle, just in case. Just in case he's still in the room, although my ears tell me differently. It's quiet, too quiet for guests and the only sound is my pulse as it throbs in my ears.

I'm lying stretched out on a bed, a bed topped with the softest mattress and the smoothest of sheets. This is no cheap student flat as I sink my head further into the pillow, aware of a slight pull on my scalp. But there's no pain, just the awareness that something isn't quite right. I let my muscles relax, concentrating on easing the sudden tension that threatens to overwhelm everything. I have to think this through, all of it and I have to do it before he comes back into the room.

There's no sign of the nausea and dizziness of earlier. Nevertheless, I take a few deep breaths before shifting back against the pillows. I don't know who he is. I suspect that he may be this Manus van der Hooke person. But, in truth, that's only a guess, a guess based on a couple of unsubstantiated texts from the most unreliable of sources, my stepsister. Who's to say he isn't just an innocent bystander that's stumbled into the middle of the most bizarre of situations? But if that's the case, what was he doing in my house? And with the staircase all but demolished, how the hell did he manage to get into the basement?

My head's starting to ache. Now all I can think about is when I last had a drink. There was that coffee, hours ago, which I never got to finish and all that delicious wine, which I never got to start.

I swing my legs out of bed, feeling for the floor, before pushing to standing, one hand still securely fastened onto the mattress as I wait for the room to spin. But, for the first time in what seems like ages, my luck holds and I soon find myself standing by the bed and taking an interest in my surroundings. The floor that looks so cold is warm underfoot. The whole house is warm, come to think of it; warm, cosy and cared for.

I turn my attention from the floor to the room and a smile tugs. There's beauty here; beauty and charm as colours, designs and taste amalgamate to maximum effect. Now that's a surprise. This is obviously not just any old guest room but something suitable for some well-loved relative, or girlfriend as my friendly little ear-worm decides to add her thoughts to mine. The furniture is old and solid, in some light wood I don't recognise. The floor is polished hardwood with the most amazing hand-worked rug thrown across the centre with a careful hand. The linen is puritan white, masculine even, as are the walls, with the colour echoed in the voile curtains and slated blinds.

But it's the artwork on the wall above the bed that draws and inspires. It's this and this alone that makes my heart thump a little faster.

There is only one painting. Most people would say 'only one'. But any more would be too many. If I owned a room like this I'd never want to leave. Yes, art to me is more important than food. I can live for weeks on toast and the odd apple. But, to go even a day without feeding my mind on streaks of colour is a day too long.

The painting stands out against the blank canvas and it's only now that I understand the absence of colour on both the walls and the floor. The only backdrop for such a display is white. I don't see white, all I see is colour. All I feel is emotion as a gasp drags from my lips. Just like the room there is beauty here. There's charm too. But this work of art is so much more than those two insignificant words. There's talent, a masterly talent I can only dream and marvel at. In contrast, my daubs are just that: the work of a child - here is the master.

I view myself quite knowledgeable on the subject of art; after all, it's both my job and my hobby. Art for me is more than just a nine-to-five. It's a way of life. There's nothing that gives me greater pleasure than traipsing through antique fairs and art galleries in the hope of finding that special piece to add to my very small collection. But I could never hope to own something like the picture in front of me; a picture he's stored away in some second-best bedroom, unless he's put me to bed in his room? What a thought, a shiver trailing across my shoulders and down my spine. But, if this is his bedroom then where are his belongings, his brushes, his books? My eyes glide over the bare surfaces. Where is he? No, this isn't his room and now a little part of me wonders which painting he has chosen for best? A Cezanne? A Titian? A Manet? Just who is my rescuer?

I've been putting it off but now I step up to the canvas and wander through the brushwork until I'm knee deep in paint, the silken folds of her gown brushing across my ankles. The image of the girl draws me in. I too can see and feel what the artist has: the luminous quality of her blue dress, the curl of her hair, the brightness of her gaze as she examines something in the distance.

What is she looking at that pulls at her brow and strains her lips? Certainly not a lover or, if it is, they've just had a row. I'll never know and yet I want to know. I must know as I squint at the corner to see the artist's squiggle. But it's too faint or I'm too tired to make out more than a random letter M, partially obscured by the ornate golden frame.

I stand back with a sigh, regretting the absence of my phone. But it's probably still where I'd left it in the bottom of my bag. I'll have to forgo the pleasure of ever seeing the painting again and I'm already mourning the loss. I turn my shoulder and head for the door, a part of me now left in the room. I'll never see her again: *Girl in a blue dress…*

The landing is like the rest of the house; warm, cosy and with a feeling of security that belies my fears. My attention never wavers from my goal of reaching the stairs without waking him. I'm so engrossed in this target, interspersed with thoughts of diffuse light and shade as it plays with the curve of her neck and the tilt of her chin that I forget the one thing I shouldn't. I forget the one thing that will catch me out. The scrabble of paws on polished wood and a short bark is a sharp reminder.

A floorboard creaks. Metal grates on metal and a door shifts. And he's standing leaning against the jamb, his hand carefully closing the door behind him with a gentle click. I glance from him to the door with a frown. I had thought we were alone. But now I'm not so sure. It seems as if he's standing guard, his arms folded across his dressing gown, a bland expression stamped across his features. No, not bland, my gaze shifting to Nigel, sitting patiently at my feet.

He's angry. At the sight of his anger my anxiety levels shoot through the roof and my knees start to bend. I can't do anger, I never could. Shouting, swearing, hitting; it's all there in my past for anyone to see, if they care to look hard enough. It's there in my career and the way I've never pushed myself towards the limelight that other, similar artists demand. After all, with success comes the threat of failure, of ridicule, of disappointment. It's also there in my relationships with men, or should that be relationship? I was the luckiest girl in the world when Robert cast his net in my direction. But, isn't it true that I've been waiting for him to come to his senses for the last ten years? In a funny sort of way it was a relief when he finally decided to leave; I knew it was coming, just not when.

'You do know it's only five o'clock, don't you? Or do you always rise this early?' his attention now on Nigel who's flopped by my feet. 'Even your dog knows the time, even if you don't,' his eyes skimming my wrist and the absence of any watch.

'He's not my dog. He belongs to my stepsister and the reason I'm here. She's getting married.'

He scrubs his hand across his chin, his look wary. I'm drawn to the stubble and deeply etched lines and shadows. I know I look pretty bad but he doesn't look much better. For all his dressing gown and slippers, I'll just bet he's slept less than a wink. Interesting. Has he been lying there waiting for me to steal away at the first opportunity? I lower my gaze as the idea presses. Did he rescue me or did he imprison me? Am I free to go or—? A shiver descends as the idea takes hold and I fold my arms across my chest for comfort.

'Hey, you're freezing. What you need is a hot drink.'

I throw him a look. 'As long as I make it.'

'As long as you…what?' his glance sharp. 'You think I'm going to drug you? Give me a break. I have more things to interest me than—' his eyes take a stroll from the top of my head to my feet.

He leaves the words unsaid but I know enough about rejection to fill in the gaps.

'Come on,' he goes to place his hand on my arm only to stuff it back in his pocket. 'You can make the drink and I'll even taste it, if you're that paranoid.'

And don't I have a right to be paranoid? But the words remain unsaid.

I follow him downstairs, my attention on the old family portraits that dot the walls. As an artist I'd have relished examining the paintings but not now. Now all I can think about is why I'm here. I want to leave. I want to leave now.

He must have read my thoughts. Before I know it, he's taken my arm in a firm hold and directed me to a room leading off the back of the hall. The kitchen is surprisingly modern with glossy white surfaces and functional, deep pine cabinets. There's a traditional stove at one end. I'd guess at it being an Aga but I'm in no position to ask about his taste in anything culinary. The room has its own appeal though, despite the modern, functional pieces. This is a family room made for generation upon generation of parents and children, huddled around the huge pine table as they share their day. I close my eyes and, instead of hearing the sound of the tap as he fills the kettle, all I hear is the distant echo of children's voices. Are they real? Are they an echo from the past or a premonition? Or am I going mad?

My eyes snap open and the sound disappears. I'm left standing in the room, prey to all kinds of thoughts, partly motivated by the weight of his stare. The words are out before I can stop them.

'Are you following me?'

'Excuse me?'

'I asked if you were following me.'

'Following you? Why would you think I'd be following you?' he replies but his eyes don't quite meet mine.

I frown at him. I don't like altercations of any kind. If truth be known I'm the very last person to push myself forward and I'm probably more surprised than he is that I've actually tackled him on the thing that's been uppermost in my mind for weeks. I take a couple of seconds to choose my words carefully. 'Because you were in that café in the arcade and then at the airport when I was dropping off my stepsister. Now you're here. There are coincidences and coincidences.'

I can almost feel his eyes as they wander a second time, a thin smile stamped on his lips. There is nowhere to hide from his intense unwavering gaze. It's as if he's boring through the layers of clothing and skin and invading my soul. I would have blushed but I don't. I'm ashamed more than embarrassed by his scrutiny. To be honest I don't know what to think. Finally, common-sense kicks in, causing me to question my thoughts. Just who in their right mind would want to follow me when there are millions of other women more suited for that purpose? However, the fact remains that Ness is missing, and this man is tied up somehow. I can almost smell it.

He laughs.

I can't believe that he's thrown back his head with laughter. He's either a better actor than I am, or coincidences do exist. No. I can't continue doubting myself. I know he was following me. As to whether he still is — that's another matter entirely. I pull out a chair and sink down. I'll wait to see what he comes up with before deciding whether it's the truth or a lie. I know it's a cope out. I know I'm letting him take the lead but years of being in a subservient relationship have taken their toll in more ways than one.

The laughter stops as abruptly as it started. He sits down, all thoughts of the drink he's meant to be making presumably forgotten.

'I can see why you might think that,' the palms of his hands flat on the table, inches from my own. 'I have no reason to follow you, no reason at all. But I do know who you are.' His voice pauses, he pauses and into the silence I finally speak.

'How do you know who I am? I have no idea who—?'

'Who I am? That's easily rectified. Manus van der Hooke at your service.'

It shouldn't come as such a big surprise. After all, it's what I suspected all along, my frown deepening. This is the man she texted me about. This is the man she abandoned both her life and her mother for and I can't even think up one question to ask him.

I stare at his outstretched hand but, instead of taking those fingers in my own, I push away from the table. I can't stay in his company for one more second. He's playing some sort of game here. The only problem is that I have no idea of any of the rules. All he had to say was *and, by the way, I'm in love with Ness and I'm going to be your brother.* It's not as if I'm an ogre or have any say in what my stepsister does with her life. There's something going on here that I can't fathom, certainly not with the remnants of my headache lingering. I'll decide what I'm going to do after a good night's sleep.

'What's wrong now?'

As if he doesn't know but I decide to play along and see where it gets me.

'My stepsister is missing. I was wondering if perhaps you knew where she is?'

'Me? Why would you even think that?'

He stares at me for a long moment, a look of pure astonishment stamped across his face and I stare straight back.

He's lying. For some reason I can't attempt to guess at, he's decided to brazen it out. I shake my head instead of answering. There's no point in me staying. The simple fact is my stepsister is missing. She's been missing for weeks. Now I need to do what I should have done all those weeks ago. If it hadn't been for that blasted text I'd have had no compunction. I need to go back to the police and push for some answers. He knows who I am, hasn't he just admitted it? But now I don't want to know how he knows. I'm afraid of what he'll come up with.

My headache is back and suddenly I'm cold in this, the warmest of houses. I fold my arms around me and head for the door, only one thought in mind, but obviously a different one to his.

'Hey, where are you going now? What about your drink?' he says, tilting his head towards the kettle merrily whistling out its tune on the hob.

'I really can't impose on your hospitality any further Mr van der...'

'It's doctor, actually and it's no imposition. I'm just reducing any further workload in your direction by ensuring you're fully recovered from your injuries.' He lifts the kettle off the heat with a tea-towel and fills a couple of mugs right to the top. 'Hot chocolate, just the thing to settle you back off to sleep.'

'I don't really think—'

'Well don't,' he interrupts, the smile back as he reaches into one of the drawers and removes a box, shoving it across the table in my direction. 'Paracetamol for that head. After, I'll walk you back to your house, if you insist. I promise,' his hand back in his hair. 'I have a busy day ahead of me and a couple of hours more sleep would be welcome.'

Apart from storming out without my shoes there's very little I can do other than sit down again and pick up the mug and the tablets. My head is banging a tap dance against my skull and all I want is to be back in the house with the lights off.

The scarf. It's the first thing I see when he directs me to the downstairs cloakroom. I run the pale, pink silk through my fingers and remember

83

the day I bought it in Monsoon as a last minute birthday gift to add to the voucher she'd asked for. I blink hard as I remember the last time I'd seen it tucked within the folds of her coat at the airport and, raising it to my nose I can still smell the lingering trace of her signature scent. The scarf is hers but why it's hanging behind his door is another matter entirely. I should ask him, but I can't, not yet. The one thing he mustn't know is that I'm on to him.

'Are you alright in there? Your coat is behind the door and your shoes just underneath.'

'I'm fine, thanks. Just coming.' I stuff the scarf into my pocket and pull the door open. I now have proof that my stepsister came to Holland and not only that. I also have proof that she was in his house. What I'm going to do about it is another matter.

I don't know what to think when I realise that escorting me home means walking beside me to the house next door. We are neighbours for the short time I plan to spend in Delft. Not a comforting thought, despite the rescue.

All is quiet and still, the only movement the sway of the trees in the gentle breeze and the slight ripple of the water that edges the street.

I put my hand in his, keen now to break the silence.

'Thank you for rescuing me.' I frown at the thought, my attention on a solitary cyclist as they make their way across the little, humped-back bridge traversing the canal. 'You never did say how you came to find me?'

'I didn't, did I? And 5:30 in the morning isn't the time. I'll pop round later to check up on you.'

'Oh, you needn't bother. I'm sure I'll be fine.'

'That was a nasty crack and I should check on that bump. *Tot ziens.*'

.

Chapter Eight

Bed beckons but I ignore the summons. I'm too nervous, too anxious and far too afraid to go to bed. I fold the scarf into a neat square before placing it in the top drawer of the hall table until I've worked out exactly what I'm going to do with it. I still have to check in with the police back in Guernsey. But at least now I have tangible proof that she was in Holland and in his house, if her texts aren't evidence enough.

I feed Nigel with the remains of the food and, cradling a mug of tea in my hands, drift from room to room, the heat from the mug seeping warmth into my skin. The cellar I ignore, apart from carefully securing the door. I don't want any more mishaps in that direction. I still don't know exactly what happened but I intend to find out, if only to rule out any suspicion that it wasn't an accident. I wasn't pushed, that I do know. But how could a solid staircase give way like that unless it was tampered with? And that brings a host of other thoughts to the forefront. Why would someone want to harm me, if indeed the stairs were sabotaged in the first place? What if they'd been damaged before? What if they were intended for someone else, like Aldert, for instance? No, surely not. I'm as sure as I can be that the little surprise in the cellar was for me and me alone. But none of it makes any sense. No one knew I was arriving except for *Meneer* Bakker, the solicitor, and I can't for the life of me believe that he'd have anything to gain in targeting my staircase for vandalism.

I curl up beside Nigel on his chair, keen now for some doggy comfort and warmth. The house is lovely, very different from the couple of rooms I'd been shown next door but with its own charm all the same. The furniture is old and solid. Heavy mahogany pieces with barley twist legs and deep curves and slashes where wood has met life head on and suffered the consequences. I feel sadness for this man, this Aldert de Wees. He's left us a house but he's left so much more than just bricks and mortar. He's left his life or, at least, the imprint that's been left from his three score years and ten. He hasn't left a letter. There's nothing that the solicitor could tell us except for Aldert's determination to leave the house to the Marsh sisters.

I heave a sigh, disturbing Nigel. I want to know about this man. I want to examine his papers and try to backtrack across his thought processes to find out why he'd chosen us. Did he make a mistake? Is there another pair of poor, unsuspecting Marsh sisters back in Guernsey that I don't know about? But, of course, there's not. It's not only that. I'd really like to know his wishes on the matter. What had he intended to be done with the house? He must have known that our lives were in Guernsey.

My hand stills on Nigel's back, his woolly coat soft under my fingers. The truth is I have no life in Guernsey now, no life worth living. I have no desire to ever see Robert again and as for Marilyn. There is too much ancient history between us for me to ever choose to be in her presence. Even now, from under the cloak of confusion, she still has the ability to slice deep.

I stand and stretch, my warm seat quickly invaded and conquered. But I don't mind. I'm becoming quite attached to this furry beast. He's lost Ness and it doesn't look as if he's going to get her back any time soon. I'm a poor substitute as a mother figure but I'm doing my best.

Nigel is soon out for the count and, while he sleeps, I start on my plan. It's not much. I'll phone Guernsey at nine, their time, and try to pin down that inspector. I need to shift the search from Guernsey to Holland and I'm going to need all the help I can get. In the meantime, I'm going to search the house.

I mount the stairs, my fingers clenching the bannisters. Will I ever be able to race up and down stairs without a thought for where my next step is going to land? At the moment the answer to that is *no*. I drag a sigh from my lungs, like a smoker on sixty a day. Yesterday left a mark far greater than the bruises and bumps hidden under my jumper.

The second floor is more functional than the lower rooms; three bedrooms with the same style of furniture and an antiquated bathroom that's seen better days. The first bedroom is dominated by a huge bed and more examples of Dutch furniture at its best. This was his room. I can see it in the silver-backed brushes resting on top of the chest of drawers and the absence of anything approaching a duvet, my eyes widening at the sight of the heavy brown blankets and old-style satin coverlet. The second bedroom is clearly only fit for boxes so it's the third room that I take more notice of. Instead of facing the long, narrow garden at the back, it faces front with views over the canal and that's the final decider.

This room reminds me of home. Oh, it's nothing like home, not really. There's no castle for a start and there's only motionless canal water instead of the ever-shifting mercurial seas that line the Guernsey coastline. But still, the distant cord of sight, sound and smell of home wraps me in its silken thread and for a second I can almost feel the sea air biting against my skin and whipping the breath from my lungs.

I shake my head and the image is gone. All that's left is a bare bed and bare walls, with no painting to welcome. I stare at the space above the headboard, a frown appearing. The walls are discoloured, the faded-to-yellow paint marked with echoes from the past. There were paintings here, lots of paintings. I want to know just what and where they are, my attention shifting to the floor. But there's nothing propped against the walls. There's nothing, just a lonely empty room in a lonely empty house.

There's one final flight of stairs left to investigate. There's bound to be an attic, hopefully with lots of boxes to rummage through. But just like everything else that's happened in the last twenty-four hours nothing is what it seems. I stare at the firmly shut door with a frown. Just who'd lock their attic, unless they're trying to hide something?

I put my shoulder against the wood, the handle twisted as far as it will go but nothing. It's stuck or locked and I have no idea which. I head back downstairs to check that the front door is locked. I'm alone in the house but there's something that compels me to ensure I'm locked in.

Afterwards I continue my search in the most obvious place, the study. The room isn't large and, with one small window covered in thick woollen drapes, it's both dark and drab. The wall-to-wall bookcases dominate everything and leave little room for the desk, which is where I head to first. I lay my hands on top of the scarred wood as I try to imagine Aldert. But there's no lingering reminder of the hours he spent sitting in the exact same position. If he had secrets, he's keeping them to himself.

The drawers contain the usual detritus of old fountain pens, worn out biros and new notepads. There is a bunch of keys, which I lay to one side before turning to the laptop and pressing the switch. But it's not going to be as easy as all that - I'm faced with a password and no clue as to where to start. I close the lid and push it to one side, my gaze travelling to the bookshelves. There must be a thousand books here, each with their own story and probably most of them in a foreign language. But it's a job I have to do...

I'm on my third cup of tea by the time the job's finished. There's no safe. There are no letters. Apart from a few photographs there are no secrets and no clues. But there are books...books which could quite happily live side-by-side my own small collection as they're mainly about art. I've even heaped a tidy pile beside the bunch of keys because they're on a topic I know very little about; art restoration or, at least I think they are. I've only been able to go by the photos but I should be able to muddle through with the help of a dictionary.

The books interest me. There must be something hidden amongst their pages as to why he chose us. But I have no idea where to start. I glance at the laptop and within seconds I've unravelled the messy coil of lead, carried it into the hall and set it on top of the table before heading back upstairs, the keyring dangling from my fingers. I don't think any of them will fit, by the shape and the size. But that doesn't stop me from trekking back up to the attic; a room that intrigues me more than any other.

The door, dark and foreboding mocks me and my feeble attempts to reveal its secrets. I finally throw a kick at its base in frustration as the little kid in me wells up. Totally irrational, I know, but I do feel slightly better for it.

Suddenly the house, the attic and memories of last night invade and press. I don't want to be by myself any longer. I need company. But, with no friends over here, I'm on my own, apart from Nigel. I'm also hungry, ravenously hungry where before I couldn't even face the chocolate bar, lying squashed in the bottom of my bag. Slinging my coat across my shoulders, I throw the laptop into a carrier bag and grab Nigel's lead. A couple of hour's delay in phoning the Guernsey police isn't going to make any difference and I do need to eat. I decide to kill a few birds with one rock by combining food, a computer shop and a visit to the local police station - there's no way I'm ever phoning anyone in Holland again.

The day is one of those rare, cool crisp days with no threat of rain. I can't face having to ask a Dutch speaker where the nearest computer shop is so instead I amble up and down side-streets in a futile search. There are shops selling everything from toiletries to ski boots but nothing that resembles anything remotely to do with electronics. My stomach finally gets the better of me and I halt in front of the *Stads-koffiehuis* which, with a bit of luck, means coffee house.

The cafe is busy, but I welcome that; the chink of china, the scrape of knives, the day-to-day chatter that makes up so much of our lives as we just let time slip away. I'm better surrounded by other people, even if they're strangers. I'm a loner by choice. My career forces me to spend long periods alone with only a paint brush for company. But there is always someone to see even if it's only Paula McDaid for my daily pint of milk and quota of home bakes. If I didn't force myself to leave my work and stroll down towards town, I could quite easily go for days on end with the four walls of my flat closing in like a prison. I need people in my life, just not very many and not very often and that's why Robert was the perfect man. Towards the end we were like those solitary ships that pass in the night, something I didn't realise until it was too late to fix. But he was still a calming presence. I had no roots, only him and no past that I cared to think about.

I pick up my mug, pressing it into my hands for warmth, for comfort. When he walked out, he took more than his paltry belongings with their fancy designer tags and hint of Ralph Lauren. He was my family and my friend, plugging the hole in my life left by absent parents and my skewed relationship with Marilyn. I had too much invested in the relationship, something I only realised when it was over. All I have left is my stepsister.

It's as if she's fallen off the edge of the planet and I have no idea how to rescue her, if indeed she's in need of rescuing. At the back of my mind is the odd murmur of discontent. What if she really is loved-up somewhere with someone called Manus Van der Hooke, a different Manus to the one living next door? I know it's not likely but, unlikely events do happen. After all, look what happened to me. The chances of me being found on those steps, in the depth of winter, were unlikely at best. I don't allow myself to dwell on what would have happened if they hadn't found me.

The spicy sausage, red onion and goat's cheese pancakes arrive, soft and gooey. I pick up my fork only to place it back on the table. For someone that's starving I'm doing a pretty poor job of satisfying my hunger. Lifting my head I realise that coming into a crowded place like this was the wrong thing to do. Being alone in company is so much worse than being alone within the confines of my own four walls. The place is mainly full of couples, of lovers, of friends, and then there's me and Nigel and suddenly I don't feel welcome.

My eyes snag on the man sitting at the next table, his face obscured by a baseball cap pulled low on his forehead and I remember that other time in the café. But I couldn't begin to draw this man; all I'd get is a touch of ear and chin.

I lift my fork again and make a stab at the pancake, but my heart isn't in it. However, I do need to eat so I continue working away, forkful after forkful until I'm staring at an empty plate in surprise. Pushing it aside I reach for my bag, patting Nigel's back in the process before withdrawing the two items I'm never without; my artist's pad and my favourite brand of HB pencil. But this time I'm not going to sketch as I stare at the last drawing, the drawing of him. I don't know what came over me, the flow of lines and shade that litter the page. With a flick of my wrist I add detail to the eyes and strengthen the jaw and, with that last stroke, it's finished - complete. Perhaps I should think of a career change as I examine the likeness for weak points. But I'm not bragging when I realise it's as good a drawing as any I've seen of its type. I'll know where to look if book illustration work dries up.

I close the pad and drain my mug. It's time to go home.

The laptop. I've only gone a few steps down the road, Nigel straining on the lead to reach the nicer smells that border the canal, when I remember the laptop. But it's too late. In the short time it takes for me to drag a frustrated dog back, the table is clear and the bag gone. I snag the eye of the waiter but it's useless. Either his English isn't good enough or he's just too busy to even attempt to be helpful. I frown at his reply.

'Yes, *Mevrouw*. The laptop, I found but your husband has taken.'

My husband? I stare at the table I was sitting at and then the empty table next to mine. Had he been there when I left? Had he taken it? But the fact remains it's gone and so has the chance of finding out any more about Aldert.

Chapter Nine

Home…

I use the word lightly, juggling a carrier bag and a dog lead in one hand and a door key in the other. But in some strange way this is home. This is home when it shouldn't be. I love it and yet…and yet part of me is frightened here where I've never felt frightened before. Over the years the full gamut of emotions has passed under my breast, especially when Robert walked out. But being frightened has never come into it. My hand stops, mid-turn, my fingers brushing against the rough woodwork where paint has started flaking off because that's not exactly true. I felt frightened that day in the café and suddenly I feel it now, standing here on the step.

Am I going mad? The thought appears but, unlike most of my fears, it can't be so quickly dispelled. I've seen the descent into madness with Marilyn. The normal, rational behaviour interspersed with odd quirks that grew both in frequency and quirkiness until quirkiness was too kind, too gentle a word for the dementia that finally claimed her as its own.

I shift my head, my eyes flicking both right and left but there's nothing, no one apart from a solitary cyclist on the bridge. But when isn't there a cyclist on that bridge? This is Holland, after all. The canal is calm, barely a ripple across its smooth, green surface. There's nothing. There's nobody and yet the fear remains just like that time Marilyn failed to pick me up from hockey practice all those years ago.

I was eleven or twelve; a far from popular pre-teen and insecure as hell. The day, come to think of it, was very much like today. One of those cold, crisp January days with a hint of frost in the air that turns breath to fog. Even the light, a glowing luminescent yellow haze, was the same as I struggled with my school bags, my hockey stick clenched in my hands like a club. It wasn't far from Footes Lane to our house opposite *L'Aumone* traffic lights but it was far enough. It was far enough to feel the weight of his eyes on my neck, the echo of his footsteps on the pavement, the faint smell of cigarettes as he crept closer and closer. I was running in the end, running to escape the hand clawing at my shoulder. The man who seemed to disappear into thin air by the time I'd reached our front door. I'd never told anyone. What would have been the point? They'd have called me a liar and a fantasist or worse. But it was the last time I'd stayed for after-school hockey practice, despite the chance of playing for the island.

I shake my head and the image dispels. A twenty-year-old fear isn't going to get me anywhere and I finally work the key in the lock before closing the door behind me with a resounding bang.

Nigel is tired. I can see it in his half-mast tail and lingering look towards his chair. I still have to contact the police but, after the disastrous phone call yesterday I've been putting it off. I know I'm being a coward but what's new. I'll get round to it, maybe after I've sorted out Nigel.

'Come on, boy. Let's get you fed first,' and he trots in front of me, giving a little growl at the stairs before the attraction of food proves too much of a distraction. I follow more slowly, my gaze now lingering where his was. I'll investigate but first I want a cuppa. I haven't forgotten that he's promised to check up on me later and I'd rather be prepared as I plonk a bottle of red and white on the counter. There are nibbles too and biscuits if coffee turns out to be the drink of choice.

I'm bending to put the eggs and milk in the fridge when the door knocker thumps. He's early or I've got the time wrong. Probably the latter as I glance at the clock, ticking along towards five, a frown pulling. I'd left the café at two and decided to take my time wandering back. But surely, I couldn't have been wandering for three hours? No, that's ridiculous and I start to lift my hand only remembering at the last minute about my lack of a watch. I need to think about the time lapse further but, with the knocker thumping for a second time I set down my mug and head into the hall.

Nigel is flaked out on the floor beside his chair, his nose in that perennial position between his paws. He's shattered but still not too tired to give a little yelp as I lift him onto his seat. 'Sorry boy, what was I thinking?' But that's the problem. I have no idea where I'd walked him. My mind is a complete blank…

'Would you like a coffee or—?'

'Ah, a glass of wine would be delightful and it looks like you've already had the coffee?' his voice holding a question at the sight of the unwashed mug by the sink and the lingering smell as I realise I must have left the coffee pot on all afternoon. I frown, my attention on the box of teabags beside the kettle. I made a cup of tea when I arrived home, didn't I? I don't remember making coffee and certainly not with that all singing, all dancing coffee machine with more buttons than sense. Coffee is something I can never face until late afternoon and the reason why I smuggled a jumbo box of Yorkshire teabags through customs. But the warm pot and dusty dregs in the bottom don't lie. I flick off the machine at the socket and turn my attention back to the wine bottles.

'Red or white?'

'Whatever you're having is fine.' He pulls open the second drawer down and removes a corkscrew, placing it beside the wine glasses I'd placed there earlier.

I push the bottle of red in his direction, my mind working overtime, the question out before I can edit it.

'You seem to know your way round the house pretty well?'

My attention is drawn to his hand and the way it curves the neck of the bottle; strong capable hands, capable of ringing a neck as easily as easing out a cork. This man would do exactly what he set out to. But would that include stalking and abduction? The truth is, I have a missing stepsister and only a couple of clues; the large Dutchman standing in my kitchen and a pink scarf.

I feel my pulse explode in my ears and the thought is back, the thought that I'm going mad. Surely I have nothing to fear? But fear has a name under this cloak of normality and the name is Manus. I shouldn't have agreed to see him this evening. It's in the hands of the police, which is where I should have left it instead of coming to Holland and acting like something out of an Agatha Christie novel. Coming to Holland was the wrong thing to do. I pull out a chair and sink down, resting my head in my hands. It's too complicated with too many traps. Suddenly I'm questioning everything. He's a doctor. But so was Crippen.

A chair is dragged back and suddenly I feel a hand on my forehead and one on my chin. Before I know it I'm staring up into his face.

'What are you——?'

'Shush. Remember, I'm a doctor, or had you forgotten?' his fingers pulling on my lower lid. 'You're as white as a sheet under that pale English skin of yours. That fall was pretty impressive. But I didn't think you'd done too much damage,' his hand shifting to my head and the bump, hidden by my hair. He leans back, his eyes searching my face. 'So, if it's not the aftermath of the fall, why are you shaking like a leaf, hmm?'

'I'm not shaking.' but he lifts my hand from where I've hidden it on my lap and the ripples chasing over my skin are clear to see.

I watch as he drags his fingers through his hair, a frown appearing. 'Perhaps I should have taken you to hospital,' his voice barely a whisper.

'Why? What aren't you telling me?'

'Ha, you English, always making the little joke.'

'I'm not English.'

'You're not English? But——?' his frown deepening.

'But nothing. I was born in Guernsey. That is I think I was.'

'You're not making any sense.' He peers into my eyes as if he's checking something – I have no idea what but I'm pretty sure it's not to admire the colour.

I sigh. I'm not in the mood to explain my roots. I'm in the mood to be left alone with my dog, the only one around here who's proved his devotion and loyalty. Dogs never lie. But the man in front of me...he's lied from the beginning.

I want him to leave but it looks like the esteemed doctor isn't going anywhere until I can assure him I'm not suffering from some deadly disease. There's only one problem; how can I reassure him of something I'm beginning to doubt myself?

'Guernsey people, people born in Guernsey aren't English in the same way that Welsh people are Welsh and Scottish people are Scottish,' I manage, my head now starting to pound. 'So, I'm Guernsey or British, if you like. Although, as I'm also an orphan there's a chance that I was abandoned in transit. I could be French, German, Belgium or even Dutch. But I think it's unlikely.'

He raises his eyebrows before promptly changing the subject. 'So, If you're not ill then why the shakes?' he says, his eyes flicking to the wine bottle, sitting innocently on the counter.

Because I'm scared out of my wits. Because I don't know who you are or what you're doing here. Because I have some burning questions crowding out all other thought and no nerve in which to voice them. I seem to have lost most of the last four hours, in addition to the means to find out more about my benefactor. I shut my eyes just for a moment as pain crescendos. *I don't know who I am any more. I thought I knew but now…now I fear I'm going mad, really crazy. And the sad truth is I can't ask you for help. You'd be the very last person I'd turn to.*

Instead of speaking I stand and reach for the wine, pouring two large measures. I push one in his direction before taking a hearty sip, both hands clutching the engraved glass like a child, for fear I'll slop it over the table. I retake my seat, placing the now half-empty glass in front of me and pushing it slightly away so that I can rest my chin on my hands. He thinks I'm a drinker, maybe even an alcoholic and a little part of me is quite happy to nurture the thought. He's not the sort of man to tolerate weakness in either himself or others.

'I wouldn't advise that you drink too much following a head injury.'

'Duly noted, doctor.' I pick up my glass and take another sip before replacing it in the exact same spot. 'You were going to tell me how you seem to know where things are in…my kitchen. Were you *Meneer* de Wees's doctor?'

'Hardly. I was both his neighbour and his friend. We spent many an hour sitting round this very table discussing every topic under the sun.'

But I only respond to the part that interests me the most. 'Why wouldn't you be his doctor? Surely if you lived so close?'

'Because Victoria, I may call you Victoria? *Mevrouw* is so long winded. My name is Manus,' and he smiles.

I nod in agreement. After all, I can't really refuse however much I might want to keep a distance between us. It's only a name, after all. A group of eight letters and I've been called a lot worse. All my friends call me Vee but that's something he needn't know.

He continues, the smile wiped from his face at my silence. 'Because, Victoria, I'm a psychiatrist and the one thing Aldert wasn't in need of was any help in that direction. He was as sound as a bell.'

Unlike you.

My vision blurs and I take refuge in my glass, the unsaid words hanging in the open space like a declaration of war. There are no prizes for guessing who's going to win any battles between us; the shy, neurotic, frightened foreigner or the consummate professional with the smug smile and snide insinuations.

Chapter Ten

If Aldert wasn't in need of a psychiatrist then what was he in need of? But instead of asking, I reach across for the bottle.

'I said I'd go easy on the—'

'I heard what you said,' the wariness back.

There's a lot I could ask this man, if I trusted him. I could ask him about the symptoms of madness. The first signs to look out for and any home remedies to keep the fear at bay. I could ask him how someone could lose four hours and what to do about the missing laptop. Or I could start by asking him about Marilyn. How long has she got and how will she cope without her daughter coming to visit? Despite the madness creeping in from all sides, she's relied on those visits. I could ask him all this and more if I trusted him. Instead I decide to ask him about the man who'd decided to leave us the house, my eyes sweeping the room.

'Tell me about him – this Aldert. What was he like? What did he do? '

He steeples his fingers, his elbows resting on the table. 'He was just some lonely old man.'

'How old?'

'Seventy. Seventy-five perhaps. Towards the end it was hard to tell as illness caught up with him. He suffered with Parkinson's; a great tragedy for someone with his particular talents.'

Now he has me intrigued. I look at the room with fresh eyes, focusing on the labour-saving gadgets that any Dutch homemaker would be proud of. But the room also holds a lingering sense of its owner; the walking stick in the corner, the box of medicines sitting next to the box of herbal tea on the shelf above the kettle.

Guilt is a funny thing. It sneaks up on one, out of the blue, side sweeping everything else away including fear. All I can think about is a lonely old man stuck in the house and being unable to do…what?

'Talents?'

'He was an art restorer, a highly respected one too. Before he retired he was employed by the Rijksmuseum in Amsterdam, working solely on their huge stockpile of seventeenth century Dutch paintings. As a young man he travelled the world working on some of the top paintings of all time. I think he even spent some time in Guernsey,' he says on a frown. 'A Renoir exhibition in the *eighties* but I can't really remember. The room at the top of the house, where most people keep luggage and boxes is where he had his studio. Something to do with the light but,' he shrugs his shoulders. 'Then again, I'm not an artist. I used to go up and watch him at work; painstaking work with cotton wool balls and acetone or some other similar solvent. He'd spend hours up there with the roof lights open, or closed, depending on the time of day and which part of the process he was working on. We'd talk about everything and anything. Aldert was quite a character, an old rogue in many respects with a keen eye for the ladies even towards the end.

I place my empty wine glass back on the table, my gaze meeting his. It all sounds so plausible the way he puts it. Their friendship and the way they used to gossip while he watched him work. I remember Robert used to be fascinated watching my storyboards maturing from a few pencil lines to the intricate detailing that I'm famed for. I still don't trust this man; there are far too many unanswered questions for that. But I might as well use him while he's here. After all, there are things in the house that I don't understand; the stairs in the cellar, the locked studio. Why lock a studio unless he kept items of importance up there?

There's something else that puzzles me, something out of sync with everything he's told me so far. Why the need for the top-of-the-range laptop? I'm no expert but the brand new Apple Macbook Pro would have surely set him back a tidy sum – the Macbook Pro I'd succeeded in losing.

My gaze lands on his face and the five o'clock shadow forming on his cheeks. Like me, he's probably in need of a good meal and a shower but I'm not ready to dispatch him on his way quite yet. My fingers toy with the fragile stem of the glass, cold and brittle under my touch; just like my life. My life, usually calm and probably a little boring, if I'm honest, is just the way I'd planned. Okay, so it's still missing a man and the couple of kids I'd always craved: the family I'd never had. But out of Marilyn's clutches, I've managed to carve a niche, albeit a small one. Now, with the arrival of that blasted letter, my life has fallen apart, literally. People don't leave strangers their house and all their belongings. Stepsisters don't just disappear into thin air and strange men don't arrive in the nick of time to rescue damsels from imminent danger, or do they?

I've made up my mind. Now it's time to act on it.

'The attic, his workroom is locked and, before you ask, I've tried the door.'

'Locked?' a frown flashing across his face. 'But he never locked it. Towards the end all he wanted to do was sit up there and watch the clouds trail across the sky and remember all those great paintings he'd worked on. The smell of chemicals had infiltrated the roof timbers, there's no smell quite like it.'

'It's locked, I tell you.' I sneak air through my lungs in lieu of a sigh. Really? If he thinks I'm going to be taken in by all this talk of him being neighbour of the year he's wrong. I'm going to use him just like he's obviously using me. A thought interrupts. Why exactly is he here? That's something I haven't quite gotten around to working out yet.

'Not locked, probably stuck,' he continues. 'Wood warps in the winter, especially in Holland with all the water that surrounds us. On a good day I'm lucky to be able to sneak a knife out of my cutlery drawer, let alone a spoon.'

He's trying to make me feel relaxed. Why? I stand up suddenly and move to the door, noting with a smile that he stands too. He may, or may not, be the reason I'm in this mess but at least he has manners.

'Come on then.' I note his bemused expression. This man needs to get with the programme. I ignore the lines slashing his eyes and the pallor of his skin. Okay, so it's my fault he's not quite as sharp as he should be, even for a psychiatrist, which I'm guessing, as a profession, only employs the sharpest of intellects.

'As you're here, you can give me a hand.'

'I don't understand—'
'I did tell you.'
We're standing in the narrow space at the top of the stairs, staring at the shut door. There's a lock but no visible key; all very strange. What's also strange is the sudden realisation that I'm standing shoulder-to-shoulder with this man, a man with more magnetism than is good for either of us.

Okay, I'll admit that he's as sexy as hell. But he's also a huge unknown and, until I find Ness and iron out all the niggly questions beating me up, I really don't want to find myself in the same room let alone the same house.

I watch as he roots in his pocket before removing a small bunch of keys. 'Here, these are for you. But you won't find the key you're looking for because I didn't know it existed.'

I stare down at the keys dangling from a split ring, my mind now a complete blank.

'Keys?'

'Yes, towards the end my housekeeper was coming three times a week to help out. He had community nurses visiting a couple of times a day, but things were starting to get very tired round here before his final illness.'

'What happened?' I ask, heading downstairs, my arm carefully looped over the bannister.

'It was something small that did it. He caught a cold, which just wouldn't go away despite the doctor visiting and medications. He stopped eating all together towards the end,' his gaze narrowing. 'He was getting increasingly paranoid about everything and everybody.' He takes my arm briefly. 'I tried to make him go into hospital but Aldert was nothing if not determined. He'd made up his mind to stay in his own home and that's what happened.'

'So, these keys? That's how you were able to help me yesterday?' I ask.

'Yes and no.'

'Yes and no?' I repeat.

'Come on. It's time I should be going anyway. Pop your coat on. I'll wait for you in the hall.'

'There.'

I'd followed him out of the front door, carefully pulling it closed behind me. Once down the steps, he'd turned a sharp right before stopping underneath the lounge window.

'These were merchant houses originally. Goods used to come up the canal by barge only to be stored in the damp storerooms, or cellars, underneath the main body of the house.' He takes a step back, pointing to the hook sticking out of the top of the house, just above the upper window. 'As with most of the houses along here the staircases are too narrow for large items of furniture so they were hoisted up the outside of the building and brought in through the large window in the attic.' He pulls a second split ring from his pocket, the key heavy wrought iron. 'Here, this is yours too,' and he slots it into the lock.

The cellar is just how I remember; dark, dank and full of corners. But now, with the door pulled back and the dull gleam from the streetlights filtering through the entrance, my fear is balanced by the size of the man at my side. I still don't trust him as far as I could throw him; not very far – not at all. But it's reassuring to have him here all the same. I hang back, reluctant to put a foot inside, my gaze finding the space on the floor under the electric panel. I could have died on that spot, my life draining away. I could even now be stretched out on the concrete, fading into an oblivion of blood, tendon and bone with no one any the wiser. I could...

'It's alright. It didn't happen.' I feel a brief touch on my shoulder and then nothing as he walks ahead to switch on the light. He turns, his eyes now scanning my face. 'You look terrible. Are you sure you're feeling alright?'

'Gee, thanks. Just what a woman wants to hear. I feel fine, on top of the world,' I manage, heading for the nearest wall and propping myself up.

Now I'm inside I can see how I'd missed the windowless door, situated as it is behind the wine racks. I'd have had to have known it was there. Was that something he'd been banking on?

'I'm just concerned for your welfare.'

I throw him a sharp glance. 'There's no need to be.'

But instead of replying he strolls over to inspect the staircase, the frown back. I watch in silence as he lifts part of the detached bannister from the wall and inspects the end, a sharp whistle escaping through pursed lips.

'What's the matter with it?' I push away from the wall and join him.

'It's been sabotaged is what's the matter with it. Look,' he points to where the end of the wood is smooth. 'Someone's taken a saw to it.'

It's my turn to purse my lips. He's either a very good liar or he's genuine. But, whichever it is, I really don't want to be in his company any longer.

'Yes, well, I'll tell the police tomorrow.' I head for the door. 'Are you coming or—?'

'In a sec.'

He finally emerges, handing me a couple of wine bottles before returning to fetch more.

'What are you doing?'

'What does it look like? Getting you more wine but don't drink it all at once. That was some crack you gave yourself,' he says, peering at me through the darkness. 'I've sorted out the central heating timer to come on at seven and stop at ten. I don't want you coming down here on your own until we know what's going on.' He takes the steps, two at a time. 'Promise me, Victoria,' his expression serious. 'If I hadn't popped down to my own cellar last night and heard you banging.' He leaves the sentence unfinished. We both know what he means.

I search his face for any hint of threat and all I can see is concern. I fear this man, the man that's been following me, don't I?

He takes the key from me and opens the door before following me into the hall, the wine bottles now stacked on the table.

'I have to go to Brussels for a few days; I really don't want you to stay here all alone with what's going on.'

'With what's—? I don't understand?'

'Neither do I and that's the problem.' He toys with my front door key before laying it carefully in front of the wine bottles, his gaze finally meeting mine. 'I'd be much happier if you went back to Guernsey and left me to sort things out over here. First your stepsister goes missing and then the staircase and even his workroom.' He grabs my hands, his eyes never wavering. 'You could be in danger and I can't be here to rescue you. Look, I'll book you a flight on the first plane out tomorrow. Just promise me you'll be on it?'

He wants me out of the way. Why? Can I trust him? That's a question I'm wavering on. He was in Guernsey, wasn't he? He was up to something over there, something he's never properly explained. Suddenly I don't know what to think. I want to trust him, I really do but how can I?

He releases my hand, only one of them, the other still hidden within his grasp as he pulls out his phone and starts speaking in rapid Dutch.

I've never been able to trust anyone, not really. The nearest I've come is my relationship with Robert and just look what happened to us. No, I can't afford to trust this man. I'll play along and, if the worst comes to the worst, I can be on that flight. I can run away and leave all this behind for someone else to sort out. There's still that policeman back home to get in touch with and the police over here. I can run away if I need to but now all I want is to be left alone. I still don't feel right. All of that wine on top of the head injury wasn't one of my better ideas. I'll smile nicely to everything he says and send him on his merry way while I think on it.

He's finished his conversation and shoved his phone back in his pocket. Now he's heading in the direction of the kitchen.

'Coffee for you first,' he flings over his shoulder as he switches on the kettle and reaches for a cup. 'Your ticket will be waiting for you at the airport. I'll arrange for a taxi to pick you up at seven o'clock.'

'There's no need.'

'There's every need,' he interrupts. 'I feel responsible. Aldert was my friend and there's something going on here I don't understand. There's no point in you staying – it could be dangerous,' he says, pushing the full cup into my hands before heading across the room. 'Make sure you lock the door after me…unless you'll agree to stay a second night?'

He must have known I'd object because he doesn't even try to make me change my mind.

He's gone and suddenly the house feels quiet without his presence; too quiet. I'm not afraid to be alone, am I? The coffee is hot and comforting, just what I need to combat the effects of the wine.

I'm back in the lounge, attaching the lead to Nigel's collar for the last walk of the day. I don't want to go out. There's something looming, maybe due to too much wine. Maybe not. I'm tired despite the caffeine. That walk earlier and my head…the headache is building, pressing, tormenting.

It's not late but the night has already drawn its heavy black veil across the landscape. I can still see the beauty that lingers through the mist of pain, the street lights twinkling their reflected glory across the quiet waters. No one's about. All is peaceful and still apart from Nigel sniffing and snuffling along the edge of the path. I could be completely alone in the world.

I pause, my gaze transfixed on the water and an inner peace descends to sooth away the pressure in my head. I love it here even though I didn't think I would. I'd always thought of Guernsey as both my place of birth and my home of choice. But suddenly I'm not so sure. You can keep the bright lights of New York, Paris and Rome. Even Amsterdam with its effervescent reputation holds no charm…

The darkness descends suddenly out of nowhere. There is no warning, no prescience apart from the lingering throb at the back of my eyes. Now I'm frightened more than I've ever been. It was dark before but this is different. This time the darkness is inside. It's almost as if I can feel the blood edging its way through my arteries and veins before pooling just under my diaphragm to press against my lungs. Breath is scarce and breathing, something I do a million times a day, suddenly becomes a chore. In-out, in-out, in-out. A door slams. Voices interrupt, their sound carried over the canal surface in ghostly whispers. I turn a complete circle, my eyes everywhere and nowhere: examining, evaluating, wondering. Where, moments before, I was enraptured by beauty now I'm drawn to the shadows. I'm suddenly more than alone. I'm alone, lonely and scared. It's irrational. It's absurd. It's madness. I twist on my heels and race back towards the safety of home, Nigel panting beside me.

The door hangs open, creaking against the breeze. Had I closed it? I thought I'd heard the lock snag but maybe not as another thought interrupts, a thought I've had before.

He knows where I live.

I remove Nigel's lead, curling it up into a tight ball before placing it on the hall table: the drawer underneath, the drawer with the scarf, lies open. The scarf is gone, the drawer empty. I can only stare at the space but no amount of staring is going to magic it back. Surely someone wouldn't come into the house to steal a scarf? My only physical evidence that she was in Delft is now gone. There are only the texts to prove any of it.

I don't feel like eating. I feel like climbing under the nearest duvet and hiding from everyone and everything, but Nigel has other plans. I sort him out with a snack and opt for scrambled eggs. I beat and stir with little enthusiasm before forcing myself to swallow a couple of mouthfuls. My stomach heaves and I end up scraping the remains in the bin before rinsing the plate. My eyes skate towards the upturned cup. I was fine before that coffee. What if—?

Time slips away again and attention drifts. I stare at the little hand reaching for the nine, not that time matters but it worries me all the same. Did he stay that long, or have I again tormented Nigel with more than his fair share of walks? It must be right. My phone will confirm it. My phone? I suddenly remember it was digging into my pocket when I was removing the books from that bottom shelf in the study. There might even be another call from Ness and I tear out of the room.

The laptop is back, standing accusingly in exactly the same spot on the desk, its lid closed tight, its lead a tight messy coil just like I remember. I forget about the phone. I forget everything except the need to get out of the room and out of the house.

The front door key is in my hand, how did it even get there? I stare, trying to remember, the metal grooves tattooing into my flesh. Where am I going at ten o'clock at night and without a coat? Ten? The clock face in the hall taunts me and my vision blurs. It was nine, wasn't it? Nine, ten, nine, ten; the numbers twisting round my mind. Where is the time? Who's in control? Not me, not me. I glance down at the drawer and the scarf is back, just how I remember, folded into a perfect square.

I'm back in the kitchen, scrabbling in the back of the drawer for batteries. How did I get from the hall to the kitchen, my eyes on the wine bottle? The clock, it must be faulty. No, not clock: clocks. Two clocks broken. Unlikely. Tic toc. Tic toc. Time shifts. No white rabbits here. The time, what's the time? Just after ten. Both clocks working – tic toc, tic toc. If the clocks are working then…no, don't say it. Don't think it. But laptops don't disappear only to reappear. Clocks run slower and slower before finally stopping, not faster and faster. Scarves don't vanish only to reappear like a rabbit out of a hat.

He knows where I live.

My head is ablaze, my forehead burning and sleep calls but there are things I must do first. What things? The door. I shield the clock face with my hand. I don't need to know the time. I don't need to know what it's telling me. I know already.

The front door is locked. I've checked it over and over. I leave the lights on and grab Nigel.

Poor dog, poor poor dog. You've lost one owner and the other one? It won't be long.

The knock on the head. All that wine. That final coffee. Maybe he's right. Maybe who's right? The headache escalates. The pain takes control as pounding pressure drives spikes behind my eyes. I manage the stairs, half crawling, one hand grabbing onto the bannister, the other squeezing Nigel so tight he whines.

'Good boy, it will be alright. It will be alright in the morning. Too much wine. Too much...' I collapse face down on the bed, dragging the blanket on top. The mattress flattens and Nigel presses up close, his tongue wet against my hand. Time stops. Thought stops. There are no dreams. There are no nightmares. There is only darkness.

Is it the thirst that wakes me or the noise? Nigel is standing beside the door, teeth bared, tail stretched out behind him. The noise? A dragging, scraping sound – my attention fixes on the ceiling and the pendant light shifting from side to side.

Breathe in, breathe out. Deep breaths. You're still alive. You're still here. That's good enough for now. I won't look at the time. All the clocks in this house lie. I'll be alright if I don't look at the clocks. There's someone in the house...

My head protests at the shift from lying to sitting but the white heat has abated. For that I'm thankful, only that.

He knows where I live and now he's here. He's here in the locked room.

The full glass of water on the bedside table is a blessing. I lift the glass and drain it in one, the cool liquid gushing down my throat like tide over dry grit. I place the glass back with a frown but Nigel's bark distracts me and the thought is gone, scattered and then merged with a thousand other disjointed memories. I'll think of it later. But by then it will be too late, far too late.

I ease the door open but Nigel's too quick and he races down the stairs in completely the wrong direction. He'll be safe downstairs. The noise has stopped. Now the only sound is from the thumping of my heart as I take that first step towards the attic.

The door to the attic is wide open and I'm finally privy to all its secrets. A tear falls, closely followed by another. All destroyed in a tangled mass of paint, canvas and blade.

Red gloss drips over the side of the workbench, bloodlike as it stretches and bends to every curve and groove. Paintings, twisted mangled faces and flowers slaughtered by a needless hand. For an artist this is worse than death. For the first time I'm glad that he's dead; that he's been spared the sight of his life's work destroyed with reckless abandon. No, this isn't just reckless. There's anger here. There's anger and the intent to destroy.

The noise is back and the pain. Is the sound inside my head or downstairs? I hear a door creak, the front door? *NIGEL!*

I run out of the room, tripping over my feet as I scrabble down the stairs. Bare skin meets ceramic tiles and I slip to the ground, my hip smashing against the floor. But I ignore the pain. The front door lies open where before it was locked. The clock ticks, but I squeeze my eyes shut and feel for the lead. I can't look at the clock. I don't want to check if the scarf is there or not. I can't lose him too. I can't. Selfish woman. Selfish, selfish, selfish.

He's nowhere or he's hiding: Nigel or the man - perhaps both. I can't think about that or I'll go…no, don't say it. Don't even think the word. My head and heart are exploding within their cavities and breathing is difficult. Air screams through empty lungs. The houses: no gardens, nowhere to hide. A lone cyclist on the bridge. I shout but he continues on his way. My attention slithers to the canal. Not there, please not there.

Nigel. My lungs expand to bursting and vocal cords stretch. A curtain twitches and then another. I drop to my knees, stone biting into my skin as realisation hits. He's gone, or he's been taken. Which? It doesn't matter. It doesn't matter. I keen back and forward just like Marilyn. I should never have come. It's too late. It's always been too late. Ness's dead. I'll be dead soon too. I hear a bark. Not loud, muffled even and then a splash. The canal, my biggest fear.

The water is cold, slimy and with a thin film of oil on the surface from all the barges that steam past. I stare down at the black surface but I don't recognise the image reflected back. Who is this wild-eyed, mad woman with sunken cheeks and dead eyes? It's no wonder Robert couldn't bear to stay with me. It's no wonder I'm on my own, all on my own without even a dog for company.

The sound of barking has disappeared. There's me and the canal and death. Dare I end it here? Dare I slip my fingers into the stygian blackness? It wouldn't be such a leap of conscious thought. After all, my soul is there already.

Something shifts across the surface, a ripple as the water tremors back to life. Recently I've been anxious, afraid even; now I'm petrified. I can't run. I can't move. I can barely breathe. The scream builds in the back of my throat waiting for the right moment…not yet…not yet; my attention caught on the slime as it scatters across the surface. The wheel of a bicycle, the spokes gleaming through the cover of darkness and there underneath - a shape.

The scream announces its arrival in a rush even as I lose my footing and slide across the muddy bank. Down, down - my hands scrabbling for the hold that isn't there. It's too late. I'm too late. I've always been too late. I squeeze my eyes tight. I don't want to see. I know what's to come. It has a name and the name is death.

Chapter Eleven
Part Three
Present

The light streams through the slated blind on this my third day; day three of the rest of my life. Did I sleep? It doesn't matter. I thought I might dream. They were hoping I'd dream. Nature's way of sorting out your problems, or that's what they've told me.

Were they expecting a miracle? There's no miracle here. I feel better but I never really felt ill. I have clothes now; not the sort of clothes that I'd have chosen as I stare down at the blue nightdress and hospital dressing gown. If I wear anything in bed it's usually pyjamas in the winter or nothing in the summer, a memory glimmering out through the darkness that is my mind.

I pull myself to sitting, the back of my hand still sore and bruised from the cannula they removed first thing this morning. The clock is stretching towards ten but time doesn't matter within these four walls. I eat what they put in front of me and swallow the handful of pills they dish out, four times a day, without question or query. They know what they're doing or I hope they do. I'm in a void where there's me but an incomplete version of me. There are so many unanswered questions. Just how I know some things and not others is a mystery and one they've told me not to try and solve. My memory should come back soon but that's all they're saying. There's no medical reason for the loss.

They've left me with a notebook and pen next to the regulation jug of water and plastic beaker on the bedtable. There's nothing else in this empty, white desert of a room apart from one chair, one wardrobe, a box of tissues and a TV that only runs programmes in a language I can't begin to guess at. The notebook is for me to scribble down any random thoughts, no matter how random, inconsequential or meaningless. The pen feels smooth against my fingers as I twist it round in a circle. I'm used to holding a pen. I'm used to writing. Clicking the end I mark the virgin page with the first of my thoughts; my taste in nightwear.

I don't know where I am. Oh, I know I'm in a hospital, a hospital in Holland but that's about it. I don't know exactly what happened. I know what they've told me but it's all so strange. Just why I'd be walking around Delft at six o'clock in the morning is anybody's guess. I had no ID, no handbag, nothing to identify me. I have no name, no age, no nothing. I'm like a new-born baby fallen from the sky and the worst part? Nobody has come forward to claim me. I've been on all the local news channels and even on the front of the NL Times, albeit a small article. I reach for the newspaper and the black and white photo of a woman I can't recognise, no matter how hard I squint down at the image. They reckon I'm anywhere between twenty-five and thirty-five depending on how well I've looked after myself but, by the state of my split-ends, probably nearer the upper limit.

They know my height, weight and blood group and that I'm running a low grade fever. But, they're at a loss in the same way I am. They suspect I'm a foreigner but even that's not guaranteed. Did you know that someone could lose a language just as easily as losing a wallet or a mobile? The brain is a complex structure or so they keep telling me. It will know when the time is right to reveal all its secrets.

I head across the room, my feet pushed into borrowed slippers. I don't want to think about who they're borrowed from. They've left towels and more clothes on the rail inside the bathroom, a selection of toiletries and even a comb; one of those cheap, black plastic jobs that's bound to rip at my hair and tear at my scalp. But I'm thankful all the same as tears, ever near the surface, start to stream.

Emotionally labile it's called: the inability to hold back emotions, be it laughter or tears. But, as I stare at my reflection, there's no laughter in this room. There's only silence and echoes; echoes of a past I can't seem to latch onto no matter how hard I try.

I stretch up a hand, fingering my cheek. The bruise has changed colour again, the blues fading to yellow and even a hint of brown: the clear imprint of a flattened hand just as the blackened eye is the shape of a closed fist. I've been used as a punch bag and yet have no memory of the punches, probably a blessing. Although, with no memory of my attacker how am I meant to recognise him, or her?

The shower is hot, the spray sharp against my skin but I relish the pain. Pain means I'm still alive. Pain means I can feel even if part of me feels dead. There's a void, a ruddy, great hole where before there were emotions, memories and feelings. There's nothing now except time as the clock ticks its way between the endless round of mealtimes, drug rounds and doctor's visits. In between I sleep. There is nothing else.

Chapter Twelve

'Ana, the doctors tell me you still have no memory of who attacked you?' the inspector says, his eyes pinned to mine.

It's day five and the nurses are getting restless. I can see it in their stares and the way they stop whispering when I walk past. Oh yes, I'm not a prisoner or, at least I'm not a prisoner here. I'm still a prisoner to my thoughts, not that there are many. Just the continued mantra of who am I?

I'm healed now, or I am on the outside. But now they don't know what to do with me. If it's anything like the NHS they're probably in need of the b... I stare across at the police inspector, my mind in freefall.

I'm English, I must be, if my wanderings glue onto the state of the English Health Service. English, the word rolls round my mind like a foreign species. If I'm English then what the hell am I doing in Holland? Surely I wouldn't have been brave enough to hop on a plane when, this morning, I couldn't even bring myself to ask for tea instead of the black coffee that arrived by mistake. I'm English but it doesn't resonate. I've been running through a list of names in my head all morning searching for the one special name that sounds right, but nothing. Unlike the norm, I've started with the letter V because the tattoo marking my flesh must surely stand for something. But it's useless. From Valerie to Victoria the syllables form on my tongue only to be discarded along with all the rest. The alphabet has been exhausted and I'm nowhere nearer to finding the name that means something. So, for now I'm known as Ana; no surname, no middle name, no prefix – just Ana – I like it.

I focus on his highly-polished, black regulation lace-ups and the intricate double knot, which must be a bitch to undo and I think *what comes next?* I continue being unable to answer even one of their questions so they get fed up and repatriate me back? Then what? Then all those niggly little questions like just who the hell I am remain forever unanswered. What if I never regain my memory? I'll end up living a shadowy existence on the side-lines of life with no friends or family to act as a buffer.

My eyes land on his face; his compassionate smile, his twinkling blue eyes. He's nice this detective. Someone to trust, someone I can trust and that feels good suddenly. In my world of uncertainties and unknowns he's been the one constant with his daily visits and kindly concerns. The nurses' change, the doctors flit in and out but he lingers, probably longer than he's meant to. He was kind on his first visit, when I was still bedbound with monitors flashing and wires, like spaghetti, stretching out from my chest and arms. He's still kind.

'No, nothing.' I finally say. 'It's all a blank.' The tears hover yet again but this time I sniff them back and stuff my hands with tissues. I was in no state to ask questions the last time he visited and I'm in no state now. But I must ask them. I must know. Then he told me nothing. Nobody has told me anything, not really. Oh, I know I was found wandering in what they call a fugue state, my body pumped full of drugs. The police and the paramedics were called; just as well when my heart decided to stop at the scene. Perhaps it would have been better to have left me to die… I shift my attention to my arms, hidden under the plain, black polo neck they've borrowed from somewhere. If I'm a druggie there are no tracks puncturing my skin, only the marks left from the ligatures - I don't want to think about those. There are no memories to match the toxicology reports. There's nothing apart from that V stamped on my skin. V for…vacant. There's no one here; no one at all.

'What do you think happened to me?'

He spreads his hands. 'Are you really sure you're ready to hear?' and he only continues when I nod my head. 'You've obviously been attacked, a sustained attack over a number of hours. It's unusual in that there doesn't appear to be a sexual motive,' he pauses to cough. 'But nonetheless, it was an extremely violent assault where drugs were used to presumably make it more difficult for you to leave. We've taken your clothes away for analysis.' He lifts his head from the notepad balancing on his lap. 'There's little point in you getting them back. They're ripped and torn. You escaped or you were released. Who knows? There's hardly anything to go on. Most crimes of this nature are committed by someone known to the victim but as you can't remember…'

He snaps his pad closed and stands to his feet. 'We'll continue working the case. I'm still waiting for Interpol to get back to me and there's the results of your DNA testing that will be back in a few days. I've asked the hospital to keep me personally informed about your discharge plans.' He takes my hand and gives it a gentle shake before handing me his card. 'I've scrawled my mobile on the back. If there's anything you remember, anything at all, please get in touch.' He smiles again, but this time it isn't a happy smile. 'I have a daughter about your age. I can't imagine…' he leaves the rest of the sentence hanging in mid-air.

I watch the door close on his back and I continue watching. There is bewilderment and fear now. They've finished with me. There's a crime here, a crime they can't solve without my help and I can't help them. I can't even help myself. At least, I wasn't attacked *in that way* but isn't that now part of the worry; part of the mystery? If it was just a robbery, and the absence of any money or phone would seem to indicate that, then why tie me up and subdue me with a fist?

I sink back against the pillows, my head in my hands as I let the tears trickle through my fingers. The world seems a very big place all of a sudden, a place I have no part in. And what's next? Where is there for me to go? They'll probably sort me out with a set of clothes and a few days in a hostel but, with no passport and no way of getting one, I'm stuck in a strange country all by myself. The thought that lingers is the thought that he may still be after me.

How will I recognise him if I can't even recognise myself?

The doctor is back, by himself this time. He flips his white coat up before settling on the regulation chair beside the bed as if he's here for the duration. This one, Doctor Brouwer, is a psychiatrist. Now that the medics have pronounced me fit, they've presumably left it to him to try and sort me out. I wish him luck.

'Well, Ana, how are you today?' He stretches out a hand, his fingers cool against my wrist as he fiddles to find my pulse.

How am I? Who am I would be more relevant but obviously he's not going to be able to tell me that. How am I? How am I meant to be?

I shake my head and renew the examination of my nails, now that I have my hand back. I start worrying a loose bit of skin, peeling back the cuticle so that I can reach it; pick, pick, pick until the skin loosens. He's watching me. I'm not sure what he's hoping to find with his scrutiny. There's nobody at home, only me and my nail as I start working on the next bit of skin.

His hand covers mine, his skin warm and I suddenly realise just how cold I am as a shiver snakes across my flesh. I'm scared. I'm scared but not of him. I'm scared of what he's got to say for himself.

'I'm not going to say it's going to be alright, Ana. How can I? But, in most cases of this type of post-traumatic amnesia, the memories aren't gone, more like buried under all the emotions and fears associated with the actual trauma.'

'So, I'm still here, somewhere?'

'That's right. It's a little like a dog with a bone. Do you own a dog?'

My eyes widen at the swift change of topic. Do I own a dog? I don't know is the answer.

'Maybe. Maybe not—why?'

'No reason.' He smiles and continues. 'Dogs like to bury things, bones and the like. Sometimes, just sometimes they forget where they've buried them and soon the whole garden gets a good turn-over in the search for that perfect after-supper snack. You're like that dog at the moment. You know the truth is buried deep inside but there's a whole lot of stuff in the way that you have to get through first. The memories will probably resurface all on their own or there may be a trigger. But there's no way of knowing what that trigger will be.'

'What now?'

'Now it's a waiting game and, in the meantime, I have someone who'd like to meet you.'

My hand clenches under his, my eyes never leaving his face. There's something he's not telling me, I can see it in the way his gaze flickers towards the door and back and the little frown pulling between his brows. He's anxious. But he's the doctor here. Surely he knows what he's doing? And then I hear the bark. I shift my attention back to the door as the handle shifts and through the gap a bundle of black skitters its way across the floor before leaping into my lap and attacking me with its tongue. My laugh, when it comes, sounds false to my ears, strained even as if I haven't had a great deal to laugh about recently. Another nugget of information I'm going to hold onto and add to my rapidly filling notebook.

'So, Ana, it looks like you might have a dog. This is Nigel,' his gaze searching mine but he needn't have bothered.

'Nigel?'

Who the hell calls a dog Nigel?

But, at the sound of his name the wriggling reaches mammoth proportions and I finally set him down on the bed, my hand on his back. 'Shush, Nigel. Settle down.' He obviously knows me as he does just that, his nose resting between his paws, his liquid-brown eyes peeled onto mine as if I'm about to up and disappear again. I have a dog, who knew?

'I take it you don't recognise him, then?' his expression serious. 'It was a huge risk smuggling him in, I can tell you. Matron would have a canary if she ever found out. I really thought you might remember—?'

I shake my head, my hand running up and down Nigel's back before tugging at his ears. 'He's lovely but he's a stranger,' my fingers reaching behind his head to his neck and the absence of a collar.

'How did you know he was called…how did you know he might—?' my frown back.

'Ah, I was wondering when you'd twig, Vanessa.'

Chapter Thirteen

Vanessa. I roll the sound over my tongue like licking honey off a spoon; the vowels elongating and softening to merit such a name. It doesn't resonate. It doesn't mean a thing.

I finally manage a smile to match his beam. He's proud of himself, this Doctor Brouwer. He thinks he's solved the case with a dog and a name. But I've got news for him. I finger the tattoo, hidden under the sleeve of my jumper. Just because the initial fits, it doesn't mean that I'll accept the first name that's thrown at me. What about Vera, Velma or even Vanka? There were any number of names I'd excluded, in the search for the ideal and Vanessa just doesn't do it for me. Oh, it's a beautiful name, really beautiful and that's probably part of the problem. With a name like Vanessa I'd need to be decked out in satin and silk with diamonds twinkling from my ears and my fingers. Instead I'm wearing mass-produced black polyester mix and scruffy denim.

'Ha, you English are always so funny with the little jokes. I'm afraid there's indisputable proof that your name is Vanessa. You were even listed as missing.'

'Missing?'

'Of course. The next time you decide to run away and get married please remember to inform your stepsister. She's obviously the worrying sort.'

'Married? What?'

The room fades in and out of focus before righting itself. I have a stepsister, a husband. I have a family; a family I don't remember. It's all very well forgetting your name or even your keys but a family?

'Ah, my tongue—my wife is always telling me to engage my brain before letting my tongue run wild.' He leans forward, gripping both my hands between his. 'Vanessa, this may come as a shock but I'd like to introduce you to your husband.'

The door, still open a crack from where Nigel pushed his way through, continues moving by some invisible hand.

This must be a joke, the only explanation. I'll wake in a minute back in my home…and there lies the problem. I can't picture up a home, or a house or even a flat. I can't picture up a family or even one measly friend. They say I have a dog and, whilst this Nigel seems a perfectly nice sort of dog I don't recognise him from Adam. In fact, if I was going to get a dog, Adam would be a more fitting moniker than bloody Nigel.

'No, really. I'm not married. I can't be.' Surely, I'd remember something as important as a husband? I drag my hands out from under his and leap off the bed only to trip on the edge of the counterpane and stumble to the floor in a heap.

Before I know it I have two sets of arms bending down and gently lifting me back onto the bed. I glance towards the doctor, a man I'm starting to like, only to find that he's blushing up to the roots of his hair and heading towards the door.

'I'll leave you now, Vanessa. Your husband is a fine man and a great doctor. You'll be safe in his hands.'

I stare across at him in horror. 'No. Stop. You can't mean to leave me with a stranger. Please don't.'

'He's not a stranger, Vanessa. He's your husband.'

'But I don't remember him. I don't remember anything.'

'But you will and a familiar environment will help. Trust me, Vanessa. You'll be fine. Your husband is a good man. Believe me when I say that I wouldn't just leave you with anyone.'

I squeeze my lids tight; willing him to turn around and take me with him. But the only sound is the slight click of the door as he pulls it closed.

The silence stretches and still I hide under the cover of my lids. I know he's there, lingering, hesitating, waiting. Waiting for what? Waiting for the inevitable. Nigel stirs, his paw creeping towards my leg and I reach out to pat his head before opening my eyes.

He's standing beside the window, staring out at the crowded rooftops and the hint of blue sky between the clouds. I can't see much. His hands are thrust deep within his pockets and his grey suit shrouds everything else. He's tall, well over six-feet and broad with it. But that's about all I can make out, apart from a head of dark brown hair just reaching the top of his collar.

'Well, what do you think?'

His voice is a shock although it shouldn't be. He's obviously going to speak at some point just as he's going to turn and find me examining him as if he's something in a petri dish. He looks normal enough, pretty handsome if I'm honest, my gaze pausing on his strong, weather-beaten profile with its fair share of lines. There are even a couple of grey hairs to accompany the lines so he's not young. He's not old either but probably older than me.

He drifts over to the bed, sitting down on the edge before idly picking up my hands. All of his attention is now on my fingers; my broken nails, the fading ligature marks stamped across my wrists. I watch, transfixed as his fingers stretch, kneading the damaged skin with such a gentle touch for so big a man. He continues speaking, his fingers shifting before linking through mine.

'That was the first thing I noticed about you, your pretty hands; so small and with a trace of veins peeping through almost translucent skin.' He flashes me a look from amber-brown eyes before returning his attention to our entwined hands and his thumb as he sets up a mini massage parlour across my flesh. 'When I came back from Belgium and you'd disappeared into thin air, I didn't know what to think. We hadn't known each other long enough for me to be confident in how you felt. Part of me dreaded finding out that you'd disappeared back to Guernsey.'

'Guernsey?'

He squeezes my hands gently, the pressure strangely comforting. 'I've forgotten that you don't remember any of it, that you don't remember me. You don't, do you?'

The question is casual, almost a throw away remark but his thumb has paused on its journey only to start up again at the slight shake of my head.

'There aren't many couples that get a chance, a second chance at this. I'm just going to have to make you fall in love with me all over again.'

'And if I can't?'

'We'll face that bridge when we come to it. After all, you're in Holland now and the one thing we're not short of is bridges.' He unlinks our hands and starts making a fuss of Nigel. 'At least this little fellow knows me, isn't that right, boy?' and I watch as man and dog start fooling around on the side of the bed.

Traitor.

'So, what happens now?'

'Now? Why now we go home,' he says, standing up from the bed.

'But—?'

'There's no need to be frightened, *liefje*. I know you don't remember a thing about me but I know enough for both of us. Come on, I've brought some clothes...I had no idea what you'd want to wear so I just brought a selection.'

Chapter Fourteen

I wait until he's left the room, his laugh still ringing in my ears. But if he thinks I'm going to strip off in front of a stranger, even though he just so happens to be my husband, he has another thing coming.

The case is one of those small brown travel ones popular with businessmen, but there's nothing business-like about the contents. With the door securely closed, I can't wait to fling off the horrible jumper and too large jeans, even though they've served me much better than the open-backed gown. However, what to wear is another matter entirely. There is too much to choose from and all of it beautiful. I've obviously got good taste and money to squander as I lift item after item of silk and cashmere onto the bed with a sigh. I can't make up my mind but I'm spurred on by the thought that if I don't hurry he'll get fed up waiting and just walk in on me standing in *the altogether*. I choose at random; shell-pink silk underwear that whispers across my skin, quickly followed by more silk. This time a plain, cream silk blouse and black patterned ankle-length skirt all topped off with a plain black coat.

I scan the room briefly for anything I've left behind but it's empty. I brought nothing to this room and I'm leaving nothing behind. My future, for what it's worth, lies outside the protection of these four walls. Oh yes, I've felt safe here, protected even. I still don't know who I am but, within the confines of this space, I was finding a new me or, perhaps remnants of the old one – who knows. I still don't know who I am or, should that be, who I was? But the new me, this Ana, is finding her way.

He's waiting outside the door. He doesn't say anything, just gives me one swift appraising glance from head to toe before nodding and taking the case from my grasp. He hands me Nigel's lead and tucks his hand under my elbow.

'Let's go home.'

Such friendly, ordinary words for a husband to say to his wife but I can't feel any comfort at the sound. I can only feel fear and anxiety build as I try to focus on my feet making their way across the highly-polished floor. He doesn't stop at the front desk or pause at the sight of the nurses halting in their tracks at the sight of us leaving the building. He doesn't see what I see, or perhaps he does.

'It will all blow over, my dear. We're a novelty, nothing more.'

'A novelty? Why a novelty?'

'You wanted to keep our marriage a secret from your stepsister until you had a chance to explain everything. We've been hiding out at home on our honeymoon but now, as you say in your country, *the cat is out of the bag.*'

'But—?'

I focus on the one part of the conversation I want to know more about. Not the honeymoon part, the stepsister part. If I have a stepsister then where is she? Shouldn't she be here if she was the one that reported me missing? And finally, if I was missing why didn't my handsome husband report it instead of leaving it up to her?

'Not now, *lieveling*. You're still not one-hundred-percent. Let's get you home and I think a rest in bed. We'll have a talk later.'

I'm half expecting to walk to his home or maybe cycle but not to be driven in a bright red Mercedes Cabriolet complete with leather seats and soft top.

'How can I not remember this?' I say, sinking down into the seat with a sigh of contentment, Nigel curled up by my feet. If his house is half as good as his car maybe I'll just try to ignore the fact that it still feels like I've just met him off the street. There must be plenty of advantages to being married to such a respected member of the community who's obviously loaded. But, at the moment, I can't think of a single one.

I shift my gaze from the window to where his hands are resting on the steering wheel, the knuckles white under his skin. But his face, when he turns it towards me, is smiling - a smile that doesn't quite reach his eyes.

'That's because you haven't seen it before. It was going to be a surprise.'

I think he's lying to me. There's just something about the car that doesn't make sense. But if he's lying to me about this then what else is my handsome husband lying to me about? I'll have to step cautiously around him. I'll bide my time and keep gathering the facts. I remember the notebook that I sneaked into my pocket, instead of adding it to the suitcase. I'll make sure I hide it somewhere he'll never find and, in the meantime…

My hand reaches into my pocket only to touch something else and I pull out a pale pink fabric. A scarf. I press it to my face before draping it over my neck, the slight lingering scent of some perfume hovering under my nose. I know that scent, something floral; floral and expensive but I can't pin a name or a price. But still, it's something to hook onto, something to investigate. There surely must be plenty of perfume shops in Delft for me to put a name to the scent. I'm itching now to be alone as my hand renews its acquaintance with the edge of the notebook. I have so much I want to enter.

The car is hot, stifling. I want the roof down and the feel of the wind through my hair but I'm too afraid to ask. I've been cooped up too long in that room and before… My hand clenches on my lap as thoughts revolve in an ever-spiralling loop. I may never know how long I was tied up or what happened to me. I may never know what he did. I may never know any of it. How could I not recognise my husband?

'It will be alright, my love.' I look down to where he's reached out a hand and grabbed mine; such a large dependable hand. I need to trust someone but is it going to be him? I squeeze his hand gently before easing mine away and tucking it under my sleeve. Only time will tell.

After the car I should have had some warning about the house. But I'm not thinking straight. I may never think straight again. The house is situated in a string of similar properties. It's tall, commanding and elegant with ornate gables and elaborate leaded windows - a tall, stately edifice suitable for such a tall, stately man. He parks the car and goes out of his way to remove my hand from the handle before walking round the bonnet and helping me out. His hand is warm in mine. I feel as if I'll never be warm again.

'I should have remembered gloves,' he murmurs almost to himself, as he tucks my hand into his coat pocket.

'It's no matter.'

'Everything matters where you're concerned.'

I throw him a sharp glance. He sounds as if he really cares, as if he really loves me. I feel absolutely nothing.

The inside of the house matches the outside in both tone and opulence. I stand in the hall, turning in a circle before finally meeting his gaze. Oh yes. He's watching me, his eyes never leaving me for an instant. I don't know what he expects from me so I decide to say nothing until asked. Instead I just shrug my shoulders.

'Come on, let's show you round,' he finally says.

Funnily enough it's not what I expected from the outside with its neatly painted blue gutters and posh planters marking the door like guardian angels. The lounge is large with patio doors leading off to a long strip of garden. But where I expected designer there's none. The sofas, arranged in front of an open fire, have been chosen for comfort while the furniture is a mismatch of antiques from an assortment of periods. There's even evidence of his work with a pile of medical journals set beside one of the chairs and a pair of glasses perched on top.

The study next door is his room, I can see it in the way he pushes the door open to let me through but waits with his fingers circling the handle. I glance over the bookshelves and back to the desk only to pause at the sight of an ornate silver frame, angled just out of my line of vision.

Is there something for me in this room, some indication of the man I married? If there is it's not immediately apparent and, with him watching, it's something I can't take too much time over.

However, I'd like to have the guts to stroll across the room and pick up the frame. Who is it he stares at when he's sat behind the desk? What is he thinking? Does he think of me or is it some other woman he sees? I summon up another smile and turn back towards the door. I won't enter again unless I'm invited, and I'm pretty sure that's not going to happen unless I spend too much of his money.

I hold onto that thought. Presumably I don't work now, or do I? Did I just give up my job, whatever it was, to live in the lap of luxury on his earnings? Surely that's not who I am? Surely I'd have wanted to keep even a modicum of independence if only to surprise him and the children at Christmas. I blink at the thought, only to stumble on the rug that runs the length of the hall.

'Hey, easy does it,' he places an arm across my shoulders and that's where it stays; a large, heavy, dependable arm belonging to a stranger, a stranger that I'll probably be expected to share a bed with tonight. Surely, he wouldn't expect me to...the thought lingers even as my attention is diverted by the sight of an elderly woman standing in the kitchen, her hands elbow deep in suds.

It's a beautiful kitchen, large and bright. But, I'm not interested in all that now. Just who is she? She must be in her seventies, her face crazed with lines as if she has the weight of the world on her shoulders. I tune back to the conversation, a smile glued in place.

'This is Lize, the housekeeper. She comes in Tuesdays to Thursdays for a couple of hours to keep on top of things.' I feel his arm squeezing my shoulder and I glance at him. He's trying to tell me something but I have no idea what. 'Lize has had a lot to catch up on after her holiday but I'm hoping you'll get on like, how do you say, a house on fire?'

I release breath from my lungs; breath I didn't know I was holding. So, she hasn't met me before, this Lize. I'm not sure whether that's good or bad, my eyes on her vacant expression. I shake her damp hand briefly before returning it to the confines of my pocket.

'Did you want me to make lunch before I go, Doctor? There's some nice ham in the fridge and I managed to pop down to the market for some of that smoked Gouda you're so fond of.'

'No, I'm sure we can muddle through. Thank you all the same.'

'Well, I'll just finish up here and leave you to it.' She pauses briefly, her eyes trained on my husband. 'Did you want me to pop in at the weekend or—?'

'Oh, I'm sure we can manage, Lize. We'll probably go out tomorrow anyway so there's no need to worry.' The arm is back, this time round my waist, his fingers gently pinching my skin. 'You don't mind, darling?'

All I can do is nod my head in agreement. For some reason, I can't begin to fathom, he'd prefer for us to be alone and that's fine by me. Any more of this display of happy families and I'll be in need of a sick bucket. I'll play along for now, after all, this Lize looks quite sweet and her being able to speak English is a huge bonus. But as soon as we're alone there are some questions I need him to answer, not least of which is where he expects me to sleep.

He continues speaking. 'There's a small dining room behind the lounge but what about a rest while I catch up on some phone calls? I had a long chat with your doctor earlier and he recommends plenty of sleep interspersed with plenty of good food.'

He picks up my suitcase from the hall and guides me towards the stairs and the rooms above, Nigel racing ahead. We stop at the top, his hand curled round the bannister and is that a blush chasing across his cheeks? I wouldn't have believed it if I hadn't seen it for myself but, funnily enough, the sight of that blush changes everything. I still have no idea who this man is, a man that professes his undying love. But his uncertainty over the situation, over us means that things aren't as clear cut as he'd like me to believe. Or maybe he's not sure of how I'll react. I decide to wait and see just what it is he's up to; if indeed he's up to anything. He's given a very good show at being a loving, attentive husband up to now. But if he does suddenly turn into a monster, Lize is still in the house.

I hover beside him and into the building silence he clears his throat before pushing open a door.

It's a bedroom, no great surprises there. A bedroom dominated by the biggest bed I've ever seen. My gaze leaves the discomfort of the pure white linen with its ruler creases and I continue my examination of what must be the master bedroom. It's a nice room as men's bedrooms go; utilitarian to the extreme with no wifely touches to soften the stark bedlinen or metal bedframe. The curtains are pale blue to match the wall-to-wall carpet; the walls white and with an enormous scrolled mirror behind the headboard. I raise my eyebrows at the mirror but decide to remain silent. No doubt I haven't had time to change anything - that mirror would have been the first thing to go.

He's loitering, not quite in the room and yet not quite out and I'm left wondering what comes next. He finally enters and avoids the bed. There's a huge built-in wardrobe that takes up one side of the room and this is where he heads next. He drops the case on the floor before pulling the largest of the doors open to reveal a few clothes, not very many and all in the same style as the outfit I'm wearing.

He clears his throat again and now I know he's nervous or lying, or both and my senses ping to high alert as he speaks. 'You didn't plan to spend more than a few days over here so we do need to get you more clothes. I'll take you shopping tomorrow.'

'Surely there's someone back home that can forward me some?'

'This is your home now, for as long as you want it to be, *liefje*. I know this is difficult for you but it's just as difficult for me.' He lets out a short laugh. 'It's not as if I've ever been in this position before and being a doctor only seems to make it worse.' He sits down on the end of the bed, his eyes now busily following the thick pile of the carpet before finally locking with mine. 'I love you and you haven't got a clue who I am,' his smile wry. 'So, for the moment let's just take it step-by-step and see if that memory of yours throws up any clues. And until then, there's more than enough bedrooms in the house for me to do the honourable thing.' He stands and opens the other side of the wardrobe before bundling together an armful of suits and shirts.

'Look, there's no need for you to do that. I'm happy sleeping anywhere.'

'This was my mother's room,' he interrupts, walking to the door. 'It's only right that you sleep here.' He pauses, his eyes searching my face. 'I missed you. I'll wake you in a couple of hours.'

I don't bother undressing, apart from shrugging off my coat and unzipping my boots. I leave the coat on the end of the bed only remembering, at the last minute, to remove the notebook from the pocket before returning the scarf back to its hiding place. I don't bother to trace his footsteps across the room to the wardrobe and my belongings for more clues. That can all come later. I'm tired, just as he said I would be. I linger by the edge of the bed unsure which side to take. But, with Nigel curled up on the left I end up sliding in and hope for the best. Slipping my hand under the pillow, my fingers touch some silky fabric and I pull out a nightdress in sheer gossamer white. It's the most beautiful thing I've ever seen and so different from the hospital gown I've been wearing although, probably just as indecent, if not more so. If he does decide to become amorous he won't have any difficulty finding me.

The room is warm and silent without even the ticking of a clock to interrupt the quiet. The shadows of the early afternoon filter through the blind and drape across the bed, the dim light hovering over Nigel and the notebook. I reach out a hand and flick through the pages. There is a lot I want to add, lots of questions I need to know the answers to but not now. I stifle a yawn as sleep sends out its siren and drags me into its greedy clutches.

Chapter Fifteen

'You shouldn't have let me sleep so long.' I struggle up in bed, glad now I'd decided to keep my clothes on.

The light has shifted, the shadows lengthening as darkness takes hold for another evening. He's brought tea and biscuits, which he's left on the bedside table before perching on the side of the bed, his legs only inches from mine. I want to shift, I want to move away but I don't, I can't. I'm alone with him now and at his mercy, despite his protestations of undying love. I grimace. I don't mind so much about the love part. It's quite flattering that someone like him could fall for someone like me; quite a feather in my cap. I have no idea who or what I am but something tells me that he's way out of my league, with his posh car and even posher house. No, what concerns me is the undying part. What will he expect? What will he demand? How much am I prepared to give?

He hands me a mug, our fingers touching briefly and I struggle not to slop tea across the sheet. If I can't cope with even the most insignificant of touches, how the hell am I going to cope with living as his wife? Oh, I know he's already set out the rules with regards to the sleeping arrangements. But sharing a house day in, day out is bound to throw us together in the most intimate of circumstances, intimate circumstances I don't want to think about let alone be party to. He says he loves me but, if he loves me that much, surely he should be able to tell that all I want is to be left alone until my memory returns. That it may never return is not a possibility I can allow myself to dwell on at the moment.

'What's going on in that head of yours? I can almost see the cogs turning.'

I lift the mug to my lips and take a long sip before cradling the porcelain between my fingers, my gaze finally meeting his. 'Oh, this and that, none of it of any importance.'

'Everything about you is important, you must realise that.' He takes a sip from his drink before continuing, his attention now on his tea. 'Any thoughts about what happened to you before you…'

But all I can manage is a shake of my head. 'I don't remember a thing.'

'Maybe that's a blessing.'

I place my mug back on the table, my attention now solely on him. 'Why would you say that? I have to know what happened.'

'Even if it's painful? Do you, do you really?' He stands up and walks over to the window, his hands reaching up to close first the blind and then the curtains. His fingers grip onto the edge of the fabric, crushing the material in his palm. 'If it hadn't been for Nigel, I think I'd have gone mad.'

'Nigel? I don't understand?'

'No, you don't, do you?' He drops the curtain and is now standing over me, his eyes searching my face. 'You don't understand any of it and I don't know how much I should—'

I lean forward, pushing my feet to the floor before leaping out of bed with Nigel yapping at my ankles. But I ignore him. All of my attention is now on the man in front of me.

'You should tell me all of it. In fact, I insist that you do. Just how do you expect me to work any of it out if you're keeping secrets?'

He goes to grab my shoulders but I back away and his hand drops to his side. 'Okay, but promise me you'll try not to upset yourself. I'll never forgive myself if you go and have a relapse. They only discharged you into my care because of who I am.'

And just who are you?

He's lit the fire, the logs crackling and spitting in the grate; light feathering round the room and throwing deep shadows across the floor. Nigel lies flat out in front of the flames, his stomach full and his coat almost glowing in the heat.

It's early evening. Manus has made me wait while he performs those chores I should probably be helping him with. But I just sit, leafing through the magazine he's left by my chair, while he potters in the kitchen.

I glance about like the nosy wife I'm not and take heart from the fact that it's a lived-in room. But it's now more *lived-in* than before. A folded newspaper has joined the stack of medical magazines and there's an empty mug and plate on the coffee table, presumably left over from his lunch.

'I thought we could eat on our laps, for once,' the sound of his voice alerting me to his presence. He's carrying a tray, which he sets down on the table before handing me a plate and a fork. He leaves a glass of wine within easy reaching distance before heading to the large armchair on the other side of the fireplace.

'Dig in. I'm not the world's greatest cook, by a long way, but omelettes are usually fool-proof.'

My fork hovers over the plate, my eyes on the perfectly folded mass of egg and accompanying side salad. I'm not hungry. It feels like I'll never be hungry again but I'm also not in the mood for an argument. I'm pretty sure I know who'd come out worse and it wouldn't be him. But instead of starting, I opt for a sip of wine, the heat from the plate, resting across my lap, a sharp contrast to the ice cold of the Chardonnay. I allow the liquid to float over my tongue in an explosion of flavours before settling my glass back and renewing my interest in the omelette.

He's watching me, his eyes tracking my every move but I'm not going to give him the satisfaction of raising my gaze. Instead, I focus on choosing that perfect mouthful, all the while waiting for him to speak. I have too many questions to know where to start - I'm hoping he'll start somewhere near the beginning.

His voice is soft, soft and hesitant. I almost have to strain my ears to hear against the crackle from the fire and the low snores coming from Nigel.

'I don't know where to begin so I'd better start from when we first met. It was at the airport only a few weeks ago. One of those chance meetings. I was in Guernsey doing a favour for a friend and you were on your way to Holland to…' he trails off.

'To what?'

I've given up all pretence at trying to eat, resting my fork on the edge of the plate, my gaze lifting to his.

'You and your stepsister were left a house, funnily enough the house next to this one.'

'That's quite a coincidence,' I interrupt, before I can help myself. But all he does is carry on speaking.

'Instead of you both coming over here, she asked you to attend to it.' He throws me a look. 'You're the lawyer in the family. She stayed back at home and looked after Nigel.'

'But he's here—?'

'Yes, indeed he is.' He pushes away his plate and picks up his glass. But, instead of drinking, he stares into the flames. 'I suppose you could say we eloped. You wanted her here but I, er, persuaded you not to wait. She arrived a week after the wedding and you...you were trying to pick up the courage to tell her what you'd done when you went missing.' He raises his glass and takes a lengthy sip. 'I went away, secure in the belief that your stepsister was safe next door and you were safe in my bed.'

'So, where is she?' I stand and in my hurry almost knock my plate to the floor.

'Here, let me take that.' He picks up the plate, placing it on the table, a wry smile hovering. 'I did tell you I'm not a great cook.'

'You know it's not that. The omelette is fine, very tasty but—'

He flicks me a glance before resuming his study of the fire. 'You know I'm a psychiatrist but I don't see that many patients these days. Apart from the odd consultation, my time is taken up lecturing both here and abroad and I had one such lecture tour planned. Believe me, I really didn't want to go with everything that was happening but I had very little choice.'

I wish he'd just get on with it but, I can see by the way his hands are gripping his glass that he's not going to be hurried.

'When I arrived back you'd gone, both of you. You'd both disappeared. I was frantic.' He raises his glass to his lips only to find it empty. Standing, he reaches for the bottle before topping us both up. 'I'll put some coffee on in a minute,' his only words before returning to his chair, nudging Nigel gently with his foot on the way.

'I thought you'd changed your mind about everything and decided to go back to Guernsey.' He pauses, clearing his throat. 'We hadn't known each other very long and that last evening we had words. I couldn't really blame you, not really. You told me... Well, let's just say that, when you didn't answer my phone calls I knew something was up. And when I returned, I found the house empty. I even went next door to check on your stepsister but there was no sign she'd ever even stayed there.' He glances at me then, his hand dragging through his hair. 'If it hadn't been for Nigel turning up on my doorstep I'd probably still be none the wiser as to what happened to you.'

'What, you wouldn't have chased after me?' I say, my gaze resting on his face to see if there's any additional information I can garner from his expression. But it's as if the mask, that slipped so briefly, is now securely back in place. I won't find out anything else unless he's determined to tell me.

'You have to try to see it from my point of view. Whilst I was desperate to find out what had happened, I wouldn't force myself on you even though we'd made a lifetime commitment. As a psychiatrist I know that one size doesn't fit all and what might have been wonderful yesterday might today be viewed as the worst possible situation. So, no, I wouldn't have chased after you but I would have made sure that you'd gotten back safely. In fact, before Nigel turned up, that was next on the list.'

'But where could she have gone?' I ask, my gaze pinned to his.

'I can't begin to guess, after all I didn't really know her. The police are investigating so I'm sure they'll keep us up to date with the search. Try not to worry too much.'

He drains his glass for a second time before gathering up the remainder of the dishes. 'I'll make some coffee before taking Nigel for his walk.'

'I'd like to come.'

'Are you sure you wouldn't be better in front of the fire? I don't intend to stay out long.'

'If you'd prefer for me not to—?'

'That's not the case.' But he doesn't pause on his way out of the room.

He's running away again. He did it earlier when he spent all that time in the kitchen. I lean back against the sofa and close my eyes, the soft flames warm against my cheeks. I don't know if he's coming back any time soon or if he's decided to leave me to my own devices for the rest of the evening. I don't even know if he's changed his mind about walking Nigel and, as that traitorous beast's paws have padded after him, I'm not going to know unless I follow and that's one thing I'm determined never to do.

I've lost my memory and now it looks as if I've lost both my sister and my dog.

Chapter Sixteen

What do married couples do in Holland is the second question on my lips when the knock on the door wakes me up and he walks in with an early morning mug of tea. The first question is answered almost immediately.

He leans down to drop the briefest of kisses onto my mouth while I'm struggling to prop myself up against the pillows without exposing any more cleavage than I have to.

He tastes of tea and toothpaste, the deadliest of combinations and he looks almost good enough to eat. It's funny that, knowing I'm legally allowed to do pretty much what I want with him, sex is the last thing on my mind. All I want, before I consent to anything more than a kiss, is one measly memory of our relationship, just one. How my mind could allow me to forget someone so gorgeous is beyond me. He's probably the best looking bloke I've ever slept with and I can't even remember something as simple as a kiss. Completely bizarre.

He's ambled over to the window and shifted the curtain back before messing about with the blind.

'It's another cold day out there. What do you fancy doing? We could try ice-skating? The canals towards the north have frozen solid or, if skating isn't your thing, what about a drive or a trip on a tram? We could perhaps take Nigel for a romp along the coast and stop off somewhere for lunch?'

There are plenty of ways I'd like to answer if I felt in anyway close to him. But the truth of the matter is that, for all his tea and kisses, he's still as much of a stranger as he was yesterday. It's like having a one-night-stand stay past their welcome except, instead of sex, there's awkwardness and a raft of questions I can't begin to ask.

I throw him a glance from under my lashes. This is the first time I've seen him wearing anything other than a suit. His jeans have seen better days as has his t-shirt, but he looks comfortable and relaxed, the two adjectives I'm certainly not. His taste in clothes suddenly reinforces just how little I know about the man I married. I shift my gaze away. It's probably about time I made some kind of an effort.

'A walk along the coast sounds great, I'm not sure I'm quite up to ice-skating,' I finally manage. 'How about I make breakfast in return for you making supper last night?'

'Only if you promise to eat it?' He strolls across the room but, instead of perching on the side of the bed like yesterday, he ends up leaning against the door frame. It's almost as if he's set out his mark with the kiss and is now unsure of how to move things forward. But I'm not giving him any help on that score. I don't know what this is but the one thing it isn't is a relationship. And there's very little chance of it being any different until I get my memory back. I've forgotten so much, so many important things...

'What's her name?' I ask, my mind going off on a tangent.

'Who's name?' His eyes leave mine, tracing across my cheeks to my lips before wandering down to my bare shoulders and where the spaghetti straps have slipped. My hands curl into the duvet, crushing the down between my fingers but I resist the temptation to drag the bedding up to my neck. After all, he's a doctor, a doctor I just happen to be married to. He's seen it all before and most of it probably younger and better looking. I let my hands relax and take a moment to pick up my mug, cradling the ceramic between loosely-laced fingers while I await his answer.

'My stepsister's.'

'Her name is Victoria,' his gaze intense. 'Why? Do you remember something?'

I shake my head.

'Victoria'. I mouth the name, almost to myself, all the hope in the world tied up in those four syllables. But it means nothing, absolutely nothing. The name is dead. I'm dead or as good as. What kind of a future am I going to have if I can't even remember something as significant as my stepsister's name? He knows, this Manus. He knows and he understands. He's accepted the possibility that he loves someone who can't remember the first thing about him. But it's different for me. I haven't known him long, not long enough for deep lasting memories to form or, at least that's what I've been telling myself ever since I learnt about my stepsister. But now…now I have to accept that I've lost a lot more than just my memory. I've lost Victoria.

Chapter Seventeen

Breakfast is a surprise, probably more for me than for him. Who knew I could cook and not only cook - that I could cook up something worthwhile from the pile of leftovers in the fridge and the large larder-type cupboard hidden in the corner of the kitchen? By the time I'd gathered together the ingredients for making pancakes, any thoughts of Victoria had been pushed aside as automatic tasks like sifting and weighing flour took over. The routineness of it all, swiftly followed by the look of surprise on Manus's face only added to the gloss of normality I'd started smearing across my life with a liberal hand.

'I usually only have toast,' he says, spearing the last blueberry onto the end of his fork with a sigh.

'You should know better. Breakfast is meant to be the most important meal of the day.'

'I'll take your word for it.'

I catch his smile and feel something other than fear for the first time since I'd woken up on that hospital bed surrounded by all those leads and beeps. It's probably only an illusion but, for the moment, I'll take what I can get. He's not demanding, this Manus. He hasn't asked anything of me except perhaps that I eat more and, with the smell of warm pancakes teasing my senses, I'm more than happy to reach for my fork and tuck in. There's no conversation, just the odd rustle as he props the newspaper up against the salt cellar and starts on the headlines. But I don't mind. It could be an awkward silence but it's not. I have too many thoughts chasing round my head to be worried about him ignoring me for five minutes.

'Is there anything interesting in the paper?' I finally interrupt, more for something to say than anything.

The newspaper lowers, and I watch as he folds it carefully. 'Just the usual. We'll have to get you some Dutch lessons - then you'll be able to read it for yourself.'

'I'm not sure I'd be very good. English is hard enough.'

'You'll be fine and most people don't mind a few mangled verbs and tenses. It's all about making the effort. Lize's English is quite good so you shouldn't have any problems in your own home.'

Here's the opportunity I've been waiting for because there's something about her that puzzles me.

'She seems nice. She's able to manage a big house like this?' I say, choosing my words carefully.

'You mean, isn't she a little old to be still working?' his gaze narrowing.

'Well, that's not what I said but now that you mention it. Surely she's well past retirement—?'

'Lize is only fifty-eight.' He rubs his jaw, his attention on Nigel before shooting me a look. 'She was one of my patients. I shouldn't even be telling you this but you probably need to know. She tried to throw herself off the top of the *Oude Kerk*... Yeah, okay, as if you're going to know what that is,' he adds, almost to himself. 'It's a church; a very high, very old church. One day, when everything in her life overwhelmed her, she paid her *two-euros-fifty* entrance fee and climbed to the top. I was twenty-five and straight out of med school with a measly MSc in psychiatry and, after six years, little practical experience. But I was on call, so they called me. Afterwards she had nowhere to go so she came here, and she stayed.'

'Why did she—?' my voice hesitant, a multitude of thoughts racing through my mind.

'Oh, the usual. There was a man. He promised he'd leave his wife but he didn't. The usual story but, for someone like Lize it was all too much. You don't have to worry. She's fine now.'

'I wasn't worried.'

He stands up and stretches and I know the conversation is over. He's shared something that he probably shouldn't and I'm thankful for that little insight into the real Manus. It's told me there's a human heart beating under that bland exterior, something I was starting to doubt. I frown. Who knows if and when he'll open up again?

He picks up the newspaper before tilting his head in the direction of the table.

'I'll sort out the dishes while you grab your coat.'

'But—'

'But nothing. That was the rule I was brought up with. Now scram.'

I pause on the threshold, watching as he gathers together the plates and mugs before filling the dishwasher, cleverly concealed behind one of the many cupboard doors. He's full of contradictions, this husband of mine. But I can sort of see why I might have married him. That's not to say I'm developing feelings for him, except perhaps gratitude, a shiver descending to chase the hairs over my arms. If it hadn't been for him rescuing me, goodness only knows where I'd have ended up.

I hurry out of the room and towards the stairs as another thought comes out of nowhere and the fear returns. I'm still in danger here, living in the lap of luxury with him. I'm in danger of mistaking gratitude for something stronger, something more permanent when, in truth, I can't see any permanency in the situation. I need to leave and soon. The only problem is where; where will I go? I need to find Victoria and then I need to find myself. He told me to give it time and that's what I'll do. But not too much time. There's a risk of me being trapped here and never finding out the truth, whatever that may be. I can sense that my stepsister must be key to all this but that's something I'm going to have to think on. Now, I have to brush my hair and perhaps find some lipstick.

My make-up bag is the first discordant note in all of this. I don't even know where to begin to look for my handbag, probably nowhere as it's probably missing, my eyes hovering over the fading marks on my wrists. It's probably been stolen along with any money and credit cards. I make a mental note to ask him if he's been in touch with the bank.

The make-up bag is beside the sink of the ensuite shower room but, with a shelf full of the most amazing soaps and bath crystals, I'd just ignored it. It's a little like being a child at Christmas and having a last minute present to open. There might be a clue, a lingering memory hidden within that will explode when I peel the zip back; either that or an amazing array of make-up that I'll have hours of fun with.

I don't know what I'd been expecting but a nearly finished stick of Boot's own brand lippy, in nondescript pink and a tube of congealed mascara isn't it. Instead of that Christmassy feeling, I'm Cinderella when her coach turns into a pumpkin. I fasten the top with a frown, before placing it back in the exact same position.

There's something missing but I can't for the life of me think what it might be. I thrust the thought away as I start pulling on the same boots as yesterday. Really, a day on the beach calls for jeans but, as I don't have any, a thick woollen skirt will have to suffice.

There's a knock on the door but this time he waits until I open it.

'Ah, there you are. Find everything you need?' his eyes flashing across my coat before landing on my hands and where I'm clutching the pink scarf. His eyes widen but before I can even think about what the problem is he strolls over to the dressing table and the little wooden box on top.

Flipping up the lid he rummages for a second before pulling out something and arranging it on his palm for me to see.

'You're not wearing your ring?'

My attention flicks from him and then back to the ring. A thin gold band interspersed with a ruby set with diamonds. My ring? A ring I've never seen before. How can I have forgotten? The possibility that there would be a ring hasn't even crossed my mind. I hold out my left hand and examine it for marks. But there's nothing, no indentation to indicate that I've ever worn anything on my finger.

'I'm sorry, I don't remember.' With shaking fingers, I push the ring in place or, at least, I try to. My brow puckers and I'm puzzled beyond belief as I stare down at the ring. My attention shifts back to his face and the brief smile touching his lips.

'Here, let me.'

He removes the ring from where it's almost swimming off my finger before lifting my right hand and twisting the ruby in place. 'In Holland wedding bands are usually worn on the right hand,' and he holds out his hand and the plain gold band I hadn't noticed earlier.

We travel by tram to *Kijkduin,* a beach resort just outside The Hague. It's a short twenty-minute ride and before I know it he's helping me down the steps and taking me for a brisk walk to the sea edge, with Nigel pulling at his lead. The cold breeze blowing off the North Sea takes my breath, making any form of conversation impossible. But, funnily enough I'm happy. He's tucked my hand in his and slowed his pace to match my much shorter one and I could have carried on walking for miles along the long stretch of sand with only the odd seagull and hardy dog walker for company.

We turn and the wind shifts to our back and snatches at my hair, tearing it loose from the clip I'd found on the dressing table. I reach up and try to gather it together but he stops me.

'No, leave it, it's pretty like that,' his gaze travelling from my hair to my eyes before pausing on my lips. His arms tighten their hold, his hands buried deep in my hair. The kiss when it comes is feather-light. He tastes of salt, of sea air, of...

The kiss deepens, the pressure increases, and senses dull as I give myself up to feeling something other than lost, lonely and frightened. He pulls away when I would have stayed, his words dragging me back to the reality of the beach, the cold. The reality of him - this man I call husband.

'Sorry, I probably should have asked permission or something but—' he says, stepping back and avoiding my gaze.

'But?' I prompt.

He lifts his hand, brushing it across my cheek, his eyes finally meeting mine. 'Remember, it's difficult for me too. This situation we're in. I feel I should be giving you time, all the time you need. When the truth of it is, all I want to do is—' His eyes stare into mine for a second before dropping away and I know the conversation is over.

'I'm starving,' Manus says. 'Let's stop here for lunch.'

We've walked the length of the beach and are now standing outside a busy little café with red awnings.

'Come on. That couple beside the window look to be going, which is lucky. They serve one of the best *erwtensoep* in Holland.'

'You what?' But instead of answering he almost wrenches my arm from its socket in his effort to secure what turns out to be the only free table in the place.

'I'm not sure I fancy this *erwten*…whatever it is. Just a coffee and perhaps a cake.'

'It's only pea soup,' he says on a laugh, unbuttoning his coat before helping me with mine and hanging them both on the back of his chair. 'No dessert before main course. Did your mother never—?' I watch as his face freezes, the teasing look wiped, only to be replaced by another frown and he grabs my hand, squeezing it gently.

I squeeze back before sliding my hand from underneath. I wish I hadn't agreed to come. If I'd stayed at home there would have been no need for this awkwardness. We don't know each other and this playing at happy families is only going to result in pain for both of us. He's desperate for me to remember him. I'm just desperate to remember anything, anything at all and my mind pings back to the one word that actually means anything.

'My mother?'

He looks haunted suddenly. It's as if I've asked about the one thing in the world he's not prepared to answer. I try searching his face for clues, but he's buried his head in the menu; avoiding my stare. When the waitress halts beside our table I can almost see his shoulders shift in relief at the interruption as he fires out our order in rapid Dutch.

'I hope you're hungry. I've ordered soup and bread,' he throws me a wink. 'And coffee and cake for afters.'

'Manus, I'm not going to be diverted. Tell me.'

He shakes his head but he can't shake me off. I'm intransient now, like a dog with a bone as I throw a glance at Nigel, snoozing under the table. Turning back. I grab his hand between mine. It's the first time I've touched him of my own accord but I'm not interested in that now. I'm not interested in the way his eyes shift from my face to our entwined hands and back again or the strength that lies under my fingers. This is not a man to battle with but I'm not giving up.

Our meal arrives, the waitress standing by the table as she glances down at our hands, her meaning clear. With mine back on my lap she places a steaming plate of the greenest soup I've ever seen in front of me along with a basket piled with rolls and butter. But I'm not interested in the soup. I push the bowl to one side and place my elbows on the table. I'm not interested in anything except the answer to my question.

He lifts his spoon but, instead of raising it to his lips, he rests it against the side of his bowl with a sigh.

'You need to eat. To build your strength up,' he says, pushing my bowl towards me. 'I'll tell you everything but only after you've finished every drop.' He leans forward and grabs my chin briefly, tilting my head so that our eyes clash. 'Please *liefje*, just for me?'

The soup is delicious, not that I taste much after that first spoonful. But I'm aware that I'm not going to get anything out of him unless I finish it.

The metal finally clatters against the empty bowl as the last of the soup settles like a lead weight. I'll probably throw up on the way back, not that he'll care. This is a strong man, a man used to getting his own way, a man that is withholding something I have a right to know.

His bowl is empty and just like me he rests his spoon against the rim before pushing it away and resting his elbows on the table, his face a smooth mask.

'You seem to think I know everything about you but that's not the case.' He manages a smile. 'We hadn't known each other that long and talking about our families was the very last thing on our minds, as you can probably imagine,' his eyes brushing mine before wandering to my lips and back. 'The last thing in the world I want is for you to be upset but I gather that you're going to hold me to the promise I made?'

I nod my head. He's the psychiatrist here. I know that he's using his skill in that department to warn me. He's firing a warning shot across my bough to alert me to the fact that I'm not going to like what he's about to say. I'm not going to like it one little bit. But I won't back away. I need to know; I need to know it all. I stay silent and wait, my gaze unwavering.

'Your mother is in a care home back in Guernsey, a dementia care home. She's been suffering from the illness now for some years.' He spreads his hands and I know that's all he's going to tell me. It's enough!

The waitress arrives with our coffees and a plate of the largest, creamiest cakes - I'm beginning to think he knows me better than I know myself because, with another spurt of Dutch she takes the plate away only to reappear moments later with a square confectionary box tied with pink ribbon.

'We can have them later,' he says, but I'm not listening.

I play with my ring, twisting it round and round, the feel of the metal foreign against my skin. It looks right, there against the pallor of my hands. It looks right when everything else in my world is wrong.

No stepsister and a mother that's ill; a mother that won't be able to help me. A mother that won't even have realised I'm gone. It's all too much, too soon. I dig in my pockets for the tissue I know won't be there.

'Here,' he hands me a napkin. 'Have a sip of that coffee to perk you up before we make our way back.'

'I'm sorry. I shouldn't have pressed you.' I manage, gulping air back into my lungs.

'No you shouldn't,' he interrupts, smoothing my hair from my forehead. 'But I would have had to tell you sometime. How about we head back and you phone the care home to find out how she is?'

That the perfect day should end up with two almost strangers walking towards the tram in silence is a bit of a let-down for both of us but, after the coffee, the truth is we'd simply run out of things to say. I'm too wrapped up in my own thoughts to worry about what he's thinking. The only happy note is Nigel, tootling along beside us with his tail wagging and his tongue hanging out.

The sun has already dipped behind the rooftops when the tram drops us off in the centre of The Hague. I swallow any questions about why we're here. He'll tell me when he's ready.

The streets, bordering the market, are a hive of activity with shoppers' toing and froing from one brightly lit window display to the next. He's tucked my hand within his and I decide to leave it there. It's comforting the way he gives my fingers a little squeeze every few minutes.

He's stopped outside a large department store, the windows full of women's fashions and I have to stop too as he's still in possession of my hand.

'I thought now would be a good time to expand your wardrobe.'

'There's really no need,' I interrupt. 'I have plenty of clothes.'

But he just stares down at me, not taking no for an answer. 'Come on, we have half an hour so let's see what damage you can do to my credit card in that time. That's an offer no woman can refuse,' he finishes on a laugh, propelling me into the shop and towards the escalator.

'Don't I have money?' I say, tugging at his arm and forcing him to stop.

But the look in his eyes says it all.

'Gone, I'm afraid, along with your bag but I've stopped all your cards.' He lifts his hands, cradling my head between his fingers before dropping a kiss on my nose. 'Don't look at me like that, little one,' his fingers brushing against my cheeks. 'I'm not short of money and I'm more than happy for you to spend it.'

What a statement, a statement that fills me with dread. I'm already too dependent on this man. I'm dependant on him for everything from food, information and even money. How am I ever going to repay him? How am I ever going to escape him when escaping seems like the stupidest of ideas? Why would I even want to?

The *De Bijenkorf* store has everything a woman could ever want, and I'm soon accosted by a sales assistant while Manus settles into a chair and takes out his phone. I throw him a glance, wondering who he's calling but, with my arms full of jeans and jumpers, I soon forget everything except the pleasure of trying on a selection of outfits. I'm determined above all else not to spend too much. He obviously thinks all women are spendthrifts but I'm the one woman to prove him wrong. I narrow it down to a pair of jeans and trousers and a couple of casual t-shirts and thick jumpers before adding warm pyjamas and lacy underwear at the last minute; the functionality of the first cancelling out the reasoning behind the second. There's also a pair of wellington boots for those late evening walks with Nigel and a smattering of make-up. I don't think I'm a great one for lipstick and the like if the sight of my depleted-looking make-up bag is anything to go by but a good face and hand cream is a must.

I flick a glance over my shoulder but he's still engrossed in his call. I wander across to the perfume counter while I'm waiting for him to finish and, with a few sprays and the sales assistant's help, we finally agree that the lingering scent on the scarf is one of Calvin Klein's more popular fragrances, Eternity.

I feel a presence by my side and tilting my head, look up at him. The frown is back although his words belie his mood.

'All done? They're closing in a few minutes. Did you want that?' his eyes on my hand and the bottle of perfume I'm still holding.

'No…really…'

But he just takes it off me and hands it over to the beaming assistant with a smile. She gets a smile and I get a frown, in addition to a whole new wardrobe as I notice the handbag and wallet he throws in at the last minute.

'There's no point staring at me like that. I know all about women and their relationship with the handbag. I'm only surprised it wasn't first on your list.'

'Yes, but—' My gaze follows the shop assistant as she lovingly places the Gucci bag in its own dust case. I decide to close my mouth and pick up my pride that seems to have dropped to my boots. I'll make it up to him this evening but probably not in the way he expects. He's going the wrong way about it if he thinks I'll ever be that grateful, my thoughts flitting to the two steaks resting in the fridge.

Chapter Eighteen

'Here,' he passes me the phone before sitting in his chair and picking up one of the medical journals, his reading glasses perched on the end of his nose.

I stare at the receiver for a moment before common sense kicks in.

'Hello, this is Marilyn Marsh's daughter. Can you tell me how she is, please?'

'If you could hold on a minute and I'll go and get the matron. She'd like a word.'

I frown at the phone while I wait to be connected.

'Mrs Le Maitre here.'

'Yes, hello. I'm enquiring about my mother, Marilyn Marsh.'

'And I'm enquiring about when you're going to pay her bill. That last top-up fee from the bank was never paid, which means your mother is now nearly two months in arrears.'

'Excuse me, I don't understand—?' I glance across the room only to find that Manus has lowered the journal, his eyes now tracing mine.

'Well, understand this. If you don't pay up within seven days your mother will be out on her ear.'

'But you can't do that. Where will she go?'

'That's not my problem, now, is it? You should have thought of that before you—'

But I never get to hear the rest of the sentence. Manus is gently prising the phone from my grasp, his palm covering the mouthpiece for a second.

'Why don't you go and put the kettle on and leave me to deal with this?'

I don't leave the room like he intends. Instead I hover by the door while I hear him placate that awful woman. I don't remember my mum, I don't remember any of it. But the one thing I do know is I don't want that horrible woman anywhere near her. I'll have to move her. I'll have to move her without any knowledge, means or money to do so.

He's writing something down on the notepad next to the phone, I don't know what. The conversation is ending on a very different note to the one it started on.

'How could you be nice to her? She said she'd...'

'It's alright. Don't upset yourself,' he interrupts. 'You know you're not to get upset.' He joins me at the door, his hands cradling my shoulders even as he pulls me onto his chest and starts stroking my hair like a child. I'm aware of the softness of his jumper against my cheek and the steady thump of his heart under my ear as he continues speaking. 'Your mother being well is the main thing, surely?'

'That woman said I owe her thousands?'

'Shush now. There's no need to worry about that. I'll transfer some money and you can pay me back sometime.'

'But what if I can't? What if I don't have it?' my voice laced with anxiety.

'You're getting all worked up over nothing.' He pushes me back gently, wiping away my tears with the pads of his thumbs. 'It's only money after all, and you are my wife - for better or worse. Now, go and pop the kettle on and after, we'll go out with Nigel. I think a breath of fresh air will help us sleep and it will be an opportunity for you to try out those new boots.'

You think that life can't get any worse and then it does. How much more am I expected to put up with and just how beholden am I going to end up? I allow myself the luxury of examining him, as he crouches down to attach Nigel's lead. There are grey hairs amongst the dark brown, only a smattering and probably only since he's met me. He has broad shoulders, rugby-playing wide but he'll need them if he intends to stay with this sinking ship.

I'm a good sort of person, I know I am. Okay, so I don't know the ins and outs but I know I'd never intentionally do anyone any harm and that I'd probably give my last pound if someone needed it more. But what about honour and integrity? Did

I walk away from Guernsey because it was all going pear-shaped, leaving my mother with unpaid bills and the threat of eviction? Is that the reason I was attracted to this man, because of his money? He's not stupid, far from it. If I married him for his money he'll know it.

He lifts his head and smiles and I manage a sort of smile in return.

'Come on, it looks like rain and when we get back, what about a nightcap? It's Sunday tomorrow so no need to rush anywhere. I've asked for an English newspaper to be delivered along with the usual *De Telegraaf.*'

He gathers up my hand and, with Nigel dragging on his lead, we head in unison towards the bridge and to the other side of the canal. We're just like any other normal married couple, although there's nothing normal about our relationship.

It's cold, my breath cloud grey as it streams from my lips to mingle and disperse into the distance. There's no one about and the canal is still, without even a ripple to break the surface. We stop and lean against the railings, our hands only inches apart, while Nigel tries to make up his mind as to the best place to sniff. I want to shift my hand, to curl my fingers into his but I don't. I can't. I'd need to know what he's thinking and that expression isn't giving anything away. I suppose he's learnt the art of masking his expression in his job, something that's filtered into his private life.

I'm diverted by thoughts of his private life. I don't think I'm very good at guessing ages, the best I can come up with is anywhere between thirty and forty. So, what is an extremely eligible man, of unknown age, doing being single?

'How old are you?' The words are out and there's no way of recalling them. I'm pleased it's dark; he won't be able to see my face turn a fine shade of beetroot pink.

'Thirty-nine.' I can hear the smile in his voice, so I decide to continue.

'And how old am I?'

He laughs, lifting his hand from the railing and draping it across my shoulders before pulling me into a deep hug. 'Twenty-nine. What's with the questions all of a sudden?'

'I'd just like to know. Tell me about you, about the man I married? Are you, were you married before? Children? Parents? I'm at a distinct disadvantage in this relationship as you know all the answers.'

'There's no need to feel like that. I'll soon get you up to speed.' He moves away from the railings and we carry on walking to the end of the road before turning back towards the canal while he tells me all his secrets.

Despite everything before and after I can pinpoint this short time, a span of minutes, as the happiest so far.

The air remains bitter, the pitch night offering little protection from its chilly fingers snaking between the layers. But, with his arm heavy about my shoulders and his voice mumbling beside me, a wealth of calm dispels all unpleasant thoughts. And with the happiness comes a sense of hope. We'll find Victoria together and continue living happily ever after.

I can't even remember his words, not exactly. He'd had girlfriends, one particular one in med school who'd gone on to marry his best-friend and after that he'd turned to his work, progressing up that proverbial ladder at break-neck speed. Until the day he'd first met me, he was all set on remaining a bachelor but it only took one look for his house of cards to crash around his ears. I don't remember his words but I remember the look on his face when he said them. A look that gives me hope.

We're standing on the bridge, his arm still on my shoulders as we stare across at the house, our house. The living room lights are just visible through the heavy curtains and a lingering sense of happiness makes me lift up my hand and brush it over his cheek, his skin rasping under my fingers.

'You need a shave.' I laugh up at him and catch his look and the world, silent before, explodes in a rush as my heart speeds up.

Do I want him to kiss me again? There, the thought is out in the open and deserves some consideration. It's still not too late to move my head, to lower my hand and allow my gaze to wander over his shoulder. It's still not too late for my attention to shift even as I feel his arms dragging me close. The truth is that I want to feel his lips on mine more than anything. But the trembling feeling building under my diaphragm isn't enough. Sex isn't enough. I need to trust him and there's still that sliver of doubt stopping me.

A light catches my eye, a light where before there was none and I have no need to force myself away - the brittle cord of feeling snaps.

I pull back, my attention now on the house opposite, the house next to ours. He'd said it was empty. He'd said... I squeeze my eyes tight, trying to remember. He'd said she'd disappeared. It was as if she'd never been. But the light? I'm not one-hundred-percent sure but as sure as I can be that there is a light now where before there was none.

'What is it, *liefje*? What's wrong?'

I chew on my lip, trying to gather my thoughts. I don't know what to think about any of it, my attention shifting back to him and the worried pull of his brow. It all comes back to trust. Can I trust him and if not, just who the hell can I turn to?

But I don't have to make a decision one way or the other. His focus shifts from me and to where the light is streaming out from the room at the top of the house.

He thinks he's going to get away with leaving me next door. He thinks I'm going to accept being dropped off like a parcel, some excuse or other on his lips.

It's too dangerous. There could be burglars. Or your stepsister might still be living next door and I've been lying to you all this time…

I know my mind is taking my thoughts on a journey, a roundabout journey of half-truths and lies mixed up into some sort of pseudo-reality but I can't seem to stop myself. By the time we've reached the front door I've convinced myself into believing that he's married the wrong sister and has Victoria shacked up in a little love nest made for two. How convenient for me to lose my memory or did I perhaps catch them in some unsavoury act? Is that what this is all about – pure un-adulterated lust?

'Try and be sensible,' he pleads. 'You're still not fully recovered.'

But I ignore him, my grip tight against Nigel's lead. I'm going into the house to see for myself just what he's been hiding and there's nothing he can do to stop me.

'Oh, very well, please yourself but don't say I didn't warn you. Just, for heaven's sake, be careful and don't go anywhere near the cellar, the stairs aren't safe.'

I nod my head but that's all he's getting until this little mystery is solved.

He produces a key and inserts it into the lock; all a little too convenient for my liking. I resolve to ask him where he's gotten it from, but the thought evaporates at the sight that greets us.

Chapter Nineteen

The house has been ransacked, or has it always been like this? Was the house we'd inherited some drug den scattered with newspaper, ripped up furnishings and other detritus? No, surely not as I bend to pick up a beautiful mahogany hall table from where it's been thrown across the hall floor like a discarded banana skin.

'No, don't touch it. Don't touch anything,' he says, his hand pulling me back.

I shoot him a look but he's right. Of course he is. If this is a crime scene then they'll want to look for finger prints. I step back and drop my hand, my fingers curling through his briefly before bending down and scooping up a disgruntled Nigel.

But the house hasn't just been ransacked. Its heart has been ripped out. We drift from room to room, careful where we step. Manus pulls out his phone and fires out orders to whoever picks up - presumably the police but I really have no idea who he's speaking to or what he's saying. That thought merges with all the others. I should start learning the language if I'm ever going to make a go of it in Holland, if I'm ever going to make a go of it with him.

I move away while he inspects the kitchen and where not even a dish, plate or glass has been spared. There's more to this than just mindless vandalism, my gaze on a cracked cut-glass goblet. Surely a thief would want to be in and out and not risk getting caught instead of wasting time on wrecking the place? I wander along the hall and into the study, Manus's footsteps hurrying to join me, not that there's anything he can do – the damage has been done and by a vicious hand. There was no need to tear every book apart, trampling the pages underfoot. Not a book is left on the shelves, not a drawer intact. It's as if someone has ripped the desk apart with bare hands and some kind of hatchet as I scrape the toe of my boot against one of the wood splinters littering the floor.

We continue in silence as we delve further into the house, stepping over the piles of carpet where the runner has been yanked from the treads. The second floor is no better with mattresses upturned and slit from side to side. The pillows have had the same treatment while the wardrobes and chest of drawers are now only fit for a bonfire. I hug Nigel to my chest, rubbing my cheek against his fur, my gaze flicking to the silent man by my side. His expression is unreadable but there's a whiteness about his jawline and lips that tells me, without the need for words, that he's furiously angry.

It's only then that I remember my stepsister. She stayed in this house. What was it Manus had said? I scrunch my eyes closed, struggling to remember.

Something about there being no trace of her when he'd checked the property on his return. I throw him another glance, less certain now about his current mood. Perhaps he's not angry at all. Perhaps he's slipped back under his bland mask in order to hide his true feelings. What a perfect way to hide any evidence of her disappearance.

I follow him into the room at the top of the stairs, less certain now. Did he orchestrate this? The day away? Pausing on the bridge long enough for my attention to be drawn to the light? I stare at his back and realisation hits. I don't know anything about the man I married, not really. Am I in danger? Where the hell is Victoria?

The last room is the worst of all. He'd said the owner was an artist of sorts, a picture restorer but obviously not anymore as my eyes scroll from surface to surface. There's nothing here that hasn't been destroyed and desecrated; an old man's life's work shredded with no thought or feeling.

'Come on.' I feel the weight of his arm on my shoulder. 'The police should be here in a minute.'

'You've reported it—?'

He stops at the top of the stairs, the frown back and he drops his hand to his side.

'Now, just where is that mind of yours taking you, hmm? Why wouldn't I report it?'

The heat builds in my cheeks under his gaze but I don't drop my eyes. Whilst he might be my husband on paper I don't have to answer his questions. To my mind, the facts just don't add up. It's all a bit too convenient that the house next door is trashed on the same day he decides to take me out. We share a party wall, after all and furniture smashing isn't the quietest of occupations. I suddenly remember the shop and his phone call, the call that seemed to go on and on. He could have been instructing the thug where to look... I frown at the thought. I was wrong in thinking that the house had been ransacked. It's been searched.

The ringing of the doorbell breaks the silence and with a final fulminating look in my direction he hurries down the stairs to the front door.

Sunday; a day of rest or, in most households, a day to catch up on all those annoying little chores like the washing and the ironing. But with the indomitable Lize due back the day after tomorrow, there's little to do apart from walk Nigel and drift round the house trying to avoid him. Oh, he's in a mood alright. The mood was there when he dropped me in an early morning cup of tea. It lingered all through breakfast and well past morning coffee. It stretched past lunch and threatens the afternoon. There's no conversation apart from an icily polite, please and thank you. There's no expression, no smile except that bland stare, which seems to be the countenance of choice. I've had enough by three o'clock and, with Nigel huddled under my coat, I sneak out for a walk by the canal; anything is better than sitting in the lounge with nothing to do and nobody to do it with.

I'm not welcome today or any day, not if my opinion doesn't match his. Well, I have news for him. Just because I have a memory to rival that of a goldfish doesn't mean that I don't have my own thoughts. I'm as sure as I can be that there's something fishy going on. It's all too convenient us meeting and falling in love. What was his plan, for all three of us to live next door to each other like one big happy family?

I stop on the bridge and stare out across the water and to our two homes; standing side by side. I know I've made a mistake in coming to Holland, probably the biggest mistake of all. My hand finds my forehead, my fingers digging into my skin as a headache builds, the first one since my discharge from hospital and suddenly I'm reminded of his advice about the need to rest. He's right; of course he is, but only in this. I'll go back to the house and shut the door in very much the same way he's shut me out. It didn't last long, our wonderful relationship. No longer than the first argument and there hasn't even been a cross word; only a difference of opinion.

Reaching the bed I throw myself on top with no thought of anything other than pain-free sleep. But sleep doesn't come easily. There's comfort and warmth only a breath away but my overactive imagination continues its wearisome thoughts as questions build, questions I should be writing down but I can't see though the pain. My mother, my stepsister, him. What is the truth and who's lying?

It's evening now, the light from the streetlamp a dim mist streaming through the blind. I remain still, easing air through my lips as I realise I'm not alone. There's a shadow beside me, an unmoving presence that's probably watching and waiting for me to make the first move. My eyes flicker closed and I aim to regulate my breathing. In-out-in-out-in…

'Ah, good. You're awake.'

The bed shifts, his hand stroking mine; the touch gentle, reassuring, confusing. I roll on my back and stare into the face of this stranger, this stranger that I'm beginning to depend on for everything. The thought strengthens. I can't remember a life before Manus. But I also can't imagine a life without him. How would I manage? Is this needy relationship what I want? Is it what he demands?

He squeezes my hand, a mannerism I'm growing to like, to look forward to. He bends his head, brushing his lips against mine. There's no pressure like yesterday on the beach. There's no intrusion, just warmth and breath next to my mouth before he leans back, cradling my face within his palm. With my heart racing in my chest, I can sort of see why I married him. The question of why he married me is something that lingers unanswered – unanswerable.

'I've been sitting here feeling ashamed of my behaviour especially in light of all that's happened. I of all people should know better. My only excuse is that I've been a bachelor too long, far too long. I've forgotten what it's like to have another person around, to have someone else to care for,' his expression rueful.

He stands, his eyes lingering on my face before turning to the door. 'Come on, the police will be back at first light and I've tried my best to make you one of those roast dinners your country folk are so keen on, although my culinary skills don't quite stretch to homemade apple pie.'

'Do they have any idea about what happened?'

I'm leaning against the kitchen worktop, sipping on the glass of wine he's just poured while he carves the chicken with the expertise of a master butcher.

He pauses briefly, the knife hovering over the breast before continuing to slice, his eyes now focused on the task to the exclusion of all else.

'They're not sure. That's why they want to visit tomorrow.'

'Why?'

He glances up but only for a second. 'They didn't believe me when I told them you'd lost your memory. Whilst I may be a respected member of the local community. I'm also your husband and they're a suspicious lot.'

'I can't believe that.'

'What? That I'm a respected member of the community or that they're a suspicious lot?' His eyes twinkle. 'Believe me when I say they gave me a grilling. They even wanted to check that we were both who I said we were. And when I couldn't produce your passport I thought they were going to arrest me for harbouring an illegal immigrant.'

I manage a laugh despite a new train of thought pushing in from the edges - no passport. If I don't have a passport then I have no means of escape. I take a sip of wine before placing the glass back down on the counter, careful to push it away from the edge. I'll be stuck in a foreign country with no money and no Dutch, not to mention no family or friends to turn to, now my stepsister is missing. No, apart from this man, currently piling my plate with a cooked dinner I'm going to struggle to eat,

I'm truly alone. But am I really thinking of escaping all this? My gaze focuses on the engraved wine glass and the pale yellow, liquid settling to stillness, before shifting to the impressive bottle of vintage wine that tastes as good as it must have cost. No, the lifestyle is fine, more than fine – it's him and the nagging feeling that he's not being entirely truthful. There's just something about him that doesn't add up.

He carries on speaking. 'They were interested in hearing more about your stepsister. It seems as if they're taking her disappearance more seriously. But I couldn't tell them much. I hardly knew her, after all. I'm afraid they're going to want to speak to you about it tomorrow, amongst other things,' his eyes flicking briefly to my wrists. 'They wouldn't take my word for it. In fact, I seem to be *persona non grata* as far as the police are concerned.' He grabs both glasses and places them on the table before reaching for the plates.

'Come on; let's eat before it gets cold.'

I manage to eat a little. I don't have much choice under his searing gaze. With the washing-up cleared, we return to the lounge with a tray of coffee. He busies himself with catching up on his reading while I stroke Nigel and watch the flames dance across the logs. And despite everything that's gone before, it's peaceful. I empty my head of all thought and drift into a somnolent state where the past and future don't matter. I feel both safe and warm. It's as if my mind, too full of everything it's taken on board the last few days, has finally decided to shut down completely. I don't notice that he's stopped reading or that he too is staring, but not at the fire. I'm lost in my own world, oblivious to everything, even him as my breathing regulates and my eyelids droop. I would have drifted off if he hadn't bent over me and scooped me up in his arms. But now I'm wide awake, awake and annoyed.

'Hey, what are you doing? Put me down this instant.'

'Shush. I'm not doing anything,' he says, shifting my weight in his arms so that my head finds that nest just under his shoulder blade, his cashmere jumper smooth under my cheek, the subtle trace of aftershave a lingering presence. 'It's after midnight so bed for you,' his voice rumbling next to my ear.

'But I'm far too heavy.'

He breaks into laughter, squeezing me tighter to his chest as he heads for the stairs. 'There's nothing to you. You don't eat enough to keep a sparrow alive. In fact, that's a good name for you.'

'I have a perfectly good name as it is.'

He pauses briefly. 'Yes, you do but you do remind me of a little sparrow with your abundance of brown hair and a gaze that can sharpen pencils at sixty paces.'

'Why did you marry me then if you think I'm bad-tempered?'

'Did I say that?' he pushes the bedroom door open before placing me gently on the bed, his eyes pinned to my face, my hair, my mouth.

The world stops but only for a second before his mask slips back and he's retreating out of the room with barely a glance, a brief 'sleep well' on his lips before the door closes with a soft click.

'Well, what was that all about, Nige? Is it me or has my husband just done a runner?' But Nigel's having none of it. He's far too busy chasing his tail round and round in circles before flopping beside me.

'I think I'll join you,' I mutter, a yawn adding weight to my words. But, when I snuggle under the duvet, sleep decides to evade me. If I'd stayed on the sofa I'd be asleep by now. Annoyance joins frustration at my inability to slip into oblivion. I thump my pillow for what must be the twentieth time and give it five more minutes as I try to empty my mind of everything except sheep jumping over canals. One. Two. Three. Four.

Chapter Twenty

I awake with a start.

Something's woken me but what? It's cold, so cold as a shiver chases across my skin and my teeth begin to chatter. There's a noise in the background…was it the sound that woke me? There it is again, the relentless drip, drip, drip.

I don't know how long I lie there, listening to that drip, while I try to drag back under my lids, but I can't. Reason dictates that I must have left a tap on – the tap in the bathroom. But reason hasn't a clue. Reason has gone mad. There's a door between the bathroom and my bed, a door I distinctly remember shutting just in case Nigel went walkabouts.

All this thought of water on top of last night's wine and brandy sets up another chain of thought as I run the tip of my tongue over parched-dry lips. I need water and a pee. But still I lie there, suddenly unsure…unsure of everything. I strain my ears for that other sound, the sound as comforting as it is familiar but there's nothing, only the drip. No heavy breathing, no little snuffles, no Nigel.

Fear is a wasted emotion that sets the pulses alight and whips air from the lungs – it's a wasted, irrational emotion for someone like me, for someone with no memory. And yet I'm afraid, possibly more afraid than I've ever been. I know I went to bed in my pyjamas, the new turquoise and cream striped ones with tiny mother-of-pearl buttons. I remember how difficult they were to fasten and that I'd given up after about three.

My breath follows my heart and catches in my throat as I bring to the forefront the thing that's worrying me the most. I'm not in my bed. I'm not in any bed. I'm lying. No. I'm not even lying. I'm half-slumped against a wall, a wall as hard as rock. There are no pyjamas, as soft as silk brushing against my skin. There is fabric but it's wet; wet and digging into my flesh.

The truth of the matter is I don't know where I am or what's happening as my heart picks up a pace and blood rushes to my ears. I still have my eyes shut. In fact, it would take quite a lot to prise them open but open them I must. I have to…I have to know where I am and what's going on even as my thoughts swing to Manus. Is he here? Dare I call out his name? Do I trust him?

Air eases past my lips and I gear myself up for the big reveal. I can do this. After all, it's only opening my eyes a little, just a slit so I can see where I am. So I can see who I'm with — so I can see who's done this to me.

It's black, completely pitch. There's not a sound except for the relentless drip and there's nothing to see except complete darkness. I open my eyes wide, terrified, a new thought rivalling that of the drip. Where is the shade, the colours of grey? Where is the light filtering under the door, through the keyhole, at the edge of the window? There's always light even when it's dark. But, with my eyes fully open, all I'm seeing is black. I'm either in a box or underground somewhere or…I'm blind.

There's panic now, wild panic as my heart explodes and breath leaves my body. I have to get away even though I'm unable to see. I must escape and that's when I realise that I can't. I can't get away, I can't move. My arms and legs are stretched out and strapped.

There's a noise at my side. A rasp of shoe against stone and I know I'm not alone.

'Good. You're awake.'

The darkness fades and light creeps in from the edges. The drip dries up and even as I wait, breath held, the next drip never comes. But there are other noises to replace it; a snore, a scratch, a snort – Nigel. I let air escape again while I wait for my heart to settle back within my chest. Other things are different. Soft replaces hard, Dry replaces wet…and where I was frightened before now I'm petrified.

I leap out of bed and switch on the light. My eyes find my ankles, my wrists and my fingers follow; massaging, rubbing, kneading. But the bruises have faded, leaving only a pale trace of memory. There's no pain, no nothing except a relentless thirst. I head to the bathroom and start scooping up water into my palm, not worrying that it's trickling down my neck and spilling onto my top. I'm home; I'm in his home – Manus, my husband. It was a dream, a nightmare. I frown. It was none of those things. It was a memory.

Grabbing the towel, I make a half-hearted attempt to dry my neck. I'd been hoping for this day like no other. In truth, I'd been hoping ever since I'd realised that instead of a past I had a ruddy great gap larger than a Swiss cheese. I want... No. I need other memories, happy memories: my first day at school, my first kiss, what I spent my first wage packet on. I need the small little fragments of life that go to make up a person instead of an empty shell. But life is never simple, certainly not mine.

I perch on the edge of the bath and worry attacks me from all sides. I have clues now, but no way of making any sense of them. There's the place I was in, a cold damp place but that's all I know. I'd hazard a guess that it's underground, it had that sort of feel about it: a misused tunnel, a mineshaft, a crypt even. Someone dragged me to that dank place before shackling me to the floor and...

Suddenly I'm racing to the toilet and heaving up the remains of my supper, waves of stomach cramps hitting like a storm surge. After, I sit in front of the bowl and feel tears press, but I sniff them back and crawl to my feet before heading to the sink and my toothbrush.

The mirror tells me what I don't want to know. A wild-eyed ghost woman stares back, a wild-eyed ghost of the woman I once was. He's done this to me, only him and I can't even recognise his voice, only his words. I could be next to him and I'd still be none the wiser. And the worst thing about it? I can still only remember a snapshot – I still don't know what comes next. I still don't know what he's done with Victoria, if anything. The thought sets up another set of shivers but this time it's nothing to do with the cold. I wander back into the bedroom. The bed looks a mess, pillows on the floor and the duvet in the biggest tangle imaginable, which reinforces that it was a dream, and a bloody awful one at that.

The clock beside the bed heads for three. I wasn't tired before but now, at the sight of the clock, a wave of fatigue envelops me. But, the stark truth is I know I'll never be able to sleep with thoughts of the dark, the drip and the man storming my mind.

The door beckons and the landing beyond. I'll make a hot drink and take it into the lounge. The lingering warmth from the fire might just be the thing to filter through the wall of ice that seems to have layered across my skin.

I hesitate, paused on the threshold, one hand on the light switch. The landing is dark, not as dark as my dream but dark enough to set my pulses racing afresh. I squint, struggling to make out the shape of the tallboy with the priceless looking Chinese vase set in the middle but it's useless. And if I can't make that out how am I meant to make out other things like the top of the stairs? All is silent. His door is closed. Unless he's awake and standing with his eye pushed to the keyhole he won't even know I've...

'Can't sleep either?'

He's appeared in front of me out of nowhere. One second, I'm facing his room and the next...I can't take it, I can't take any of it. Where before I'd managed to hold back the tears now they stream in a torrent and my knees buckle. But I don't land in a heap on the floor. Instead of carpet there's warmth and the light smell of soap as he cradles me against his chest, his hands warm against my back.

I don't know how long we stay like that. My tears subside into a trickle before drying up altogether but still he holds onto me and I let him. It's comforting. It's safe. For the first time he feels safe.

'There now, what was that all about, hmm?' He leans back slightly, one hand still on my back, the other tilting my chin so that he can stare into my face while gently wiping away my tears. 'You're as white as a sheet and trembling too,' and he hugs me even tighter.

I find I'm trapped under his gaze and all sensible thought flies out of the window, all thought except just one. Do I trust him? The answer evades me still. I'd like to, I really would. He makes me feel safe. I'd even go so far as to say he makes me feel loved but trust is a different emotion altogether. There are still too many question marks surrounding his behaviour to make that sentiment come easily.

'I...I...had a dream, a nightmare,' a sort of truth if not the whole one. 'I'm sorry for disturbing you.'

'Don't be silly, *liefje*. You couldn't disturb me if you tried. Come on, let's get you back to bed and I'll make you a warm—'

'No, really. I'm fine,' my eyes flitting to the door and the one room I can't bear to be in at the moment. 'I'll just sit in the lounge for a bit.'

'Now, you really are worrying me.' He searches my face. 'Something about your room?' he asks unexpectedly and I know that it's impossible for me to hide anything from this man. For some reason I'm an open book, a salutary lesson and one I can't do anything about at the moment except perhaps file for future reference. He raises an eyebrow, presumably waiting for me to reply but I just shake my head. He sees too much. He knows too much. Any words I say he'll know to be false and I'm certainly not prepared to tell him the truth.

His finger traces along my cheek briefly and, before I know it he's shouted to Nigel and lifted me up in a repeat of earlier.

'Hey, I can walk.'

'I know. But I'm tired, sweetheart, and if the only way I can get some sleep is for you to be in the same room as me, then so be it.'

Within moments he's placed me on the edge of the bed, his bed – a bed that doesn't even have a wrinkle or a crease. He picks up Nigel and with a pat to his back heads to the door. 'Will warm milk do?' and he's gone without waiting for an answer.

I pummel the pillow with a sharp fist. It would serve him right if I went back to my own room. No. I can't do that, not now with my brain still reeling from those images, from all that dark. So I prop myself up against the headboard, with the duvet pulled up to my chin like the shy virgin I'm pretty sure I'm not. I'll sleep in his room but that's all.

Chapter Twenty One

The dream intrudes again or is it reality? I can't be sure. Soft has again been replaced by hard and warmth by cold but now it's different. Now there's pain.

I can't see him, I can't see anything but I know he's beside me, leaning across my body, his breath warm on my cheek. I try to remain still but obviously not still enough as the next thing I feel is the sting of his open hand as he slaps me across the face.

'Where is it, bitch? You'll tell me if I have to prise it out of you with a wrench.'

He's grabbing my shoulders, jarring my head backwards and forwards like a puppet even as the ties binding my wrists bite into my flesh; searing, grinding, twisting. It's clear now, perfectly clear. Somehow I'm back; I'm back in the same dream I was before.

'I...I...stop, please stop.' The words dragged from my lips. 'Tell me what you want.'

'I want what's mine. I deserve it.' He forces a bottle against my lips, spilling liquid down my throat with a heavy hand. 'I'll make you drink the lot if you don't tell me where it is. I have to have it.'

'What? What do you have to have?'

'How many times do I have to tell you or are you as stupid as your sister?'

His hands are now about my throat, squeezing tight but, despite the distance of only a couple of centimetres, I'm still surrounded by dark. I can't see. I can't see him but I can smell. I can smell the fear building up beyond the wall of black, the odour of sweat mingled with the pervading air of damp. He's afraid, this man, petrified even. I have to play it cool or it's the end. There has to be some way for me to escape and, even as the thought filters, my fingers feel the outline of the bottle he's discarded. It's cold under my touch, cold and hard. The thought of using a broken shard of glass scares me but I'll do anything to get away. With a wriggle I've shifted it into my side - I hope he doesn't notice.

'My stepsister must know. Why don't you ask her?'

'You don't ask the questions, my pretty,' his voice softening to a whisper, his fingers starting to crawl over my neck with a relentless determination. 'You don't get to do anything other than tell me where it is and after—I might just let you go.

The scream is still in my throat as I stare into the eyes of a stranger. No, not a stranger. Manus.

Did he rescue me? It feels as if he's rescued me. I collapse against his shoulder, breath gasping into my lungs. I'm safe. I'm safe here with him, only him as his arms pull me closer and I return the hug. I'm back in bed, his bed but I don't care about that as I squeeze him tight. All I care about is being out of that place. All I want is to stay here wrapped in his arms where it's safe. No. I want more than that now. I want to feel something different to being afraid. I want to feel loved.

There's a dull flickering light from his alarm clock and the restful sound of Nigel lying at the end of the bed. Finally I feel my limbs relax into the comfort and security of the mattress as Manus shifts his arm to tuck the duvet back before dropping a kiss against my cheek. Or, at least, that's his plan, a plan I decide to scupper. I twist my head in time to capture his lips.

I need more from him now than a brief hug and an even briefer kiss as he tries to break away. I've been starved of affection for too long. We're married and yet he's been avoiding me, I know he has. It's as if I'm a threat and I want to know why. Maybe he's decided he doesn't want to be married to a mad woman but I'm not mad, not really. Or perhaps it's simply that he doesn't love me enough. He could have made the biggest mistake of his life when he proposed and I accepted. After all, we hadn't known each other more than five minutes before tying the knot; a knot that seems to be unravelling at break-neck speed.

I frame his face with my hands, defying him to break away, his skin warm against my fingers. We stare at each other for a moment, a message hidden within his gaze that I choose to ignore. Pushing him back against the pillows I roll on top, my knees clenched around his waist as I continue my inspection of his lips. He responds just like I knew he would but something's missing. While his mouth is participating his hands are just lying by his side and I know he's placed a band of steel over his emotions. For some reason, best known to him, he's forcing himself not to join in with anything other than his lips.

No woman likes to be ignored, certainly not at a time like this when she's literally throwing herself at her man. I have no pride, no shame, no self-respect. No, I lost all of those things when someone drugged me, tied me up and did goodness only knows what else to make me lose my memory. But this ends here. I won't be ignored. I won't be ignored by someone that's meant to love me above all others.

I break the seal, my eyes scanning his face, a face I'm learning to recognise as well as my own; the colour of his eyes, the shape of his mouth, the angle of his jawline, the way his hair sits across his forehead. I'm even getting to know his expressions and the bland one is back. Well, we'll see about that as I start on the buttons of my top before peeling it off my shoulders and gathering his hands to my breasts.

'No, really. I can't.' his gaze avoiding mine, his hands trying to shift from where I have them pressed up against my flesh.

'What, you don't want to?' my voice sharp.

'You don't understand. It's not right. You don't remember.'

'I don't need to remember.' I release his hands and something snaps inside as I feel them drop to his sides. He doesn't want me, nobody wants me. I'm all alone despite his overtures of concern and affection. I was beginning to think we had a chance despite my amnesia. I was beginning to think I could make a real go of it with him over here in Holland. I was beginning to learn to trust again.

Muscles relax, shoulders drop and eyes fill. 'I just wanted to feel, to feel something other than…'

I struggle to roll off and back to my side of the bed. But now that I've decided to abandon the idea, his arms come up to span my waist, his hands warm against my rapidly cooling skin.

'*Liefje,* you need to be sure that this is the right thing for you,' his gaze studying my face. 'I don't want you to regret a thing and you could, you know. You could wake up tomorrow hating me.'

I could never do that…

Is it the alarm clock that rouses me or the ringing of the doorbell? Whatever it is, I regret the disturbance. It's early, it must be. There's light streaming through the chinks in the curtains but a dull, hazy light with less strength than a forty-watt bulb. I don't want to move. I'm both warm and comfortable with the heavy weight of a stray arm and leg pressing into me and a memory, a new one, a pleasant memory that brings a smile to my lips and steel to my bones as I try to prevent him from leaving the circle of my arms.

He relents and presses a deep kiss against my lips, his hands brushing the hair from my face but it's only a brief reprieve. Soon he slips out of my grasp and reaches for his pyjama bottoms.

'Do you have to get up so early?' I say, stretching shamelessly, aware of his gaze lingering. 'Come back to bed and after, I'll make you some more of those pancakes.'

'You're a temptress, a wicked temptress,' he murmurs and he leans in for another kiss just as the bell starts up again and causes his frown to return. 'I'll bring you up a tea and take you up on that offer.'

Now that he's gone I stretch again before jumping out of bed and heading for the shower. It's a long time since I've felt so alive, so rejuvenated. Memory is a funny thing or that's what Doctor Brouwer told me and, along with those dreams of last night, now I remember other things. Oh, not a lot and nothing of any importance. I still don't remember who I am but there are other things, little things that are more familiar. For instance, the make-up bag with hardly any make-up isn't so much of a mystery as I don't usually wear any apart from the occasional slick of lipstick. I used to suffer from eczema as a child and the indignity of tar baths and shampoos, when all of my friends were messing about with fancy oils and conditioners, left a lasting impression.

I turn on the shower and allow the spray to flood my skin, instinctively reaching for the soap, his soap before tracing the path his hands followed last night. He's an expert lover, I'll give him that, certainly a lot more experienced than me but then again I was never one for stray relationships. I was too busy with... I shake my head as I reach for his shampoo, relishing in the fragrance, his fragrance. The doctor had also said not to force it. The memories will come when they're good and ready. So, I try to think about something else, something happy like what flavour pancake I can cobble together at the last minute. It's Monday so presumably he's got work but he might be able to meet me for lunch.

I step out of the shower, only to find he's standing in the doorway, a towel in his hands and the bland expression is back. I thought I'd managed to make that look disappear but obviously not. I try a smile of sorts. After all, I'm stark-naked and he wasn't immune to my charms last night, far from it. But his words freeze the smile on my lips and I ignore his hands as he starts rubbing me dry. Seconds ago I was imagining dragging him back under the sheets for a repeat performance but not now. Now his touch is impersonal and almost unwelcome. I step away and start dragging on the clothes he's carried through from the other bedroom, his words echoing through my mind.

'It's the police. They need to speak to you. They've found a body.'

Chapter Twenty Two

Is the room cold or is it me? It feels that, despite the thick jumper and socks he's brought to accompany the jeans, I'll never feel warm again.

I'm sitting by the spent fire. A mug has appeared, I couldn't tell you from where but I welcome the heat permeating through my fingers all the same. It's the only part of me that feels warm.

There are two of them sitting opposite with similar mugs in their hands. I recognise Inspector de Groot but, despite my best efforts, I can't muster up even the semblance of a smile. There's a stranger with him or at least a woman I don't recognise. She could be my best friend and I'd be none the wiser but I don't think so. She's young and pretty with the bright flush of youth still lingering against her cheeks. She's sad too. I can tell she's sad by the way she just can't quite manage to catch my gaze. And Manus, where is he? He must have made the tea. He must have placed it between my fingers before handing out the rest of the drinks.

'My husband—?'

'He'll be back shortly. He's just popped out with the dog.' He leans forward, placing his mug on the floor beside him before resting his hands on his knees and I know he's asked to see me alone as surely as if he's told Manus to clear off in front of me. I want him here, I need him but I don't say anything. What would be the point? Suddenly I have the overwhelming feeling that the man in front of me doesn't like my husband. I don't know what makes me think that but the thought remains. He's gotten rid of him and he's not about to tell me why.

'I'm afraid I have some bad news for you,' he finally says, his voice low in his throat, his expression solemn. 'We found a body a few days ago, the body of a woman and we believe it to be that of your sister, Victoria.'

I knew it was coming, of course I did. Who else could it be? It's not as if I know anyone over here except Manus and even he's a stranger.

There's no mistaking my reaction to the news because the mug falls from my fingers and smashes in two, tea spilling everywhere. I probably should be leaping up to grab a cloth to prevent any damage to the beautiful, hardwood floor and it's testament to my state of mind that I ignore everything except his words floating through my head.

Victoria, the girl I can't remember. And that somehow makes it worse. There are no tears, not yet. They'll come but only after I've had time to allow the news to sink in. I feel numb to the core.

I vaguely hear the inspector say something to the other officer and suddenly we're alone.

'I'm sorry to have to break it to you like this...Vanessa. We only got confirmation yesterday and, along with the break-in at the De Wees property, it's all very worrying.' He leans across and pats my hand briefly. 'How are you coping with the situation?'

His question; the pace, the tone, the look say more than the sum total of his words. I shoot him a glance. I know what he's asking. He's inquiring, in the blandest way possibly, if Manus is treating me well. How should I answer? If I'm honest I'd have to say that he's a moody bugger but considerate to my needs and fabulous in bed. But I don't think that's quite what the fatherly figure in front of me wants to hear. There's still the fact that I don't feel I can completely trust my caring husband but that's probably to be expected after what I've been through. Or that's what I keep telling myself. There are still those niggly little questions that keep cropping up, questions I can't fathom the answers to - like where was he last night, if his bed hadn't been slept in?

Instead of replying I decide to answer his question with one of my own.

'I get the impression that you don't like my husband, Inspector?'

He studies me for a moment, his face giving nothing away before finally giving voice to his words, words I can see he's choosing carefully.

'I have nothing against him, Vanessa, and he is a well-respected Delft citizen without even a parking ticket to his name, in addition to being a good friend of the chief commissioner,' his voice wry. 'But I don't like coincidences, coincidences worry me.'

The other detective arrives back just in time to interrupt the conversation. Has she been standing just outside the door waiting for the most opportune moment to enter? Of course she has.

With the floor now clean and the broken china in the bin I settle back in my seat, my gaze now on the clock. I'd like him here and he isn't.

I swallow hard. 'Where was she—?'

'Found?' he interrupts. 'She turned up in one of the canals on the outskirts of the city. We had thought it was accidental drowning. It does happen, you know. But then we noticed the marks on her wrists and ankles, the same wounds that you...to repeat, coincidences worry me.'

'And when was she found?'

He pauses. 'The same day you were released from hospital. They were ice-skating on the canal, something they do if it's cold enough. One of the skaters tripped and fell.'

'I get the picture,' I interrupt, trying and failing not to imagine the scene. The cold air. The happy, smiling skaters. The body just under the ice.

I frown. Surely there'd have been something on the news or in the papers? I know I've been pretty wrapped up in my own problems. But it's not as if I've been living in a vortex, or are there that many unexplained deaths over here for it to be an everyday occurrence? My attention swings to the window and the view beyond of the quiet canal. That's something I can't believe. No, it would have been on everyone's lips and I hadn't even heard a whisper. I remember the newspaper Manus gets delivered each morning, the newspaper he reads from front to back but always tidies away afterwards. Just who exactly is he trying to protect? Him or me?

I bite down on my lip, trying to focus as another thought hovers and I run Inspector de Groot's words over again in the silence of my mind. I liked this man from the beginning and I like him now, despite the news. I'd even go so far as to say I trust him. I flash him a look, my thoughts now wandering into dangerous waters but I let them wash over me all the same. I trust this man more than I trust Manus and, reading between the lines, this man knows it and he's not surprised. There's something about my husband...I suddenly recall his words of last night.

Am I going to end up hating him?

'You. You called her my sister. But she's not a relation, not in that way. She's my stepsister. Manus said—'

'The doctor is mistaken.' He pats my hand again. 'When you turned up, wandering about confused and with no memory, we did a DNA search. It's routine procedure for unidentified...' He pauses briefly. 'Unidentified persons. Nothing came up on any of the databases so you have no need to worry about being on Interpol's most wanted list.' He hazards a smile, which I can't return. 'Well, anyway. We did the same for your sister and it's definite that you share one parent. So, to be exact, she's your half-sister.

I search his face, trying to delve for further clues. I'd like to know what he really thinks about the situation – my situation. But a cardboard box would be easier to read. I can't really take it in. To someone in my position the difference between sister and stepsister is negligible. Will it make a difference in the scheme of things? I'm sad, of course I am, or should that be devastated? I've lost my only link to the past with the news, something I need to think about.

There are more questions that need to be asked and I heave a sigh. 'What happens now to my sister? I don't know about—'

'You don't have to worry about that.' And his kindly smile is back, one I manage to return. 'Normally we'd be calling you in to verify the…em well. To verify your sister but, with your little problem, I believe that's not possible?' He waits until I nod my head before continuing. 'We'll get onto Guernsey and fly someone over that knew her. You just work on getting well again and leave the police to continue looking into what happened.'

There's a noise outside, a scuffle at the door. 'Ah, it looks as if your husband has returned.'

I stand, aware of an increase in my heartbeat at the sight of him filling the doorway, a ghost of a smile on his lips. There's an unexpected silence and the room is suddenly crammed with more testosterone than can be found in the centre of an average rugby scrum.

My attention flicks to Inspector de Groot and the expression on his face, quickly masked, before I turn back to Manus. I try not to let last night intrude but it's difficult not to remember every glance, every kiss, every caress. I need his support. The simple truth is I need him, even as another thought strikes – an unwelcome one. I don't know how he's managed it but he's made me dependent;

dependent on him. If I didn't know any better, the cynic in me would say that he's gone all out to make me financially and emotionally reliant. But to what end? If love is at the centre surely the fact of me being dependent shouldn't matter? I frown as I try to recall his words from last night, words issued in the heat of passion, all of them in Dutch and all of them unrecognisable.

The inspector heads for the door, the other officer following behind.

'Well, I'm sure you have a lot to discuss. We'll see ourselves out.' He throws me a final look before giving Manus a wide berth.

You'd think that they were both vying for my attention. But, whatever the reason for their behaviour, they both need to get a grip. I'm married to one and the other is old enough to be my father – whoever that may be.

Chapter Twenty Three

What is there to say when your greatest fear is realised? What is there to do? The stark truth is that my sister is lying in some morgue or other and my life goes on. There will be things I'll have to organise over the coming days but, just at the moment, all I seem to be able to do is sit, curled up in front of the fire and stare into the open flames. I'll make a list of all the tasks I'll have to perform but later. Now it takes all my energy to respond to Manus's entreaties to eat and drink whatever he puts in front of me.

He's worried, I know he is. It's there in his hushed tones and the way nothing is too much bother. He's even tried to prise Nigel away from my lap but, for some reason Nigel isn't budging. It's as if he knows I need his doggy comfort now more than ever.

The day goes by on a tide of apathy and, before I know it, the shadows have lengthened and the day has darkened. Manus and Nigel have gone out for their walk. They hovered by my chair, an anxious looking pair if ever there was one - I don't respond. But, as soon as the door clicks behind them I'm on my feet and almost running up the stairs. I want to be in bed by the time they return. No. By the time he returns. I want to be tucked up with the duvet secure and my lids closed. A repeat of last night isn't an option. Not now.

I still haven't decided where I'll sleep as I push my bedroom door open. The bed has been made and with no Lize today it must have been Manus who fixed the pillows and righted the sheets. Tucking my hand under the pillow I search for my pyjamas only to return empty-handed, images of last night springing to life – images I squash back with a dousing of reality. He's muddying my thoughts, something I can't allow to happen. I'm not afraid of him. After all, he is the man I married. No. I'm afraid of myself.

He's made his bed too. There are even hospital corners and the edge of blue peeking out from under the pillow. I've come here to gather up my pyjamas and I have to be quick. But it's not the pyjamas that hold my attention. It's not memories from our night of passion that seem to linger despite everything that followed. It's what's hanging on the wall above his bed.

How could I have missed it last night? Was I that wrapped up in my own tragedy to miss such beauty only a whisper above my head?

The colour entrances me. The way the artist has defined her face, her lips, her dress and with a palate limited to what looks to be only four colours; blue, red, yellow and flesh tones. My gaze wanders across her face; the shading across her cheeks, the way the light dimples over red plump lips. This is talent. This is beauty. This is a surprise.

I'm on the bed now, the pyjamas forgotten, my feet crushing the smooth duvet underfoot but I don't care about that. I hardly realise that I'm standing on the middle of his mattress, my eyes pinned to the painting, absorbing every line and curve. I have no thoughts about what he'll say if he finds me. One part of me wonders about how he came to hide it away in the spare bedroom. But the other just accepts it for what it is. There's an M in the corner and a squiggle and that confuses me because suddenly I know who the artist is.

My legs give way and I sink back against the pillows, my eyes still riveted to the painting of the *Girl in a Blue Dress*. But I'm not in Holland now. I'm not sitting in the middle of Manus's bed with pyjamas twisting under my fingers. No, I'm back in the *Guille Alles Library* searching up my Year Ten school project.

The library is warm, too warm, especially after the January artic blizzard that chased me down Mill Street and towards the market. I drag my grey cardigan off my back and dump it on the hard chair beside me, trying to make a mental note not to forget it. If I lose another one there'll be hell to pay. My pad is open and with a selection of pencils to hand I turn the first page of the first book on the top of the pile.

This is a chore, only that. I'm not into old art with their muted colours and boring backdrops. Dead people on canvas are a drag and as for bowls of fruit – give me a break. I'll race off the five-hundred words on seventeenth-century Dutch artists and the couple of sketches necessary to prevent a detention before heading into town and the CD racks in Woolworths.

It only takes one look, one glance and the cardigan is forgotten. The boy with the winsome smile and sticky-out ears, at the next table, dissolves as does any thoughts of spending my pocket money on the latest album by Taylor Dayne. All I can see is the painting in front of me, a painting I know, a painting that haunts me. Is it the translucency of her gaze, the tilt of her head or the surprise on her lips that draws me? Who knows?

The painting is everywhere; on every billboard and every talk-show and TV slot. It's no surprise that the art teacher picked up on it for the Trinity Term art project, no surprise at all. But the big screen version of The Girl with a Pearl Earring doesn't do the painting justice. Oh, that actress, what's her name, is beautiful, probably more beautiful than Vermeer's model but this isn't about a painting of a beautiful woman. This is so much more than a chocolate-box depiction of beauty. This is a master-class on the use of texture, light and shade of oils on canvas and executed to the nth degree.

The desk fades as does the library and I'm collapsed in the middle of his bed with a lump in the back of my throat that threatens to turn to tears. I feel like Scrooge after a visit from *The Ghost of Christmas Past* but, unlike him, there's nothing I can do to rectify my mistakes. The memories are coming, just like Doctor Brouwer said they would, but they hold no substance and little clues. Just how many am I going to have to live through before my memory returns in full?

I scrub my hand across my face, and push my hair out of the way, my attention back on the painting. There is little I can do about my amnesia but the painting is a different challenge altogether. I know it's by Vermeer but how do I know? My gaze wanders over his use of light on the side of her cheek, her nose, the folds of her gown. Fifteen years is a long time to remember the contents of a piddly five-hundred word essay, especially for someone with my diagnosis, but I do remember that he wasn't prolific. He ended up with only a handful of paintings to his name and all catalogued to death. So if this is a Vermeer then the likelihood is that it's an undiscovered...

'I see you've found my little secret.'

I'm so engrossed in the painting that I lose my balance and would have ended up toppling off the bed if he hadn't been there to stop my fall.

I'm sitting on the edge of the bed and he's looming over me, his hands on my shoulder. Something shifts but nothing moves, except perhaps my heart as it starts up a little tap dance all on its own. It's a traitor just like Nigel, who's looking up at us with his tongue hanging out. Maybe I've got it wrong. Maybe the pressure of his hands hasn't just changed from a desperate grip to a sensuous hold. Maybe the air that seconds before was filled with a couple of swears (one Dutch and one English) hasn't become heady with desire. Maybe his eyes haven't darkened or my breath hasn't caught in the back of my throat.

I clear my traitorous thoughts with a frown. He might be my husband but last night I more than fulfilled my marital duties. Now there are more important things on the table: the death of my sister for one and the painting.

Easing back is difficult. Firstly, of course, is the undeniable fact that I find I'm happy just where I am. It wouldn't take much, perhaps a little eyelash fluttering, to push him over the edge but do I really want that now? Okay, so the answer is yes but I have to be strong; for Victoria but also for me. I wriggle out of his grasp.

'Your guilty secret?' I finally manage, my voice barely a whisper

'Yes.' His hand is dragging through his hair again and I know he's anxious or upset – possibly both. 'Your…benefactor gave it to me to mind before his death. I didn't know what to do with it afterwards. It's yours, of course. I just shoved it in here out of the way,' his expression wry. 'It was the only room with a hook sturdy enough.'

'What about insurance?' I know it comes out as an accusatory squeak but I'm shocked at his response not least because it looks like I'm the new owner of a painting that is probably worth millions, tens of millions even.

'Well, it will be covered as part of the house contents.' He's looking at me again, but the frown is back, and I know without him saying the words that he thinks I'm barking. 'So, you think it might be worth something then? I can always up the insurance by a few—'

'Million.'

'Million? What? Surely not?' he says, both eyebrows raised. 'It's only something Aldert picked up on eBay for a couple of hundred pounds. One of his bargain-basement buys to keep him out of mischief when he retired. He was always bidding for paintings that no one else wanted. Sometimes he'd make a few euros at one of the local Dutch auction houses but mostly he did it for fun. This though,' his hand reaching to finger the gilt frame. 'He was so proud of this. He bought it as a joke, nothing more. Someone had daubed over her face and dress, there was nothing left to see of any worth apart from her hands, which they'd forgotten to overpaint.' He joins me on the bed, moving closer to the painting, leaning in to study the entwined fingers. 'I don't know how he spotted that the hands didn't match the face but then again he had an amazing talent.' He rests back on his heels, throwing me a glance from across the bed. 'It was the only painting he ever asked me to look after. Maybe he knew something and didn't want to say? After all, if I'd known it was worth something I probably wouldn't have agreed to mind it,' his voice soft. 'So, you think this painting is important? I thought you said you were a lawyer, or were you holding out on me? Don't get me wrong. I'm actually delighted. What the hell do you buy a lawyer for her birthday anyway?'

I throw back my head and laugh. 'Ha, if I knew when my birthday was I'd tell you. A little thing like amnesia isn't going to let any husband of mine off the hook.'

'Any husband of yours? So you have more than one. Oh, God, now I'm married to a bigamist.'

'If I can't remember the first wedding how do you think I'm going to remember any of the others? In fact, if this memory thing persists I'm going to have to insist on another.'

'And no doubt another one of these,' his finger tapping the ring and where I've left it ever since he'd twisted it in place.

'No, I love my ring.'

He smiles, his eyes twinkling. 'I was hoping you'd say that. It belonged to my grandmother,' his gaze lingering on my mouth. 'It's a deal. I'll stand you a wedding that you'll never forget but only on one condition.'

'Which is?'

'That I get to plan the honeymoon.'

Is this us flirting with each other, his eyes on my face, my eyes, my mouth? Is this what it's like to have a relationship with someone; with a man I can trust? More questions than I can answer but I do know it feels good to be sitting here beside him. It's probably what half of the couples in Delft are doing right now, exchanging chitchat about their day while they prepare for bed. But I have to break the connection, or we'll end up doing more than I planned. I don't need company now the memories are coming thick and fast. With this last one, I wasn't even asleep when it intruded.

I take his hand, trying to ignore the way his fingers curl around mine or the warmth of his touch as I drag him to his feet. If anyone walked in now they'd think us mad, or perverted, standing there in the middle of his bed like a pair of hyperactive children in the days before the trampoline. But I can't help that. The only way to see the painting is up close. The only way to stop me pushing him back against the mattress is to stay focused. With these thoughts uppermost, I return the conversation back to the subject of art.

'I'm pretty sure I know squat about art or, if I do, it's buried deep. But I do remember about an art project in secondary school, would you believe, on Dutch artists?'

I expect him to laugh but he doesn't. Instead his brow wrinkles and the interrogation begins.

'These memories. You've had more? How often? Are there headaches to accompany them?'

I'd forgotten that he's the doctor here, a doctor and a psychiatrist. He's obviously going to be more interested in my mind than he is in some stupid painting if the state of his house is anything to go by. Oh, I'm not criticising. It's a beautiful house and full of beautiful things but I'd hazard a guess that it's all inherited. There's no soul here. There's no hint of the man except for the books on his shelves and the picture on his desk, a picture I still intend to see.

'I've only had three.'

'So, two others?'

I feel the blush but ignore it. Instead I lift my chin. 'That's right, about my school project. The painting—'

'No, sweetheart. I want to hear more about this memory. The painting, lovely as it is, isn't important.' He takes my hand and helps me to the side of the bed before sitting beside me, his hand still in mine. 'How long was it? Was there any warning? Was it a dream, a memory or a vision? How did you feel after?'

'Whoa. I don't know. It was short, seconds' maybe but it felt longer. The library was hot, so hot. I left my cardigan behind.'

'Interesting. So, it was a flashback rather than a memory.' He must have caught my look of confusion. 'With memories and dreams we sit outside the experience, watching if you like. But you relived it as if for the first time. There was no disassociation between you as an adult and you as a—?'

'Fifteen-year-old.'

'Exactly.' He drops my hand only to pick it up again, this time messing about with my fingers. 'It's good, you know. Very good. This type of amnesia tends to come back in full. Soon, you'll remember – you'll remember everything with absolute clarity.' He forgets my hand and shifts his attention to my face, his warm palms cradling my cheeks, his fingers stroking my skin. 'That includes all the bad things…all the things that have just happened to you. I'd like you to promise me something. I'm on your side even if it doesn't feel like it sometimes. So, please promise to tell me when you know…everything. Promise me *liefje*?'

I have no idea what he's going on about, which must be perfectly clear from my bemused expression but I nod my head anyway. After all, I can't see a reason why I wouldn't want to tell him. Apart from that policeman, he's the only there for me.

The tone changes and he shifts away, the swift change in tempo and conversation both awkward and puzzling. I go along with it, I have no choice not to. But, for someone with my condition, this rollercoaster approach is the wrong way.

I meet his gaze, trying to concentrate on what comes next.

'You were telling me about the painting?'

He has his listening face on again as he prepares to play the attentive husband. A thought flickers, joining all of the other ones with doubt at their heart. Is he the dutiful, loving husband or is he just playing a part and, if so, to what end? He says I'll remember, I'll remember everything so what is there to be frightened of? I can't change what's happened to me or indeed to my sister, no matter how much I wish it. I can't change anything. Surely the truth will be better than the ruddy black hole where all my memories are meant to be hiding?

So I play the game, his game. If there are rules, I'm in blissful ignorance.

I pull him closer, directing his attention to the upper left-hand quadrant of the canvas. 'You see that funny M with the letter I in the centre?'

'No, but carry on,' I throw him a glance, but he's scrunched up his face into a squint and I remember the glasses he usually leaves beside his chair.

'It's there, believe me. And it's important. In fact, you could say it's vital.'

'Sweetheart, you're killing me. Just what do you think I have hanging on my wall?'

'A Vermeer.'

Of all the responses I'd expected, laughter wasn't even in the running. I'd expected bemusement, confusion even and maybe denial but humour? Humour seems an insult. He throws back his head and roars, exposing his thick column of throat and almost all of his teeth. I'm not impressed by his behaviour, not one little bit, something he probably realises pretty quickly as I shift off the bed and head for the door.

'Hey, where are you going?' his laugh just a lingering hoarseness. 'I didn't mean to—'

'You didn't mean to—?' I stand, hands on my hips, my expression neutral as I await his explanation.

My gaze softens, my eyes drawn to the woman over his head. His derision can't take away from the fact that the painting is the one good thing that's happened. My thoughts drift and my mood drops; the euphoria of seconds before fading to a bare shadow.

The painting doesn't matter, not really. It's not as if I need the odd fifty-million. I wouldn't know what to do with even a fraction of that sum. Okay, so maybe I'd be able to pay back Manus for sorting out my mother's care home fees but that's paltry in comparison. Money can't bring happiness and you can't take it with you. Money doesn't matter to my sister now, nothing matters and the worst of it is there's no one to grieve except me...and I can't even remember what she looked like. I have a sudden urge to find out more – to find out everything.

He goes to speak. 'I didn't mean to...' but I stop him with my hand and my voice.

'What was she like?'

I think he's going to ask who; what was who like. But he doesn't. Instead he rests back on the bed, his eyes never leaving my face.

'As I said to the detective earlier, I didn't know her that well. We only met a couple of times.'

'Please, Manus. Tell me,' I whisper. 'Did she look like me? Can you see any likeness?'

'If you're asking me if she was pretty, I really didn't notice. But you could say that there was a family resemblance,' his voice soft. 'The way your hair curls over your ears, the length,' his head tilts to one side as he continues his comparison. 'She was about the same height, maybe a little shorter and about the same size, I guess. But as for the rest,' he heaves his shoulders. 'I'm a man and I knew she was your step…sister. I wasn't going to threaten anything about our relationship by looking too hard at another woman, especially her.'

Chapter Twenty Four

'Lize will be here in a minute, *liefje*,' he says, taking both my hands. 'I don't want you leaving the house by yourself unless Nigel is with you. And remember to keep the door locked.'

He's gone, the only reminder a tingling pressure on my lips. I'm left alone in this big house with only Nigel for company. Whilst I wouldn't be without him, he doesn't fill the void after the door shuts on Manus's back.

I know his time isn't his own. He has patients to see and lectures to give, all things he's either put off or postponed since returning from his trip to Belgium. I can't demand any more from him than he's able to give even though I want to. This tall Dutchman has gotten under my skin both literally and figuratively. I can't remember a time without him but, more worryingly, I can't envisage a future without him by my side. I trail around, with Nigel at my heels, wandering from room to room, all except his study, which is a room I won't go into by myself. I know it's foolish, but I'd feel the same if I found him rooting in my underwear drawer. There's nothing secret amongst the piles of lace, cotton and silk but what's there is personal to me and it's the same with his study — out of bounds.

The last flight of stairs leads up to a room, a room similar to the one next door but that's where any similarity ends. This almost secret room sequestered at the top of the stairs holds another secret, a secret hobby and one I'd never have guessed at, my lips parting into a smile.

Instead of art he's chosen astronomy. But, whilst most home astronomers would probably cope with something small and discrete, his telescope fills the space. There's a small table, which holds a pair of industrial-looking binoculars and a stool set precisely. He must spend hours here, wandering amongst the stars and planets. It's probably where he came last night, come to think of it, as I continue puzzling over his wrinkle-free bed. The simple solution would be to ask him but I couldn't possibly do that. I trail a gentle finger up to the lens but I'm far too short to see through the eye-piece, not that there'd be anything to see at this time of day.

I throw a lingering look at his tools for star-gazing. It's a beautiful room, with a high wooden ceiling and a crisp, clear light filtering through the large Velux window. We could sit here, hidden away and no one would know we were even at home. All it needed was a sofa, perfectly angled and perhaps a side table to hold the inevitable glass of wine and we'd have the most perfect night imaginable. The most perfect night with him.

I'd probably have stayed there all morning if truth be known, pottering amongst the small shelf of books hidden under the eaves. But I'm dragged out of my reverie by the sound of the front door slamming even as Nigel decides to hide behind my legs.

'Great guard dog you're turning out to be.' But I scoop him up and press my cheek next to his warm fur. I need him, just like he needs me. We're a right pair of scaredy-cats. We descend the stairs together only to find Lize man-handling a couple of bags of shopping into the hall.

'Here, let me help,' I race down the rest of the steps at top speed, much to Nigel's annoyance. Although, if he knew there was food in it for him, he probably wouldn't be grumbling quite so much, my eyes on the box of dog biscuits sticking out the top of the first bag.

Helping Lize with the shopping takes all of five minutes but I can see she doesn't want to chat. So much for the coffee and gossip I was hoping for. I grab my coat and Nigel's lead and hurry out of the door, remembering at the last minute to pick up the spare bunch of keys Manus had pressed into my hand before he left. Whilst she might be a treasure and devoted to Manus there is obviously some wariness around his new wife. I know I should stay and stand my ground but, in truth, I can't be bothered. If she doesn't like me that's her problem and if it continues I can always say that, now he's married surely the services of a housekeeper are redundant.

With that thought uppermost, I wander down the street and cross over to the canal. The day is one of those crisp, cool days with no sign of rain. In fact, glancing up, the sky is free from clouds for the first time in days. All there is overhead is miles upon miles of the deepest bluest sky. The beauty of the place whips the air from my lips and challenges my soul. If I was an artist, if I was Victoria, I'd be dragging out my paint pots and hitting the cerulean blue with perhaps a touch of titanium where the sky bleeds into the background. My lips still at the thought, at the thought of her lying cold and stiff. She'll never enjoy the beauty of this. She'll never be able to pick up a brush and take pleasure in choosing the exact colour for that perfect stroke. She'll never be able to do any of those things again and that's the tragedy.

I stand there, eyes swimming and make a silent promise to her, the sister I can't remember – the sister I can't remember yet. There will be no more living life in the slow lane. There'll be no more sitting in the back seat while I watch the world race past my window. Life is for living and, for me, the living starts now. I heave a sigh. I've made a decision, a huge one for me. Memory is a funny thing. Whilst I have no idea about the ins and outs of my life, I do know what type of person I was. But that's not who I'm going to be now. Now I have two lives to live – hers and mine, my fingers instinctively going to the tattoo embellishing my inner arm.

Nigel interrupts, the ground at his feet obviously not as interesting as the lampposts trailing the canal border and I acquiesce, my mercurial thoughts fading like the cold grey mist dispersing from my lips with each breath.

If it wasn't for the freezing temperature I could be forgiven for thinking I'm in the height of summer. I wonder where I was last summer, probably in Guernsey in the middle of some *legal eagle* case or other. I'm more interested in next summer. Will I still be here, tracing the same footsteps across the bridge or will I be some other place? Will I still be with him?

I jingle the keys in my pocket for something to do, part of my mind counting them. So many keys to his house - so many secrets to lock away, to lock away from whom? Not me, a smile tugging as I remember he handed them to me with a brief hand on my shoulder. I knew then that I could have made him stay. I knew by the way his eyes were reluctant to break from mine and the softness in his gaze, so at odds with his size and strength. Whatever my doubts and, yes they're still there, persistent and dawdling long past their sell-by-date.

Whatever my fears, I know now that his bland countenance is an expression I can conquer. I don't even know why it's there but this tall, strong Dutchman is mine for the taking. I'm still undecided if I want him.

I look up only to find that Nigel has led me back home, but not to my home – to the house next door.

'No, you don't live here anymore, sweetie.' But he pulls at the lead, determined in his own doggy way to climb up the steps.

I don't want to go in after what's happened. The police were meant to be here today to examine the place, but something has obviously interrupted their plans. The keys are still pressed in my palm. I pull them out and study them. It's unlikely he's left a key but…

The first key fits. I flick a look over both shoulders but there's no one about – not that it should make any difference. As her sister and presumably her legal next-of-kin, then all of this belongs to me.

The hall is just how I remember; everything smashed, crushed, desecrated. There's a faint powder residue lingering and I'm pleased now that I'm still wearing the gloves he's lent me. Nigel barks and I run to his side, shushing him with a whisper. There's no one to hear but still the whisper remains. I don't feel safe. There's something almost haunting about the place. I kneel, hugging his warm body to my chest. He barks again and starts scratching the leg of an overturned chair, his gaze fixed.

'You want to sit here?' and I turn the chair back to upright and flip over the cushion to hide the rip. Standing back I watch with a smile as he sniffs and twists before settling down for a mid-morning snooze. Whilst he might not be much of a guard-dog it's good to have him by my side even if he's happy to sleep in a chair only fit for the rubbish heap.

I trail from room to room, trying not to touch anything but drawn all the same. The kitchen is a death trap, the sound of broken crockery and glass crunching under my feet. This is the house my sister stayed in. She drank from these cups. She sat on these chairs. He's even ripped the doors from their hinges in his need to find…what? My hand pauses on the door handle. What could he be looking for? Did he find it?

The study is next, a room that seems very much the heart of the house and not just because of its central position tucked between the kitchen and the lounge. It's here the damage is at its worst with everything ripped asunder. I make a half-hearted attempt to right the desk, forgetting that I shouldn't touch anything. When I remember, I place it back down on the floor before tucking my hands in my pockets. There's nothing retrievable, nothing at all. Even the fountain pens have been ground underfoot in a case of sheer malice. Why would someone do such a thing?

I wander about, sometimes remembering not to touch, sometimes forgetting, hoping above all else I'll find something to prove that she was here. I breathe the same air and walk in her footsteps. But there's no trace of her presence.

The attic breaks my heart, not because the damage is any worse. The damage is the same. But this room was central to who Aldert de Wees was. The room he must have spent hours in, practicing and honing his craft until he was able to rediscover work the quality of the *Girl in a Blue Dress...* I stumble on a discarded canvas but manage to prevent myself from falling. Of course. How stupid. The only thing of value is the painting, the painting hanging on the wall next door. I stare at the room with new eyes; the red paint dripping to dry like blood icicles, the trashed canvases, ripped and torn. He was searching like a crazy man and what would someone be searching for in the house of a picture restorer if not a picture? But the picture was never here, not really. As soon as Aldert realised what he had on his hands he tried to get rid of it but, by then, it was too late. Someone had seen, but who? The only one who visited surely was Manus and perhaps his doctor.

I walk downstairs, still searching; an earring, a glove, a lipstick. I can't believe she stayed here two days without leaving a trace, unless someone obliterated all evidence – their first act before starting their search.

My head starts to ache and suddenly I'm reminded that I'm only a few days out of hospital. He told me to take it easy. He probably expected me to spend a lazy day pottering in the house. After all, neither of us managed to get much sleep last night what with one thing and another, colour warming my cheeks. I sink onto the bottom stair, and rest my head in my hands, the thought of a snooze now uppermost. I had so many plans when I pushed open the door and all I've managed to achieve is a headache and some crazy idea that whoever did this was after a painting. Really? Delft, from what I've seen up to now, is a charming town with a small village feel about it. It's not the kind of place for a major art heist or whatever it's called. I could be wrong, but somehow I don't think I am. The truth of the matter is my knowledge of art is probably postage stamp in size and my knowledge of Vermeer, in particular, is a good fifteen years out of date.

My hair drapes across my face. Dragging it across one shoulder I start fiddling with a hair bobble and that's when I see it. Hair forgotten, I make my way across to the hall table and, with no thought for any of the *scene of the crime* precautions, stand it upright. There's a drawer too, it's four sides stamped flat but that's not what's caught my eye. I shift the drawer and place it gently on top, my attention on the sheet of paper partially hidden underneath. Why I should be interested in this specific item when the floor is littered with similar detritus is a mystery. I drop to my knees and reach out a hand that's shaking where before it was still. The paper isn't lined and that immediately sets alarm bells ringing. It reminds me of an artist's pad. My fingers touch the corner before flipping it over.

I'm looking at a drawing of a face, a face so familiar and yet so different; an impression of how the artist sees him. There's no softness here. There isn't even a hint of bland. There's anger rising from the page, anger and so much more. I stare into his eyes, the eyes of a stranger. A stranger who just so happens to be my husband.

The room fades and where before there was the unsettling hush of an empty house now there's noise, lots of noise: the scrape of chair legs on wood, the clatter of cups, the sound of laughter.

'Hello, Vanessa. I wasn't sure if you'd be able to make it.'

'Oh, you know. It's only work after all and they get more than their pound of flesh. God, it's freezing out there and all

those Christmas shoppers are doing my head in. At least the coffee's hot.'

Silence invades as we both take a sip, the hot liquid a panacea but also a reprieve. There's nothing to talk about, not really.

'Well, I must dash. I'm going to try to pop into that travel agent on my way back to see about tickets.'

'But—?'

'But nothing, darling. Let me sort out this one little thing after that no-good tosser of a boyfriend of yours did the dirty. He may be God's gift but, ever since he's pulled the boss's daughter he's been a right pain in the arse.'

Robert. How could I have forgotten about Robert?

Chapter Twenty Five

Mindful of Manus's entreaties to be careful, I head next door only to find a man on the doorstep, one arm raised as if he's about to bang the knocker.

I raise an enquiring eyebrow, my Dutch not up to more than a brief hello. He holds out his hand and I see he's clutching a brown envelope. Air seeps through my teeth. He's here on business.

'*Goedemorgen*. I'm Sem Bakker. *Meneer* de Wees's lawyer. I'm here to offer my condolences on your loss, *Mevrouw* van der Hooke,' he says, pulling out a tissue and blowing his nose. 'I had wanted to meet you and your sister earlier but I've been away on business.'

I step back from the door and beckon him through before closing it behind him when all I really want to do is close it in his face. He's looks harmless enough with his brushed-back grey hair and three-piece suit but I'm not in the mood for company.

'Come in. Would you like a drink? Tea, coffee?'

'Coffee, if it's not too much trouble,' and he's following me into the kitchen.

I had planned on taking him into the lounge but now I gesture to the table with a sort of smile. 'You're lucky to have caught me in. I've just been out for a walk.'

He remains silent and I suddenly wonder just how much of my gabble he's really interested in. He's obviously here to do more than just offer his condolences.

I hand him his mug, placing sugar and a teaspoon within easy reach. I don't really want a coffee, but I make one before joining him at the table, all the time wondering why he's here. I don't have to wait long.

'It was quite a surprise when I heard about your marriage to *Meneer* van der Hooke?'

'Oh, you know. One of those whirlwind romances,' I say with a frown. It's really none of his business.

'Ah, the youth of today although, of course, the esteemed doctor isn't all that young,' and he chuckles to himself before tapping the envelope he's placed on the table. 'I know it's probably not the time but when is,' he says, spreading his hands before pushing the envelope towards me. 'If I could leave this with you? It's the valuation and offer for the house I wrote to you both about a few weeks ago. You really should look at it, it's a great opportunity. In times like these, cash offers are a gift.'

I finger the edge of the envelope, his words running through my mind. 'So, you didn't get to meet my sister when she was across?'

'No, I didn't have that pleasure,' he says, clearing his throat before standing. 'Well, I must be on my way,' he adds in a rush. 'If you ever feel in need of a friend, I'm always on the end of the telephone. I'd be happy to take you out to show you the sights. Holland is a very beautiful country.'

I glance up and find him raking me with those pale eyes. He unnerves me and I wish I'd never invited him in. I know my fear is irrational but he's arrived on the back of my experience next door and that drawing. He smiles for the first time and my fear intensifies. There's just something about him that makes me want him out of the house. I almost laugh out loud at the thought of this weak ineffectual man being a threat. I'll be afraid of my own shadow next. But still I want him gone. I pick up my mug and drain it in one, burning my throat in the process.

The door knocker bangs a second time and I quickly place the mugs in the sink before pushing back from the table.

'Thank you for the coffee,' his voice stilted. 'I'll leave you my number, both at work and home,' and he pulls a pen from his top pocket and quickly jots down a couple of numbers on the back of the envelope.

'I'm not sure what I'm up to but thank you,' his footsteps echoing mine as I head for the front door.

It's Manus. But the smile on his face fades at the sight of my visitor. I make quick introductions before ushering *Meneer* Bakker to the door.

'Thank you again.'

'You're welcome, and don't forget my offer. If you need anything, anything at all,' his attention now on the doctor, 'I'm happy to help.'

I shut the door, my hand lingering on the wood, all the time aware that Manus has taken up residence against the bannister, his cool gaze centred in the middle of my back.

'Offer?'

We're standing in the kitchen and I can see his attention drifting round the room. This man, for all his slumberous gaze and laid-back demeanour, doesn't miss a trick as his eyes flick from the back of the envelope and the telephone numbers before focusing on the mugs in the sink.

'He was Aldert's solicitor. He came to offer his condolences.'

'I wonder how he knew that you'd be here?' his frown back.

'I have no idea. He's also offered to take me sightseeing,' I add, my chin up.

'Has he now—?' He leaves the sentence unfinished and hanging in the air.

'He was only trying to be kind. I might even take him up on it,' I fling back, in a fit of pique. I have no intention of ever seeing *Meneer* Bakker again, but Manus doesn't need to know that, my thoughts returning to Victoria's drawing.

It's unsettled me, I know it has. There's just something on the edge of my vision. If I twist my head it's almost as if I'll be able see it staring me in the face but, when I look, it stretches and fades into the distance, as elusive as all of my other memories. I decide a change of subject is probably the best thing.

'Where are your keys?'

'I have no idea. I have another set somewhere if mine don't turn up.' His eyes search my face but seemingly he's content with what he finds because he turns away with a smile, a smile that freezes when he sees what I've forgotten.

'This is new, isn't it? Should I be flattered?'

He's picked up the drawing, the drawing of him that I found next door. He stares hard and I wonder does he see what I see? Does he see an incredibly handsome face, with strongly defined features and hooded lids that conceal far more than they reveal? Or, like me, does he feel the fear skittering under his breast at the heavy lines, so heavy that she's almost broken through the paper with the thrust of her pencil.

'I don't know, should you?'

He places the drawing down, his finger straightening the edge so that it lines up with the side of the worktop. 'So, it's not just your half-sister that can draw then?' his voice soft but, despite the lack of volume, there's still an underpinning of steel.

I laugh, I can't help it. I throw back my head and giggle until my eyes smart. 'Oh, that's funny, so funny. You think I drew this? You think I moped around all day waiting for your return and in the meantime picked up a pencil so that I could have your image to hand. I don't think so.' My laughter stops as quickly as it starts and, instead of humour, there's silence as the words ebb and flow but don't quite disperse.

What's said can't be unsaid and I've just made the elementary mistake of actually saying what I think. I try to backtrack. 'I'm sorry, that came out wrong...'

'No, don't apologise. You said what had to be said.' He stands there with his hands in his pockets, staring down at the floor as if he's stepped on something unsavoury and I know I've hurt him. I've hurt the man who has gone out of his way to be everything a woman could ever want and I don't know how to put it right.

He finally moves but towards the kettle, almost ignoring me but not quite. His manners are far too good for that. 'I had thought we could go out for dinner but it's probably a bad Idea. I have some work to catch up on anyway. Would you like a coffee while I'm making one?' he shoots over his shoulder, but his gaze doesn't meet mine.

'No, I'm fine. Manus, I'd have liked to…'

But he interrupts again. 'Lize has left a lasagne and salad. Help yourself, I'll probably eat at my desk,' and he's gone.

It's a lonely evening sitting in the lounge with only Nigel's snores and my thoughts for company. He hasn't left the sanctuary of his study all evening. It's as if he's retreated back into his shell and there's no way for me to entice him out. The truth is I'm a coward. I should just storm in and demand to be told what the problem is. But I can't, for fear that he'll actually tell me. He might even decide that he can't be bothered with someone like me - someone who can't even remember one single solitary thing about him.

At eight o'clock I scoop up my courage and make him a coffee just the way he likes it. But all I get for my efforts is a grunt. He barely raises his head from the book he's reading.

I leave Nigel's walk for as long as I dare but, with the clock creeping towards eleven, I fling on my coat with little enthusiasm and head for the bridge. All is silent along the canal and many of the houses have locked up for the night. I don't dawdle despite a sudden restlessness about what comes next. We've been sharing a bed for a couple of nights now; we've been doing a lot more than just sharing a bed. But things will have changed, my words will have changed them and, for the thousandth time that evening, I beat myself up for allowing my thoughts to air.

The house is just the way I'd left it, the pale glow from the hall light flickering across the chequerboard floor. Nigel doesn't wait to be told. Once his lead is off he goes lumbering up the stairs with a swish of his tail and a doggy intent that rivals and overtakes thoughts of food and walkies. I follow at a much slower pace, switching the lights off in the lounge on my way. The stairs beckon, bed beckons and, despite his mood, I've decided that I want to sleep in his room. I can't be alone, not now – not with the threat of more dreams only a breath away. I said I wasn't a coward, I lied.

I ignore the stairs for a moment. Instead I tiptoe past his door, I don't know why. It's not that I expect him to be doing anything illegal or even a tad suspicious. It's just that I want to see what he's up to. After all, he's missed out on taking me out for dinner not to mention the lasagne that remains untouched in the fridge – there's no way I'm eating alone. No, there must be a reason for his behaviour that sits outside of my words: a problem at work, a problem with a patient? Surely I can't have upset him that much but, with eye pressed up to the crack, where door meets frame, I realise that's just what I've done.

He's not working. He's not reading. He's not doing anything except staring down at the drawing in his hand; Victoria's drawing of him. I shift my focus from his hand and back to his expression. There's no sign of the perennial bland mask now I'm not in the room to see it. There's sadness, a great deal of sadness, which to my mind seems worse somehow than anything. I make a silent retreat before heading upstairs and to the bed I haven't slept in since that very first night.

Chapter Twenty Six

My first thought on waking is one of relief. Then I turn to the empty side of the bed, empty apart from Nigel and my relief soon changes to discontent. But there's nothing I can do about it, not now. So, instead of brooding about something I can't change, I chase the thought away and swing my legs out of bed.

It feels late but I get a shock when I see that the clock on the landing is heading towards ten. I've obviously missed breakfast just as I've missed him but that was probably intentional. Who'd want to breakfast beside a mean-minded shrew without a good word to say about anyone? Nigel, for all the late hour, is content to stay by my side, which is more than unusual. It's unheard of. So he must have sneaked in while I was fast asleep. He couldn't speak to me last night. He couldn't bear my company and yet he was still prepared to sort out Nigel so that I could have a lie-in. Perhaps it isn't quite so hopeless after all.

I push the thought aside to the realms of fantasy-land and head to the kitchen in search of tea and toast only to find Lize ensconced. Up until that moment I'd forgotten about her but it takes one look at her downturned mouth to realise that I wasn't being paranoid in thinking that she doesn't like me. I've done something or not done something or maybe it's just that she doesn't like the idea of her beloved employer marrying someone like me. But, whatever the reason, I remember what he told me about her background. No one knows what kind of a life she led before Manus rescued her and, for someone who can't remember last week let alone last year, I'm prepared to be generous.

'Good morning Lize. I'm sorry we didn't get round to eating the lasagne last night, it looked delicious. I plan to have some for my lunch,' I say, with a smile. 'I'm just about to make myself a drink. Would you like one?'

'No, thank you, *Mevrouw.*'

And that's it. The end of the conversation. I watch her turn her back and head into the larder cupboard. She might as well have slammed the door behind her just to make it perfectly clear how unwelcome I am. As far as I'm concerned, she can stay in there all day. I pop a couple of slices of bread in the toaster and rummage in the fridge for butter and milk. I've made the effort to be nice, more than nice and she's as good as thrown it back in my face. The toast pings and I grab a plate and my mug before escaping into the lounge. Oh, yes. There's no doubt about it. Whilst it's meant to be my home too, obviously it's only a passing acknowledgement. It would serve them both right if I shifted lock, stock and barrel next door and left them to get on with it.

The idea festers and grows as I plonk down on the sofa and attack my breakfast as if food is going out of fashion. Crumbs wiped, I place my mug tidily on top of my plate before placing it on the coffee table. Nigel is snoozing again, when isn't he? But that leaves me time to catch up with writing in my notebook, something I've been neglecting since that first day.

Ten minutes later and I'm at a loss. I distinctly remember placing it in the top drawer of the dressing table. I find I'm even searching the floor just in case it's fallen behind. But no, it's gone and, as I know I didn't move it, someone has taken it. It could only be Manus, couldn't it? Perhaps he took it this morning to read when he collected Nigel. He is a psychiatrist, I remind myself with a frown. Maybe, after what happened yesterday, he's trying to gauge my state of mind. All paltry excuses really and I slam the drawer closed. It's private and none of his business. I continue to search in vain before heading next door. But his bedroom comes up a blank, a complete blank. I avoid the bed completely, instead focusing on the chest of drawers and wardrobe but there's nothing visible and I'm reluctant, after last night, to start rummaging in his cupboards…

Oh, for God's sake get a grip, woman. Your sister is dead and you're still standing back. What is the very worst thing that could happen? A row with Manus? Big deal! It might even clear the air.

Within seconds I've pulled out all the drawers and opened the cupboard doors and, despite the continued absence of the notebook I feel better than I've felt in a while. I've stood back for pretty much all of my life and look where it's gotten me? Absolutely bloody nowhere. At twenty-nine I think it's time for a rethink.

I stand still, noticing the one thing I should have spotted straight away. The Vermeer has gone; the only thing to show that it was ever there the heavy-duty hook standing proud against the backdrop of white.

I forget about the notebook. I forget my new-found backbone. I forget about everything except the sheer disbelief at its absence. I glance at the space under the bed, but it won't be there. It won't be anywhere as convenient as being hidden under the bed or stashed away in the back of the wardrobe. It won't be anywhere that I can find. He's hiding it; surely not from me but, if not from me then who?

The thought lingers only to be replaced by another one. His missing keys. If someone took his keys then they'd have access to the house, wouldn't they? They could have easily taken both the painting and the notebook while I was hiding away in the lounge although why they'd want my notebook…

I fling myself back down the stairs and into the lounge, looking for the bag he bought me. The keys are still in the inside pocket exactly where I'd left them. I don't like it. I don't like this not knowing what's going on. The painting is missing. Manus's keys are missing. Someone has taken the painting.

The obvious answer is to phone him but I'm not going to do that. I can't. What if it's him all along? The doubt remains. It's always there. There's something about him that I still cannot trust. I know it's senseless. I know he's been kind to me from the beginning but there it is. However, there is one man I know who's on my side. A man I know I can trust. A man I should have been hounding from the very beginning for answers. I just hope I haven't left it too late.

I leave the lounge. I leave my plate and mug sitting on the coffee table, where before I'd have carried it back into the kitchen and placed it in the dishwasher. But I have more things to worry about than appeasing stroppy housekeepers.

I have no idea what a policeman's schedule might look like but I'm determined to be at the station before the start of his lunchbreak.

The police station looks nothing like the one in Guernsey. But once through the doors, all differences fade and, if it wasn't for the language, I could be forgiven in thinking that I'm walking up to the front desk of the St Peter Port station. He's in but I have to wait. He has somebody with him.

The chairs are of the hard-plastic variety, which businesses presumably choose so that their visitors don't stay past their welcome. There is nothing to do except read a copy of the local newspaper that someone has left on the bench in front of me and, as it's in Dutch that would be a no. I'm left staring at the four walls trying to translate the numerous posters dotted about. I'm still struggling with a poster on drink driving when I hear my name called.

'Ah, hello, Vanessa. I believe you know Robert Quevatre, your sister's fiancé?'

Chapter Twenty Seven

'Ex-fiancé. Inspector.'

'What was that?'

'I said he wasn't her fiancé.'

'Really? That's interesting, very interesting. When the Guernsey police put us in touch with her landlord that's what they told us and he certainly didn't deny it just now.' He throws me a swift glance before turning his attention back to Robert's inert body slumped before him. 'I was about to take him along to verify your sister's body but I think perhaps it can wait until I can verify his relationship with the deceas…your sister.'

We've managed to half drag, half carry Robert into one of the interview rooms following his collapse. I stare down at him and feel nothing. I thought I knew him; his past, his present. I wasn't interested in his future. But, after all these years, I suddenly realise I didn't really know him at all. He'd always come across as the cool, calm and collected type but, at the first sign of a crisis he'd just crumpled into a heap at my feet. If it had been me I'd have left him there to block the entrance. He means nothing to me, absolutely nothing. I stare down at his death-pale face and the way his floppy fringe, boy-like, begs for a female hand to sweep it back. There was a time I fancied him rotten. There was a time I'd have done anything for him but not now. Now I'm detached from reality. It's as if I'm in a big bubble and someone has just walked up and prodded it with a pin – bang. My world has just come tumbling down for a second time. But the repercussions of me regaining my memory will go on far beyond the expected.

Oh, yes, that elusive of all entities has decided, with the arrival of Robert, to explode on the scene and whitewash everything in a cloud of clarity that defies logic. I don't remember it all, far from it. My memory, about what actually happened when I went missing, is still a blank. I can remember everything up to my arrival in Holland but after that it starts to unravel. There are glimmers of truth but so many lies that I'll need more than the time I have now to undo the knots.

'I think that would be best,' I say, zoning back into the conversation. 'In fact, why don't we leave him to recover? It might give him the shock he deserves, waking up to find he's all alone in here.'

He laughs, his eyes twinkling. 'I take it you and him don't get on?'

'You could say that,' I grin back. 'But, anyway, it's immaterial because my memory has returned, or at least most of it has. I'd like to pay my respects to my sister one last time, if I may?'

'Of course, of course,' He throws a quick look back at Robert before shrugging his shoulders. 'I dislike liars nearly as much as I do lawyers, present company excepted. It will probably serve him a lesson, as you say. It's just a shame I can't lock him in, he'd probably sue.'

Outside the heavy steel door of the morgue he pauses, any trace of humour wiped from his face. 'Are you sure you want to? Perhaps I should get your husband to accompany you?'

'He's not my husband.'

Chapter Twenty Eight

There, I've said it out loud so it must be true. No, there's no must about it. I know it's true. Whilst my memory isn't intact, far from it, I do remember meeting him and there was nothing romantic about it. He said it was love at first sight. He said he'd fallen in love with my hands, my face and finally, with me. That may be true; I'm in no position to judge. But I certainly didn't return his feelings. That part was pure fabrication. He lied to me and I can never forgive him for that.

'Not your husband—?' his look anxious, his hands now on my arm as he holds me back from entering the room. I smile up at him but it's not a happy smile. There is sadness and tears lingering on the brink, but I won't cry, not now, not with him. I'll do this one last thing for my sister and then...there is no then. There are no more thoughts, only feelings.

I know I'll have to face him, to hold him to account, to hear his side of the story. I'm sure it will be a good one. But it's not one I'm going to believe, however good he makes it. He can't change the fact he lied and that's central to everything that followed. I squeeze my eyes tight, shutting out those other memories, the ones I thought happy. We were happy then. No, I was happy. He was being a bastard. He was only right about one thing the whole time I spent with him as his wife – that I'd end up hating him. I hate him more than anything.

'Yes, let's do this. I'm sure Nigel is driving your desk Sergeant bananas by now.'

It looks as if she's asleep. She's so peaceful and without a mark on her face. I didn't know what to expect but I certainly didn't expect this. They've even combed her hair so that it frames her face. She'd have been pleased about that. She was always going on about the importance of good grooming. There's nothing here for me now. There's nobody left now she's gone, apart from Marilyn and that's another tangle I'll have to sort out

I dig deep in my pocket before pulling out the scarf, the scarf that has never been far from my side since that day in the car. Lifting it to my nose I can still smell the gentle trace of her perfume. I wrap it round her neck and press one last kiss onto her cold forehead.

There. Done. Over. I don't know what comes next.

'Right then, young lady.' He's not so confident now. I can see it in the way he doesn't quite meet my gaze but he continues speaking all the same. 'We probably should rescue Mr Quevatre. However, before then there are some things we need to discuss.'

I shrug my shoulders before following him into the lift and up to the offices above. I knew he wasn't going to let me escape that easily.

If I'd spared a thought for what his office would be like it would have been exactly like this. There's not a free space on the desk and even the chairs are piled high with files. He apologizes profusely, shifting the folders from the chair to the floor with a wry smile. 'There's never any spare time for filing in this job,' he says, taking up his seat with a sigh.

'I like it, it's homely,' I reply, turning away from the family photos that litter his desk. Other people's happy families are the last thing I need right now.

'I have a form somewhere that you need to complete. It's pretty straightforward, just a confirmation that follows every formal identification.' He opens all the drawers on his desk before returning to the top and shuffling under a pile of red folders. 'Ah, here it is.'

The form looks simple enough, probably similar to many of the forms I've had to complete throughout my life and he's even gone to the trouble of insuring that it's in English but it's wrong all the same.

'Do you have another one, a blank one this time? I'm not sure but I think it's illegal to bury oneself or, if it's not, it should be.' And I rip the form again and again until torn paper litters my lap.

'To bury oneself? I don't understand?' He's given up any pretence of being in charge of the situation, his jaw dropping wide.

'Oh, you know. It's printed pretty clearly on the top of the form, nice handwriting by the way, that the deceased's name is a Victoria Marsh. My st…sister…I'll have to get used to calling her my sister,' I continue, conversationally. 'She's been my stepsister for so long.' I throw him a smile, one he doesn't return. 'I really don't know how the mix-up happened, Inspector. But the person you have downstairs isn't me. It's Vanessa, or Ness for short. She hated her name.'

'They told me you were dead.'

'Well, I am, as far as you're concerned.'

But he just carries on speaking. 'One minute the Inspector is asking me if I've ever seen a dead body before and the next thing I know I'm staring into the face of a corpse.' He tries to grab my arm but I twist it away just in time. 'It's too much, it really is. I think I'm going to put in a formal complaint against the Dutch police force for incompete…'

'Don't you dare!' I turn on him, forgetting that I'm standing in full sight of the desk sergeant. 'They've been exemplary through all of this fiasco, which is more than can be said about you. What parallel universe do you reside in where you're prepared to tell the authorities that we're still engaged? I know I've had a problem with my memory but I do seem to remember a fiancée. Ah, yes, Crystal, the boss's daughter. Or isn't one fiancée good enough so you have to come sniffing about after me again?'

'You were meant to be dead and, anyway,' his look glum. 'Crystal and I have broken up. She wasn't the right girl for me.'

'Girl is right. What was she, all of eighteen?'

'Nineteen, but I haven't come here to talk about her.' He takes my hand and this time I'm too wrapped up in what he's about to say to stop him. 'Can't we try again? I've even brought your ring; I thought you'd like to be buried wearing it.'

'You thought that I'd—?'

Of all the cheek. I can't believe this man. I can't believe myself. I wasted ten years, probably the best ten years of my life. Certainly, the last few weeks haven't been a barrel of laughs.

I forget he's holding my hand. I forget everything as memory after memory hover; the crappy presents and missed birthdays. The long lunches and even longer dinners where I was never invited and, on the odd occasions when I was, the frantic trips to *Le Pollet* to buy something I wouldn't normally be seen dead in.

'What's this?' and he grabs my other hand.

'What's what,' I snap back. All I want to do is pick up Nigel and leave. Okay, so I have nowhere to go except perhaps my house. I smile. It's mine, really mine and I still have the keys. He won't find me there, not if I keep the lights off and bribe Nigel with some more of those chicken dinners he's grown so fond of.

'That is my wife's ring, not that it's any concern of yours.'

Chapter Twenty Nine

Robert's hand drops to his side in an action that mirrors his jaw and, for the first time in weeks, I wish I had a pencil and paper. I could do some real damage with that look if I had the time.

If I wasn't so angry I'd laugh at the sight of all the *hurly burly* Dutch police officers converging in front of the entrance just in time for the show. Well, as they're here looking all manly and formidable, I decide not to let them down. What better way to get rid of two sleaze balls than in front of the *boys in blue*.

I stare down at his hand, Manus's hand and where he's taken the mantle of wrist holding from Robert, his fingers gripping mine. The hands that were such a comfort and joy in the depth of night when I had no one else to turn to.

A silent sigh fills my lungs, before trickling down towards my legs and my body says stay. Stay, we can sort this out. He's a good man really. With hands like that surely he has to be good and kind. But my brain tells a different story, a story it's sharing with my feet. Run; run away as fast as you can. He's dangerous, this Manus van der Hooke, more dangerous than you can ever know.

It started with a ring, his ring so that's how it will end. I lift my hand, the one I've been hiding behind my back just in case he tries to grab that one too, before slowly prizing his fingers from my wrist, my eyes never leaving his face. He opens his mouth to speak only to close it again as he watches me remove his ring and hold it out to him. There's nothing to say. There's nothing he can say. I can see by the expression on his face that he knows the game is up.

I'm fading fast but there's one thing left for me to do. After all, politeness dictates that this pair of tossers get the formal introduction they're due.

'Manus, I'd like to introduce you to Robert, my ex-fiancé. He's come squirming back into my life after dumping me like a used tea-bag. Robert, this is Doctor Manus van der Hooke who, for reasons known only to himself, has been pretending to be my husband.'

The inspector moves forward with Nigel straining on the lead and I welcome the interruption. It's been one hell of a morning with one thing and another, a morning I never want to repeat. Home calls but not his home. It will have to be our... No. My home, although I don't think that's something I'll ever be able to call it. I remember everything now and there's something about that house and cellar that scares me silly.

'*Mevrouw*, can I be of assistance? Perhaps one of my men could drive you?'

'I'll drive her,' Manus interrupts, only to pause, his eyes not quite meeting mine. 'To wherever she'd like to go.'

'No Doctor. You won't.'

'Excuse me, Inspector?' his eyebrows arch and the bland expression is back.

'Your...*Mevrouw* Marsh has made some serious allegations against you, allegations that it's my duty to investigate. If you could follow me, Doctor. The sooner we can get this little misunderstanding sorted, the better for all concerned.'

'What allegations?'

'Do you really want me to go into how your behaviour is in breach of Article Eight of the Human Rights Act? I haven't even started on any accusations she might make of sexual assault or even rape if you happened to be foolish enough to consummate the union; bearing in mind we are still standing in reception?'

'I'd like to speak to Patrick van Lees, the Chief Commissioner.'

'I'm sure you would,' his eyes bright. 'This way, Doctor, if you please.'

I'd forgotten all about Robert, standing silently while they lead Manus away for questioning.

'Well, now that he's been taken care of why don't I escort you back to your house? I know you probably don't feel like telling me anything about what's happened,' his gaze lingering on my hand and the indentation the ring has left. 'But I really think you owe me. I've come all this way only to find—'

'Only to find that I'm not dead? Is that what you were going to say?' I wrap Nigel's lead more securely round my wrist and head for the door and the police officer that's waiting to give me a lift. 'Robert, I owe you precisely what you left me with when you walked out on our relationship. If I find you've followed me I'll report you for harassment.'

'*Intimidatie, Mevrouw.*'

'Excuse me?' I say, throwing a smile at the taller than tall policeman as he escorts me to the car waiting in front of the entrance.

'In Dutch, yes?'

'Yes,' I reply firmly, all the while thinking no. I'll never learn the language now. There's no point. But this nice young man, so eager to please with his golden blond crew-cut and bright smile doesn't need to know that. He doesn't need to know that the first thing I'm going to do when I reach Manus's house is throw what few belongings I have into a bag before heading to the relative security of next door. But I won't be there long, only long enough to book a taxi to the nearest British Consulate in order to obtain a replacement passport. I still have a wad of notes left over from the pile he shoved into my bag and I intend to use them. I'll pay him back, every cent.

Is it only twelve-thirty? It seems much later but the clock tower on the *Oude Kirk* can't be wrong. I've lived a lifetime in the last couple of hours, more than one. I've had to say a final good bye to my sister in addition to ditching my husband and that's before I even get started on Robert. Poor Robert, travelling all this way and for nothing. If I was more interested I'd have asked him what happened between him and Crystal but, in truth, I couldn't give a damn. I should never have dated him for so long and as for getting engaged...our relationship fizzled out a long time ago and Crystal was a blessing. It's just a shame I didn't realise it at the time. I'd have prevented a lot of heart-wrenching in addition to saving what was, after all, a perfectly good dress shirt.

I stand on the steps of his house and survey the scene; a scene I've grown to love more than anything. There's complete stillness on the water, there's stillness everywhere as people in Delft head inside for their lunch. Apart from the perennial bicycle propped up against the bridge, indicating that someone's about, I could be forgiven for thinking that I'm the only person in this little piece of paradise. Guernsey is beautiful with its rugged cliffs and majestic castle rising up against the tides of change. It's where I was raised and it will always be a part of me. But, for me, it's tainted with the sadness of both my birth and my upbringing.

Happiness – that pure elemental feeling of joy that expands the lungs and swells the heart is something that has been denied me for most of my life. Being abandoned at birth is probably right up there with dumping puppies at the roadside or drowning kittens in a stream. Okay, so I was left somewhere relatively central but that's not the point. As a beginning it sucked and I learnt from a very young age that happiness was something only found in others. I was never happy with Robert, not really. It was only in Delft with Manus that I reached that heady status. No. I pause, my fingers on the key, my thoughts raging. I found happiness with him and that's why I have to leave. I have to leave the place I adore because of the monster in the white coat that made me lo... I squash down the words and turn the key in the lock before closing the door on Delft, on him and on any future I might have had here.

The house is silent, which is unusual. Lize, for all her quiet ways and lack of anything approaching charwoman chatter, has either gone or is still hiding in the cupboard, as humour again comes to my rescue. I can't be interested in her now. Her thoughts, feelings and attitudes are her problem. Perhaps he'll have more luck with his next wife but

I very much doubt it. Another thought crowds in, a thought that belongs in the same place as those abandoned puppies and kittens. But that doesn't prevent the image of him standing at some alter or another from claiming my attention. It hurts, it hurts so much, and it will probably continue hurting for a very long time.

Nigel settles on the rug in the lounge and I take the opportunity to head upstairs and into the bedroom. There's not much for me here, not really. I pull out drawers and survey the piles of silk and satin that he must have bought on that first day before collecting me from the hospital. This isn't me, any of it, my fingers trailing through the gossamer soft fabrics. He'd gone to a lot of trouble with his deception. But the one thing he could never know is the real me. He might have been able to make a fair guess as to my size; he is a doctor after all, but I'd never wear something as impractical as a silk shirt or indeed as expensive. If I haven't bought it in either George or Peacocks, it's not mine and there's nothing here to fit that bill. I tense at the thought and I wonder what happened to my rucksack. There wasn't much but none of it is either here or next door. Just like the painting it's disappeared.

I leave the clothes. I leave everything he's bought me. My own clothes must be somewhere but I can't be bothered to search. The only thing that's mine is my tatty washbag, which I hug tightly. If I have to turn up at the consulate in my knickers then so be it although, as he owns those too… He owns everything except me - that's one thing he'll never own.

The study is just how I remember although it feels empty somehow without him sitting behind the desk. I shouldn't be here, I know that but the drawing is the only thing I own, apart from Nigel and the washbag and that's what I'm going to leave with – that and the clothes on my back, which I'll mail back to him as soon as I'm able along with every penny he's ever spent on me.

It's there, just where I'd last seen it and I waste minutes I don't have staring down at his face, a face I know better than my own. It's his expression I don't understand even though I'm the one responsible for that look. There's anger there, lots of anger but what did he have to be angry about? I examine his features and the clear look of reproach stamped across his face. My finger traces the angle of his jaw, the curve of his cheek, the set of his lips. I can't rid myself of the feeling that there's more here, there's something that I'm not seeing under his mask of reproof. But, of course, that's something I'll never know: one of life's mysteries, another one because I'm never going to be able to ask him.

I lift my head and then I see it, the photo-frame angled away from the door, the photo I'd so wanted to see on that first day. This is what he can see when he's sitting behind his desk; the bent head, the hair partially covering her face - my face. He must have taken it that day in the café on his phone and had it professionally printed. Probably for appearances sake just in case I ever started asking awkward questions like where the hell our wedding licence was. I feel a tear weave down my cheek. I believed him, I believed every word he said and they were lies, all of them.

What else? What else is there of mine here? It's a short answer – nothing. I'll take the money from the bag he bought and stuff it into the pocket of my jeans and, apart from that…food. My thoughts travel to Nigel. I'm not hungry. I don't think I'll ever be hungry again but the cans of dog food will only go to waste. It's only then that I remember Lize.

She's in the kitchen just where I'd expected her to be all along. But instead of standing by the sink or hiding in the larder, her sightless eyes are staring up from the floor, blood seeping from the back of her head. There's nothing I can do, it's far too late for that but it doesn't stop me from trying all the same. I touch the side of her neck, my fingers repelled by the still warm skin. There's no pulse, there's no signs of life. I know I shouldn't but I shift my hand across to her eyes and gently slip her lids back in place.

I rest back on my heels, my gaze resting on her motionless body. There's no sense of urgency now. All that's gone: all thoughts of leaving have disappeared into the cacophony of confusion running inside my head. Someone's done this but I'm at a loss to understand any of it. I should move. I should shift towards the door, grabbing Nigel on the way and run as fast as I can. There's danger here, I can almost taste it as my tongue flicks out in an attempt to add moisture to suddenly dry lips. I sit there for seconds, minutes, hours. Time leaves no trace and has no meaning. I would probably still be there now if it wasn't for Nigel's growl swiftly followed by a yelp of pain. Then nothing but silence as darkness invades.

Chapter Thirty

I'm back in the dark.

One minute I'm in the kitchen, the remnants of Nigel's scream tearing my soul to shreds and the next I'm confronted with all that black again. But not only that – the drip is back. There's another difference. Now I don't want to know what's happening to me. Now my only concern is for Nigel. My heart pumps to bursting as I relive that yelp. He's my only link, the only thing I have left and there's nothing I can do to save him. I'm stuck here; helpless, while heaven only knows what's happening in the house. I squeeze my eyes tight, not that it makes any difference. The darkness remains. Tears slide down my cheeks to drip onto the floor. This place can't hurt me now. It's done its worst in taking my sister and now Nigel. Nigel is dead, I know he is. I'm probably going to die too and there's nothing I can do about it. Soon, very soon, my inner light will go out for good and, in truth, it won't be a bad thing. The tears continue to slide, for her, for him, for me.

I'm lying stretched out, manacled by my feet and hands as dream again collides with reality and reality wins. I furl my fingers up, my nails digging deep and the resulting pain is no surprise, not now, not now I know the truth. Now I know what he's capable of. Now I know that there have already been two deaths.

'Ah, good. You're awake, Chloroform isn't an exact science.'

Chloroform? How he got me here in the first place. Memory pushes back the fog and I recall that night when I'd thought I was going mad. The clocks. The reappearance of the laptop. The man stopping to help me back up the side of the canal when I'd lost my footing. I ease air into my lungs, trying to work it out but the haze of drugs, working round my system makes it an uphill struggle. He obviously still hasn't found the painting, which isn't good because it's the one thing I can't help him with. He tore Aldert's house apart and murdered two people and he's still hunting. How many more people is he going to have to kill? My thoughts turn to Manus, the man I suspected of a lot more than pretending to be my husband. I couldn't have been more wrong.

'Have a drink,' he says, and I feel the top of a bottle being pressed up against my lips. I don't want to drink but it's impossible as he prises my mouth open and forces water down my throat. It's drugged, I know it is, probably with the same concoction as before but who knows. It's hopeless, completely hopeless. I try to resist. I try to spit out the water, but he holds my head back until I finally swallow. I'm going to end up in the same place as my sister.

'Now that we've established just what I'm capable of, I'd like you to tell me where the Vermeer is and don't lie to me, please.'

'I'm not lying. I don't know where it is.'

I expected a slap, of course I did. He's slapped me before and it had hurt then. Instead all I get is a sigh, a heavy sigh.

'You don't seem to understand. I don't want to kill you. I really don't, just as I didn't want to kill Aldert.' He's moved away, his footsteps loud against the hard floor. 'Such a silly old man. He was so chuffed when he was telling me about his find, less so when I offered to buy it from him. He was a stubborn fool, wanting to leave it for his daughters, women he'd barely met. I tried to dissuade him but he was adamant. It cost him his life.'

I try to think but it's difficult with the drugs clawing up my veins. My fingers bite into my palm even harder as I struggle to gain a foothold on reality. I can't see him but there's something about the voice that I've heard before, some intonation that I recognise. He said Aldert wanted to leave it to his daughters. Does he mean Ness and me? Another thought filters through the grey murk that's clogging up all my senses. Manus. I have to keep him safe from this madness. He's killed three people now. He's going to kill me too…if I can just keep him talking long enough for Manus to find Lize.

'He died from his disease,' my tongue too thick for my mouth.

'Ha. That's what I wanted everyone to think, especially that interfering husband of yours. I nearly bumped into him on several occasions, but he never caught me. He obviously wanted the painting for himself but I soon put a stop to that. I had you chasing over here for their wedding when the truth of it was they'd never even met. You were so easy to fool.' I feel his hand trailing over my arm. 'I didn't want her to die - such a pretty woman. If de Wees had told me where he'd hidden it, there'd have been no need. Even on his last breath he refused to relent. Stubborn old man. He said I'd have to rip the house apart, brick by brick…and with that husband of yours next door, that was something I couldn't do unless I owned it.

Think. So, he doesn't know about Manus and me and he can't, not now. He'll use it against him. I must keep him talking, after all it always works in the movies.

'What about my sister, how did you—?'

'I picked her up from the airport. It was simple, really. Everyone trusts their solicitor, don't they? It's just a shame she didn't bring you with her because then I could have forced you both to tell me where the painting was.' His fingers have shifted up to my neck and to my jaw. 'I didn't want her to die, I really didn't. I had it all planned, my sweet. She was going to tell me where the painting was and then I was going to let her go. But it didn't work out like that. She couldn't breathe. I tried to save her - I didn't want her to die.' He draws even closer, his stale breath warm on my cheek. 'You're lucky, did you know that? It could so easily been you in that morgue, awaiting the worms. I got the shock of my life when I heard you'd managed to escape and married *van de Hooke*. I couldn't wait to pop round to see how you'd managed it. If you'd just accepted my original offer for the house, none of this would have happened. All I wanted was the painting, nothing more.'

His fingers have reached my cheek, tracing the curve of my face, his voice now tucked beside my ear. 'I really don't want to hurt you, Victoria, I really don't. Just tell me where it is, and there's no point in pretending it's at your husband's because I've already searched.' His hand stills, lingering against the back of my neck and I force myself not to recoil from his touch. 'I don't want to kill you, just like I didn't want to kill Lize. She had the most beautiful golden hair down to her waist. We had such fun when she was younger, before she found out about my wife.' He pauses, his fingers massaging my skin and I struggle not to scream. 'She was determined to tell Manus about me searching his house and that's something I couldn't allow. You will tell me, won't you, Victoria? I'd hate to have to end it for you,' his hand shifting to my hair, smoothing out the ends between his fingers. 'Maybe, when all this is over, I'll drop in for a coffee when your husband's left for work—'

I stare up at his face, so close that I can almost make out his silhouette in the darkness. Oh my God. He's mad, completely mad. He's just admitted to killing Lize and there's no regret, no sense of remorse. He's going to kill me before he's through or worse and I think I'd prefer death to any other plans he might have in store. Manus; that's the only thing I can think of now. I have to protect him at all costs. Bakker thinks we're married, which is good and something I have to use and soon before the drugs take a further hold.

'I don't think my husband would approve. He's quite protective.'

'Ha, really? I could tell you a thing or two about your lovely husband if I had a mind to. Love at first sight, was it or did he marry you because of the painting?'

'The painting would mean nothing to him.'

'You'll forgive me if I don't believe you. Money is everything.' There's a pause and I hold my breath for what comes next. 'All I need is for you to tell me what I want and I'll release you.'

He's lying. I know he is. He can't afford to let me live now that he's let slip who he is. I knew there was something about him when he visited the house. The only chance I have is to keep him talking. If I can stretch it out there's more chance of someone following my trail. Poor Nigel, he'd have found me. I know he would. Losing him will be my biggest regret in all of this. I shouldn't have brought him with me. I could have boarded him somewhere instead of putting his life at risk.

Another thought flickers as memories of that last day sweep in from all sides.

The scarf. How did Manus get the scarf if he'd never met my sister? And despite everything, does it mean that he's tied up in all this?

'The scarf?'

'Ah, you've discovered my little joke.' I hear him chuckle. 'There's nothing I like better than a little joke like clocks changing time and scarves appearing as if by magic. A little LSD smeared round the rim of your mug to spice things up and you had no idea what was happening.'

'How did you manage to—?'

'It was easy enough to get Lise to help me with the scarf. After all, she still had a key to de Wees's house. Poor, poor Lise,' he sighs. 'Still infatuated with me even after all these years. The rest was easy. I was tucked away in the one place you'd never dream of looking. I had such a hard time trying not to laugh at the sight of you rushing around the house like a mad woman. I was there the whole time hiding behind the door of the—'

'Cellar,' I interrupt. 'I don't understand. Why would you want to?' my voice fading as the drugs in the bottle find their target and the world slows. I'm conscious of my heart thumping in unison to the drip and my breathing, something I've managed all my life with amazing regularity, now seems laboured and forced. I have to do something before it's too late. It's now or never. I can't move. I'm tethered like a rabid dog. But I have my mouth. I have my lungs. I have my voice. I know my time is coming to an end. I know he can't let me live no matter his words. My senses dull and my hearing, fed up with being left in the lurch, starts to play tricks. I hear the sound of a muffled bark. But Nigel's dead. I heard his squeal.

Bakker's voice continues as if from a long distance. 'It doesn't really matter. Tell me where the painting is?'

It's now or never. I close my eyes to the darkness. I close my ears to his nasally voice droning on. I close my thoughts to what comes next. A slap? A punch? A blade? I open my mouth and scream.

Chapter Thirty One

The sheets alert me that something's different. I'm in the exact same position, my arms and legs outstretched. But, instead of the drip, there's the squeak of rubber soles and the continuous buzz and bleep of machinery. I'm back in hospital. Is this a memory or is this reality?

'Ah, Victoria, you're awake at last. Forgive an old man but I keep wanting to call you Ana…'

'Ana will be fine. It makes me feel special. In fact, I may even change my name. How do you think Victoriana sounds?' I reply, my voice sounding hoarse to my ears.

I recognise him, of course I do. It's that nice psychiatrist, Doctor Brouwer, come here to try and sort out my life for a second time.

'Very good. At least you haven't lost your sense of humour, something you're going to need over the coming days.'

I hear papers rustling and then silence. I have no idea what he's up to and, in truth, I don't really care. In the same way I trust the inspector, I also trust him. I've sort of managed to piece together bits and pieces and if not come up with a finished jigsaw then, at least, part of the middle is complete. I was rescued and, just like the last time, I'm back in hospital to be pumped clear of drugs before being turned loose on the world. But, unlike last time, I now have a name and a past. The one thing that's missing is a future but, as the saying goes, you can't have everything.

It's dark now. Not the blackness of before. There's still light: the glimmer of the heart monitor, the strip of yellow glinting through the bottom of the door. I'm not frightened, not like before. It only takes an indifferent shade of grey to filter through the black for my heart to surge with relief. I don't know the time and I don't care. Day or night, time is irrelevant. The nurse has just been in and I can still feel the shape of the needle she slipped under my skin. 'Just something the doctor ordered to help you sleep,' and I acquiesce – after all, I haven't the strength or inclination to do anything other than follow instructions.

I'll do as I'm told like a good girl until they let me leave and if they want to keep me longer I'll discharge myself. Because you see, even after everything that's happened, I still have to get away. I'm finished with Delft. There are far too many memories of him for me to stay. Getting that letter from *Meneer* Bakker was like dropping a penny in the ocean, the ripples spreading and growing into tidal wave proportions. Without the letter I'd still have a sister and Manus would still have Lize. Without the letter I'd be in Guernsey practicing my art in the only way I know how, my life following the expected pattern of middle-age as an aperitif to retirement and dotage. Without that letter I'd never have met him, something I can't regret, no matter how wrong our relationship was.

My thoughts, never the most reliable, are still in the hands of the drugs racing through my system. They've given me an antidote and a continual flush of fluids into my veins but things are distorted in my mind. It's like looking at my face in one of those carnival mirrors; nothing is quite what it seems. I'm alone or am I? I'm not even sure of that. I can't see enough to make out any images but there's a shadow by the window. I squint but it's useless. There's no sound except my own heartbeat thumping in my ears and the whoosh of the machine by my side. The drug she's given weighs down my eyelids and dulls my thoughts as sleep reclaims what's left of my mind. It's useless to fight it so I don't. My breathing regulates and my senses switch to the off position. In that last second before sleep I feel him near, his aftershave a dull reminder of our shared history. Is it my imagination or do I feel the gentle pressure of his lips on mine just as darkness fades to black?

'I've someone here who's desperate to see you.'

It's early. I'm becoming an expert in guessing the time without the hands of a clock as a guide. The nurse with the six o'clock meds is closely followed by my morning cuppa. Before I've even finished my drink the detective strolls in as if he doesn't have a care in the world. The nick on his chin, from where his razor slipped and the shadows bruising his skin, tell a different story.

Someone eager to see me? It can only be Manus and I can't see him, not now, not ever. But my expression must have told the Inspector of my reluctance because he's by my side in an instant, weighing down the edge of the bed with his burly frame.

'The nurses will tell you off. The one on this morning eats babies for breakfast and as for her lunch menu…' I manage a pull of my lips and he replies with a short laugh. He knows the nurse I'm speaking of, he must. She's sweet really under that bluff exterior and sergeant major frame but I still wouldn't mess with her.

'I don't think so,' he says, changing the subject. 'You led us on a wild goose chase, young lady. I must have aged a decade in the last couple of days. If it wasn't for that mutt of yours coming to the rescue I don't know where we'd be.'

'Nigel?' I whisper, all thoughts of overbearing nurses flying out the window. I'd have jumped off the bed except for the bag of fluid dripping into my arm. Instead I have to be happy with leaning forward and grabbing his hand in mine. 'Tell me, please.'

'Well, I'm not really a dog person, never enough hours in the day as it is without having to walk a dog. But I have to give it to him for his bravery. Your…er…Doctor van der Hooke found him when he returned after—' He twists in his chair, crossing his legs before continuing and I can tell he's feeling awkward. 'Enough said about that the better. Let's just say that Nigel was determined to help in the search when we realised what must have happened. He's outside, special dispensation even though dogs aren't allowed. Doctor van der Hooke's orders. He's outside too in case you'll agree to see him?'

I shake my head. I can't see him now.

He squeezes my hand gently before placing it back against the sheet and heading for the door. 'Try not to get too upset. Nigel has been injured quite badly but, with a little care and attention, they say he'll be as good as new.'

He's barely recognisable, my beloved Nigel but I'd still know him despite the bandage wrapped around his back leg and, more to the point, he knows me.

'Careful now, boy.' The inspector places him on the bed and I get licked all over by a tongue that smells decidedly of chicken before he finally settles down on my lap in the guard dog pose I'm starting to get used to.

'He's broken his back leg but luckily there's nothing internal. The doctor has been looking after him, if that's all right?' his expression cautious all of a sudden. 'As he knows him we all thought it best until you're back on your feet.'

I close my eyes briefly, a soft *okay* on my lips. If it's best for Nigel then so be it. It means I'll probably have to see him one last time, something I'll have to steel myself for. He continues speaking and I try to concentrate on his words.

'I've had a long chat with the Chief Commissioner, Victoria and he's led me to believe that I was wrong about your…the doctor. He was trying to protect you.'

I shake my head a second time. I can't listen to this now, later. Much later. Now all I want to do is get better and leave. There have been too many people injured in all of this for me to think of anything else.

'We got the toxicology reports back on your sister,' he continues after a moment. 'It was lorazepam in the end.'

'Lorazepam?'

'It's a very common sleeping tablet over here. She had an allergic reaction and would have died almost immediately.'

'Thank God!' I see his look of surprise and I don't blame him. But he doesn't have to live with the guilt that's flooding my veins. I left her. I left her for six weeks and did nothing when she went missing. I believed in the fairy tale that Bakker spouted about Vanessa finally finding her happy ever after and, for that I'll never forgive myself. It doesn't matter if the outcome couldn't be unchanged. Marilyn and then Robert certainly did a number on my self-confidence but I should have had the guts to do what was right, what was necessary and, hanging around walking Nigel wasn't it.

I glance at the drip still running into my arm. He probably used the same drug on me and I lived. If we'd just agreed to sell the house then none of this would have happened. It was his fault but it will always feel as if I'm to blame.

'What about *Meneer* Bakker? Do I have to worry about him now I'm free or—?'

'He's dead, which is probably a blessing. If he hadn't fallen and fractured his skull in the race to evade arrest he'd have ended up being locked up for life, if the drug cartel he was tied up with didn't get to him first.' He throws back his shoulders with a sigh. 'Such a waste of a life. He was into them for thousands. The one thing we can't figure out is his motive. Apart from the house, *Meneer* de Wees didn't have much worth having. But I've set my best team on it.'

I throw him a sharp glance. He doesn't know about the Vermeer and I'm not going to tell him. It makes sense now, all of it. He must have seen the painting in the attic before Aldert gave it to Manus and that's why he wanted the house. So many lives lost and all because we didn't sell.

Chapter Thirty Two

It's the daffodils' fault. Their blaze of yellow-headed glory and long necks, bent in regal acknowledgement of my return and the tears that have been hovering for days launch in a deluge. The taxi driver is beside himself and Nigel, damper by the second, just presses tighter against my lap, his nose cool against my wrist.

Why now? But I already know the answer. Everything for me has changed over the last three short weeks. But it's taken the humble daffodil to reinforce that everything will be different now. Too much has happened for me to ever reclaim the strands of my former life. I've come home to a magnificent welcome but the brilliance of yellow mocks because, of course, this is home no longer. Delft wasn't home, how could it be? But it felt like home. It felt like the only place I ever wanted to be, despite my attachment to Guernsey.

I ask the taxi to pull up along Havelet. I want to lean against the grey granite wall and reclaim my castle but even that has lost all attraction. It's not mine, not anymore. The sea air teases my nostrils but a lungful of the freshest air can't dispel the image of my canal, my bridge, my home.

The flat is cold and with that damp smell reminiscent of old raincoats and musty wellingtons. I wander from room to room and I know more than anything that I don't want to be here. After Robert moved in it felt more his than mine and, as far as I'm concerned, he can have it. He's probably in need of a place to live now she's booted him out and where better than here. I pause on the way to my studio, wondering for the first time just who did the booting? Crystal, for all her youth, exuberance and money surely would have recognised most of Robert's faults and her father, as owner of one of the island's largest law firms, would have recognised the rest.

I have a sudden yearning to start again. I don't need much, only a few clothes and my artist's materials. But first I'm in need of a cuppa. I head to the kitchen and open the fridge, forgetting for a moment that I'd stripped it of all perishables before I left. With Nigel a trip hazard, stubbornly glued to the spot where his bowl should be, I quickly realise that the first thing I need to do is make a trip down the road to catch up with Paula McDaid and her choice of doggy treats.

'Hello stranger. I thought you'd deserted us for the likes of Waitrose and the Co-op?'

'You know I'd never do that, Paula.' I laugh, grabbing a home-baked loaf and a slice of her extra-chocolaty gateau. 'I see you're still trying to ruin my waistline. So, when are you entering MasterChef?' I ask, unable to resist adding an apple turnover to my steadily increasing pile before turning my attention to the dietary staples of milk and dog food. I'm not lying in my praise of Paula's skill in the kitchen. She was born with a rolling pin instead of a silver spoon. If it wasn't for the proximity of her little store, tucked down a lane off Pedvin Street, I'd have survived off white-sliced instead of the mouth-watering selection of designer breads and artisan bakes she made in her flat above the shop. In truth, she probably knows that I'd been avoiding her in the weeks following my break-up with Robert. But kindness was the one thing I couldn't cope with. Now it's something I crave.

'Get away with you, Vee,' but I can see by the way her cheeks bloom that she's pleased. She clears her throat and her colour fades. 'I had that ex of yours in here earlier asking when you'd be back.'

'And what did you say?' My attention split between her words and the two varieties of dog food in my hands. Nigel wasn't going to be a happy boy. I sigh, placing both cans on the counter before adding a carton of eggs and some apples.

'I said I'd tell him when I saw you,' her eyes gleaming. 'It's just a shame I seem to have mislaid my glasses, luv. I never was any good at distinguishing faces without them.'

I laugh, my attention now on dog biscuits so I don't notice her pause until an awkward cough reminds me that the conversation has hit a hurdle.

'I had that other man in looking for you too.'

She has my attention, all of it. I place both boxes on the counter and root in my pockets for the bag I'd stuffed there earlier. I know who she means, of course I do. There's only one man it could be, the man I'd been avoiding despite his daily bouquets of tulips, always tulips and always cream. The doctors and nurses were beside themselves when they realised I wasn't going to allow him to visit. It was unheard of. Such a distinguished doctor and one that was obviously interested in me in *that way*. Mmm, a distinguished doctor he may be but he's still not someone I can trust despite my heart, that most unreliable of organs, doing a hop, skip and a jump at his mention.

'Really?' my attempt at nonchalance falling far short of the mark if the smile on Paula's face is anything to go by.

'Yes, really! Now, there's a man, if you don't mind me saying. I didn't half get a creak in my neck checking him out. Any taller and I'd have asked to pause the conversation while I fetched the stepladder from out back,' she chortles.

I match her laugh with a smile, choosing my words carefully. 'What did he say?'

'Only that he was a good friend of yours.' She frowns, starting to scan my items. 'Funny that he came all this way when he could have just picked up the phone?'

'I lost it.'

'That explains it. Now, let me see, I want to get this right,' her frown deepening. 'He said that he'd wait for you in the café, like before. He's here until Friday,' her gaze now searching my face. 'I liked him, I liked him a lot, Vee.'

'Yes, well. It's all a little awkward at the moment.' my eyes snagging on a bucketful of cream tulips shining out amongst the other bouquets. They really were a beautiful flower and I decide, at the last minute, to add a bunch to the lilies I'd already rested on the counter for tomorrow's duty visit to Marilyn - a visit I'm dreading.

'They're beautiful, aren't they? My favourite flower, not that anyone ever buys me any.'

'I'm not a fan of lilies myself but—'

'No, it's the tulips, I mean, and in cream too; very popular with Valentine's Day around the corner and a cheaper alternative to roses.' She throws me a sharp glance. 'Be careful who you give them to, in case they get the wrong idea.'

'Wrong idea?'

'Aye, you know...or perhaps you don't. Red roses say I love you but cream tulips say so much more.'

What a load of poppycock. But I don't say anything other than to wish her a quick goodbye before starting to lug the shopping, including two bunches of flowers and far more dog food than he'll ever eat, back to the flat. As soon as the shopping is put away I click open my laptop and there it is in black and white - or should that be cream? I scroll down page after page of the Victorian art of floriography, each one telling the same story. Give someone cream tulips and you're telling them you'll love them forever.

I'm afraid all of a sudden. He's here in Guernsey. He's followed me. A thought comes unbidden, a thought I'd forgotten. Oh, I know my memory has sort of flooded back like a tide returning to shore but it's still an imperfect record. Bits and pieces of information appear as if out of nowhere to shock and scare me like the one just now.

He knows where I live...

Chapter Thirty Three

It doesn't take long to pack up my belongings. After all, there's not much left after all those bin bags I'd thrown out before losing my sister, before my trip to Holland, before everything. Life has thrown lemons at me, the bitterest of lemons but there isn't enough sugar in the world to turn my life into lemonade. If life, as you know it, has been smashed beyond repair there's no choice but to start again. But there is no plan for a new life, no great scheme of things. He knows where I live and that's enough for now – now I'm going to escape to somewhere he doesn't know.

The flat looks empty, deserted even but I don't shed a tear as I slam the door on the remains of yesterday's life, his painting resting against my leg. There's nothing I want from here now. I'll phone a charity to pick up the rest before getting in touch with the letting agent.

Nigel is confused, and I don't blame him one little bit. I scoop him up under one arm and make my way to the car. Walking is difficult with his leg still in plaster but he manages. He's doing exactly what I'm trying to do if the likes of Manus and Robert will let me - just get on with it.

Ness's flat is just how I remember. Situated in the centre of the recently rejuvenated Glategny Esplanade and with views across to Herm, it's a far throw from my little corner of Guernsey. She bought it on a whim, after a larger than average annual bonus and the difference in our financial circumstances certainly shows. I furnished our place with an eclectic mix from the Red Cross while she shopped in those small boutiques along Mill Street. It's lovely with its feather cushions and hand-woven woollen throws in tasteful shades of sea-blue and caramel. It's lovely but it's not home. However, it will do for now.

I head to the kitchen in search of a bowl for Nigel and caffeine for me. I'm not sure I'm meant to be using the apartment, but I'll sort it out in the morning, a wave of tiredness creeping in from the edges and slamming against my skull. It's only seven p.m. Far too early to go to bed but that doesn't stop me from placing the perishables in the fridge and the flowers in water before making my way to her bedroom.

I pause on the threshold of her private domain, tastefully decorated in pale pinks and greys. But it's not the sight of her wallpaper that finally clutches at my throat and squeezes my heart. It's a memory from childhood, another one. The tatty teddy bear missing one eye that's lived on her bed for as long as I've known her. Funny how it takes such a little thing like a teddy to flood my mind with memories, all good and all of her. Yes, we'd had our differences as we'd grown older, but she'd always been there for me. It's that loss I now grieve more than anything. I forget about getting undressed or even cleaning my teeth. Instead I help Nigel onto the bed and cuddle up beside him while I wait for sleep to come.

The question of what to do about Marilyn has been trembling in the back of my mind ever since I'd regained my memory. She's now my responsibility and one I'm balking at. The truth of the matter is I'm still no better off understanding how Ness and I can be sisters. Oh, don't get me wrong. I've obviously worked out that we share the same dad but just how did it happen? How could he abandon me on those steps and where is my mother in all of this? I just don't get it and, without Marilyn to tell me, it looks as if I'll always be left in the dark.

The care home is the same. In fact, it's probably the same auxiliary that leads me to Marilyn. In a clear case of *de ja vu* she's wearing the same jumper and the same blank smile. There's no tell-tale sign of recognition and I can see by the droop of her mouth and the spittle gathering in the corner of her lips that her condition has continued to deteriorate. I sit there with a cooling mug of weak tea and let my thoughts wander. There's no point in me visiting; none at all. But still I sit, watching her rolling her hands, her nails yellowed and cracked with age - she's not yet sixty.

I promised I'd stay half an hour and the clock hanging above the door has only ticked ten minutes. It's futile sitting here for the sake of it so I get up and drift round the room, lifting up a box here and opening a drawer there. Everything is utilitarian down to the stout walking shoes and musty-smelling raincoat that she'll probably never wear again. Except for her clothes there are no personal belongings. There aren't even any photographs apart from the solitary one of Ness on her eighteenth birthday that sits beside the bed. I pick up the frame and smile as another memory hits; us sneaking away from her birthday meal early and ending up the top of Fountain Street to get our first and only tattoo each, my finger now on the V etched into my arm. They were the good times before work, men and life got in the way.

I place the frame back, tilting the angle so that she can see it if she turns her head. I won't visit again, there's no point. She's always hated me; it's just a shame I'll never know why. I'll ensure that she's able to stay here despite the top-up fees. There's nothing I can do for her except perhaps find some up-to-date photos of Ness for her room.

The drive back to town takes me past Duquemin Le Page and Associates, Ness's place of employment, and some impulse finds me making a sharp swerve at the traffic lights by *Camp du Roi* and into their carpark opposite the school. It's possible that I'll meet Robert but what the hell. I'm going to meet him again at some point so better sooner than later. He's out but Mrs Duquemin is in and I'm directed straight to her office.

'Call me Ruthie,' she says, and we shake hands. 'I was so sorry to hear about the death of your step…'

'Sister. She was my sister, not my stepsister.'

'Oh, sorry. I didn't realise,' her glance sharp behind her glasses. 'She was a huge asset to the firm.'

At the sight of her smile I let out a silent sigh of relief. I hadn't been sure how to take this smartly dressed woman when I'd met her face-to-face at Ness's apartment. It's very different chatting to someone at a work's Christmas bash to actually meeting them in person and Robert was always in awe of her success. But one glance at her desk, plastered with photos of her husband and kids and I realise that she's no different from me, except perhaps in the brains department.

'That's good to hear.' I say, trying to gather my thoughts. 'This is all new to me. I want to bring her back to bury her. She'd have wanted that and…I don't know about money or a will or anything. It's such a muddle.'

'If we can be of any help?' She pushes a box of tissues in my direction and waits for me to grab a handful before continuing. 'She did make a will. It's all part of the package as a member of the firm and I have it here if you'd like to—?'

'Only if I'm allowed?'

'I think it may come as a surprise,' and she pushes across a tightly-worded document.

I must have looked bemused because she joins me on the other side of the desk, a friendly hand on my shoulder as she points out the relevant parts with a bright red nail tip. 'It's pretty straightforward despite the jargon. In brief, she's left everything to you with the proviso that you continue paying for her mother and look after Nigel.'

'Why would she do such a thing? She didn't even know that we were sisters?' I say, my eyes filling.

'That's something I can't help you with but, if you'd like me to assist with seeking probate, in addition to sorting out her repatriation? *Pro bono*, of course,' she adds, with a smile. 'What are you thinking of doing with her apartment? The property market is about to fly again so if you'd like me to help?'

I leave her office with a huge boulder lifted off my shoulders and onto hers. Nothing had been too much trouble. All I'd had to do was sign on whichever dotted line she'd thrust at me and, in the way of all fairy godmothers, Ruthie would sort it.

Chapter Thirty Four

I've walked past the entrance of Dix Neuf or, at least, my imagination has. I've strolled up to the door and looked in through the glass, my breath steaming up the window. My gaze has wandered through the perennially-filled room, lingering on each table; hovering, searching until I've found his bent head, his hands curled round his cup while he waits.

Today, Friday, is his last day. Tomorrow he'll be gone and I'll be able to start afresh. But there's something looming and hesitant; unfinished business that I must do before he leaves. So, here I am, filling my lungs to capacity as I don't think I'll be doing much breathing over the next few minutes.

It's not as I expected or imagined. I'd thought that he'd be sitting at the same table, cradling the same cup and with the same frown settled across his features. But that's what imagination gets me. I've scanned every corner and, unless he's hiding out in the toilets, he's not here. I choose a table, any table and flop into the chair. There are things to do, lots of things but all the energy and nerve I'd built up waiting for this moment has seeped away. I couldn't take another step if my life depended on it.

My coffee arrives in a flurry of activity as the table gets wiped and a polite word is shared. But I don't want conversation with her. I've psyched myself up for this meeting, a meeting that appears to have been cancelled without warning. Now that it's been cancelled I have to sit awhile and rearrange my day, my life, my future. I still have no plans. I've been reluctant to make any apart from the day-to-day ones of whether to have tea or coffee and where to take Nigel for his walk. I'm not *au fait* with the back streets behind the Esplanade but he knows the way. He's on familiar territory and I'm soon learning his favourite haunts and lampposts, his gammy leg tucked well out of the way as I carry him from spot to spot. He's so trusting, his gaze solid and steadfast. His life, like mine, has changed beyond belief but he's doing a sterling effort in reshaping his future to include me instead of her. I struggle to sleep at night and, if it wasn't for his morning face wash, I'd find it impossible to crawl out of bed. Loneliness wraps me in a blanket of apathy, its folds inveigling through all the layers - I can't seem to lift out of its heavy veil. Without Nigel I'd be lost.

I reach out a hand to push away my coffee, the smell dragging a feeling of nausea from the depths, only to find my fingers taken and held within a silken glove. A tear escapes, just one. I manage to gulp back the rest.

'I'd given up hoping you'd be here.'

I recognise his voice; the timber, the tone, the shape of his words. But I don't recognise him. My eyes are fixed, glued to his hand, my hand – our hands and another thought breaks – a thought that has been looming on the horizon ever since I'd first met him. I squeeze it back down for later, much later. I can't think about it now, not even for one second for fear that he'll guess my secret, if indeed it is a secret. But he's not going to allow me to escape. His free hand reaches out and lifts my chin, his gaze searching mine. It's the sight of the tear that forestalls him, diverting him from the truth.

The café fades and everyone and everything in it as we share a silence. I'm not scared now. I'm not scared of him. I look into his face, his eyes. He's tired, wretched looking; the lines etched deep and his skin tinged with grey. I'm the one that's been through hell and yet he looks worse than me.

When the silence stretches to breaking he finally speaks.

'How's Nigel? I thought he'd be here.'

'He's as well as can be expected. He's been hurt enough so I decided to leave him at home. I can't stay long.'

He drops his hand. 'I won't take up any more of your time than I can help,' the bland expression back. But instead of launching into the reason for his visit he orders a coffee, his eyes never leaving my face. 'I thought I'd better explain about why I...'

'Lied about being my husband? Yes, I'd quite like to hear about that.'

'It's not what you think.'

I rest my chin in my hands, my gaze unwavering. 'You have no idea what I think.'

'No, very true. The Chief Commissioner and I—'

'Oh, very good,' I interrupt. 'So, does the whole of Holland know about this travesty of a marriage or is it just everyone in Delft?'

'Don't be like that, Victoria. I'm trying to explain.'

'Well, get on with it then,' and I lift my head to glance at the clock on the wall behind his head.

I know I'm being a bitch but I don't care, not now. Seeing him again has sparked a fuse and, if I don't douse it with cold water pretty quickly, it will fan into a flame. I should have known better than to think I could cope with sharing a *friendly* cuppa with this man. There's nothing friendly about our relationship. We've gone far beyond friendship. In fact, we've bypassed that part of our relationship altogether.

He shoots me a look but carries on all the same. 'Aldert made me promise to go to Guernsey to check you both out; sort of a deathbed promise,' his voice grim. 'He was adamant he was going to leave everything to you and Vanessa. But part of him also wanted to make sure you were both who you said you were. You have to believe that's all it was. It was pure coincidence that we happened to travel back on the same plane.' He pauses and takes a sip of his coffee. 'When you arrived in Delft, I recognised you immediately. But you worried me, holed up all alone in that house and with Vanessa missing. Something wasn't right with you. I couldn't put my finger on it but there was that problem with the cellar for one thing. I wanted to scoop you up and move you next door where I could keep an eye on you.'

I frown, trying to pull a thought out from where it's hiding. 'The keys? You gave me your set that night after my fall. And yet you opened the house when it was trashed?'

'I did, didn't I,' his lips twitching. 'I wasn't prepared to give you the only set so I had copies made. I was wondering when you'd work that out. You were so suspicious.'

'And your behaviour proves that I was wrong?'

'That's as may be,' his jaw tightening. 'When you disappeared, I was frantic. The Chief Commissioner and I had sort of guessed something sinister must have happened to Vanessa. There was no trace after she left the airport. I myself had seen her getting into a car but I was too far away to notice anything out of the ordinary.' He clatters his cup back into the saucer before continuing, his eyes now on the table. 'We don't know how you managed to escape from the church crypt or what possessed you to drift towards the canal. But, if it hadn't been for an off-duty paramedic pulling you out, the same fate could have befallen you. They said it was only the effects of the cold water on your system that saved your life after your heart stopped.'

'I know all that. You're just covering old ground, Manus. What I really want to know is what happened next. Just why did you marry me?'

'Primarily to protect you,' the corner of his mouth pulling into the semblance of a smile. 'We knew then that something was up but not what. Someone wanted something from Aldert's house and they were prepared to go to any lengths,' his gaze flicking to mine. 'They even tried to confuse matters by removing any trace that you'd ever been there apart from your washbag and scarf.'

'It wasn't my scarf.'

'Not your scarf, but——?'

'I found it hanging up in the bathroom the first night I ever stayed at your house. It was Nessie's. He said he'd forced Lize to give him your keys. He would have had access to both properties.'

His face hardens but he continues all the same. 'The stakes were high. It was only later that I realised just how high when you drew my attention to the Vermeer.'

My God, I've forgotten all about the painting. I'd searched the house and it was nowhere to be found. Just where the hell had he hidden it? I'd looked everywhere.

He throws me a brief smile and I know he's read my thoughts. 'In the attic, liefje.'

'But I looked?'

'I'm sure you did, but perhaps not in the barrel of the telescope? It's lucky that I happen to have an APO refractor, which can easily accommodate a loosely rolled-up canvas without damage to either. I'm storing it in the bank at present until you tell me what you want me to do with it.'

I continue staring at him. I just want him to finish. I want him to tell me the rest of the story and then I can leave.

He must have sensed my impatience. 'I've long believed that Aldert's death was hastened unnecessarily,' his words blunt. 'The way he wouldn't eat towards the end. He wouldn't eat or drink anything except for our nightly glass of Jenever. It made no sense to target him; an old man with nothing except the house, a house he'd willed away. But we couldn't prove a thing. I have to admit we didn't think to suspect Bakker. I knew Aldert had called him in to change his will but that was all. The Chief Commissioner agreed, albeit reluctantly, that I should pretend to be your husband, if only to confuse things. If we could get him to believe that there was no reason to target you...' He spreads his hands wide, his eyes finally meeting mine and there's something in their depths that I don't want to see, a softness that reinforces everything he's said and more. He's trying to tell me something without speaking. He's shouting out the words behind still lips, words I want to believe, but I can't. There have been too many lies, too much heartache for me to believe anything from this man. Hasn't there?

'You seem to have gone out of your way to carry out a...what was it? A deathbed promise? Surely this commissioner friend of yours could have—?'

'He's my uncle.'

I wave his words away with a flap of my hand. 'Whatever. How the hell did you think you could get away with it? We look nothing alike.'

'But you couldn't remember what you looked like. I, on the other hand had no difficulty in distinguishing between you both. Why do you think I never called you Vanessa? You were Victoria from that very first day. You'll always be Victoria.'

I squash down his words. They don't make any sense. 'You still haven't replied to my question? I've watched quite a few crappy made-for-TV movies in my time. There are other ways; witness protection, round-the-clock police surveillance. You lied – You did more than lie and I can't ever forgive you for that. Tell me why you pretended to be my husband or I'm leaving,' and I punctuate my words by gathering up my bag.

Manus's silence is all the answer I need.

'I can't.'

'Fine.'

I go to stand only to be trapped by the weight of his hand on my arm.

'Because I fell in love,' he murmurs, lifting his head, his eyes finally meeting mine. 'I fell in love with a girl sitting alone in a café, her head bent over her notebook as she puzzled over her sums. There was something endearing in the way she bit on the end of her pencil, her forehead pulled into a frown. I wanted to remove the frown and all the worries that went with it. I wanted to remove the pencil from her grasp and pull her into the tightest embrace. But I didn't. I ran away because I was afraid.' He pauses, his hand dragging through his hair. 'My life was set and I was quite happy with it, thank you very much. I had my work and as little leisure as I could cope with and then you exploded on my life to ruin everything. After the initial shock and anger had worn off, I realised that you were in danger and something drastic had to be done to save you. I know I was wrong, completely and utterly wrong. I blew it in the biggest way possible and all I can do is apologise. But there's no way back from this, is there? You're never going to be able to forgive me.'

He stands, pushing back from the table before piling far too many notes under his saucer. 'I'd just like to say how very sorry I am for everything.' He lifts a hand to my cheek, cradling it briefly before turning and making his way to the door and out of my life.

Chapter Thirty Five

I have some decisions to make, some little, some stupendous. But that doesn't make getting up from the chair any easier. I know I should move. The café is suddenly heaving with people pressing for tables and still I sit - my full cup the only excuse for staying. There are more reasons to leave than there are to stay, Nigel being the most important. But that doesn't spur me on. It would need a hurricane or, in this case, the sight of a heavily pregnant woman laden down with shopping to drag me out of my stupor. I finally stand and offer her my table.

Boots is busy, but I ignore the shoppers browsing the tightly packed aisles. I'm on a mission and reluctant to ask for help. The clue was there, as far back as that second day, but I was too dim to twig. The thing that was missing from my washbag, the thing I should have spotted. The thing that should have stopped me in my tracks.

I needn't have worried about Nigel. He's just where I'd left him, as warm as toast with the central heating on full blast. Nigel will be fine, more than fine. It's me I have to worry about now as I stare down at the little blue horizontal line looking back at me.

There's mixed emotions; surprise, horror, anxiety and finally joy. I'd be lying if I said I didn't think about him. I haven't stopped thinking about him, not really. He's filled my life to capacity and taken hold of my thoughts. He's even occupied my dreams and with the sight of that blue line he's now set to invade my future. How one man can make such a difference is beyond me, but there it is. I'm going to be a mother just like he's going to be a dad. It hadn't even crossed my mind in Holland because we were married in every sense of the word except perhaps the most important one. I should have looked for proof of our marriage; a photo, a dress, a certificate. I should have thought about birth control tablets. I should have thought of all of those things but it felt so right. It wasn't right. It was wrong. It was wrong on all the levels.

'Shove up, Nige,' and I curl beside him, his doggy warmth the only thing I need right now. No, that's a lie, another one and there have been too many lies so far. I need him more than I've ever needed anyone and I've finally driven him away. I'm going to be the one thing I'd always sworn I'd never be. I'm going to be what my stepmother made such a hash of. I'm going to be a single mother.

Sleep is meant to solve a multitude of problems but no afternoon nap, no matter how long, is going to solve my life for me. I wake refreshed but still clueless as to what comes next. There is so much to think about; home, job, childcare and I can't even decide what to have for supper. The one thing I do know is that I must eat. I grab Nigel and my bag and head out to fill the cupboards with the kind of food I should be eating and after, I'm going to search Ness's flat for a pen and paper and make a list.

The list isn't a long one in the scheme of things. The only problem is there are lots of questions jotted down and very few answers. I flick through the entries and tick off what I can. My flat in Hauteville is sorted and it only takes a quick ring to arrange to hand back the keys now that the place has been cleared. At least I won't have the stress of having to think about cobbling together the rent each month and I still have somewhere to live. But not for long. Ruthie has been in touch about Ness's apartment and she's already found a potential buyer in the lawyer that's arriving from Jersey to take her place. There'll even be money left over after the mortgage has been repaid; a nice tidy sum that will act as a buffer for when I won't be able to work.

It's the rest of the list that's full of don't knows. Where do I want to live? Do I still want to persist with my art? My gaze wanders to his painting, propped up against the mantelpiece. It's good, really good. So good I could take it along to that little gallery up Mill Street and get a valuation. But it's the one thing I can't sell, not now. There's also the issue about the house in Holland. I still need to get in touch with someone to arrange both the clearance and the sale. There's nothing salvageable and living next door to him would be the worst of ideas. And finally there's the painting, that wonderful piece of art currently lurking in some bank vault. I need to decide what to do with it. I'd like to keep it, of course I would. But that would be both impractical and cost prohibitive. The insurance would run into thousands.

I push the list away and sip on my herbal tea. I'm off coffee for some reason. The kitchen is warm and cosy with the homely smell of shepherd's pie filling the air as I continue with my promise to look after myself. But there are things I can start now while the cheddar cheese that I've grated on top continues its glorious transition from gloopy to crispy golden crust.

The apartment is open plan and minimalist to the extreme. Ness wasn't a hoarder and, as she used to say every time she deigned to visit, if things weren't either functional or beautiful, they were toast. The black bin-sacks are where I'd expected them to be, hidden under the sink and I start in the lounge. There are no knickknacks and few books but what there are get placed in the bag closely followed by her collection of DVD's and paintings.

I leave the bathroom, after all, no one is going to want half-used soaps and shower gels. The guest bedroom is simply that; empty, functional, drab. I strip the bed linen and set the washing machine on before heading into the main bedroom and where Nigel has stretched out across the centre of the bed.

'You're the laziest thing,' but all I get for my trouble is a brief wag of his tail before sleep reclaims him.

The built-in wardrobes line one wall and I know that it's in this part of the room that I'll have my work cut out. This is where she'd stored all of her documents relating to work and every other part of her life. I ignore the left-hand side and start on her personal belongings; racks and racks of designer suits, silk shirts, boots and shoes that all have to be examined and sorted before being placed into the relevant bag.

I tackle the kitchen next and soon it's empty apart from one glass, one plate, one bowl and one mug – I don't intend to have any visitors up for coffee. All that's left are fifteen bin bags cluttering the entrance hall and the left hand side of the wardrobe. I'm tempted to ask Ruthie to come over but that would be the cowardly way out.

It's mostly work related and therefore easy to sort. The pile for Ruthie grows as I separate old school books and notes about client cases and invoices. There are old birthday cards that I keep to one side and a shoe box full of old photos but the big reveal that I've been dreading isn't here. There's nothing from my mother. No old letters revealing a last-minute truth about my father. No letters *only to be opened after my death*. There's nothing to help me find out just why he left us the house. I add her birth certificate on top of the box of photos and head into the lounge.

The lounge has been stripped bare apart from the furniture and Nigel, who's now asleep in the middle of the sofa. I race through the cards but there are no surprises. Nothing but old birthday messages from an assortment of names I don't recognise and they all get relegated for recycling.

I'm more hopeful that I'll find something amongst the photos. Ness was a great one for holidays; Tenerife, Greece, Ibiza and there are plenty of images to trawl through. I start three new piles; photos to discard, photos for Marilyn and photos to keep. The discard pile grows as I cherry pick the best for Marilyn. The pile for me is very small, almost non-existent; her first day at school, one from her eighteenth and finally one of us together as toothy six-year-olds before life intervened to smash our baby teeth along with our hopes for the future. Towards the bottom of the shoebox the photos change as do the people. These aren't Ness's. These are Marilyn's – the only thing of hers from her flat clearance that hasn't been chucked.

I'm eager now, my breath caught in my throat as I scan through grainy images of her with her parents; dim distant figures I can barely remember. She was pretty in her youth with the same glossy sheen of hair and dark eyes that were Ness's trademark and I can see that she would have never lacked for male partners. The box is empty and the table littered with images. But there's only one that interests me; a photo of her standing with her back against a wall, a fag in her hand as she laughs at what's being said to her. In itself it's similar to the ten or so other images in the pile except for the fact that this one has been folded over, the plastic coating coming adrift where the crease has done its worst. I smooth it out and now she's standing beside a man, a man I recognise from the images I'd found in his study. Aldert. I flip it over and there's writing, writing so faint I can barely make out the words.

Cheating bastard.

And with those words a memory from months before.

You're just like her...that tart of a mother of yours.

Chapter Thirty Six

The Dutch house looks the same; comforting, familiar, homely. I would say welcoming but after so many weeks I have no thoughts on that front. Too much has happened for me to be certain of my welcome, my hand hovering across my stomach and the soft swell concealed by the drape of my jacket.

I've lost a sister but reclaimed a past, a past that's given me a father even though I'll never get to meet him. Yes. I've finally come to accept that Aldert was my father, mine and Nessie's. With the discovery it now makes complete sense that he'd leave us the house. There are things I'll never know; things that, with Marilyn's decent into the grips of dementia, I won't be able to ask. I remember Manus telling me about Aldert being a likeable rogue with women falling for his blue-eyed charms. I suspect that he probably had a string of women on the go and my guess is he found out he was going to be a dad twice over. With abortion not available in Guernsey at the time he'd ended up with two babies and an increasingly jealous, untrusting and unfaithful partner. He went back to Holland, leaving me with a woman who had every reason to hate me.

I try not to think about my mother; the woman who must have abandoned me on that doorstep.

I'll never know for sure what happened. But now that I'm single and pregnant I don't have the heart to think badly of her. She could so easily have travelled to the UK to end her pregnancy. For that I'm thankful.

There's nothing left for me now in Guernsey. Ness's apartment has been sold and my flat re-let. All I have is a couple of suitcases and a painting, which I shift from one arm to the other. Oh, and Nigel. How could I ever forget my faithful friend who is now back to normal following the removal of his plaster cast. So, I've come back to Holland to reclaim what's mine. My house.

I'd like to say that I've also come back to reclaim Manus but he was never mine in the first place, not really. I've spent the last few weeks reliving every look and word between us and the reality is I don't know what to think. I know what I feel but that's different. My feelings don't come into it. The truth of the matter is I let him walk away in Guernsey, something he'll probably never forgive me for. But here I am anyway, not on my doorstep but his, my hand again flitting to my stomach before reaching for the door knocker.

There have been too many secrets over this business for me not to have learnt from their example. Secrets and lies hurt and there will be none of that between us. I'll say what I have to and take it from there.

My heart shifts at the sight of Manus, standing in his shirtsleeves, his tie draped around his neck. But it's not his clothes I'm drawn to. It's his expression. Did he ever stare at me with that bland look stamped across his features? It's not there now. Nigel barks but I don't hear. I hear nothing except the sound of my heart drumming in my ears. I feel nothing except the pressure of his arms as he wraps them round me in the tightest of hugs, his lips finding mine.

We break apart. Of course we do. We have to speak. We have to sort out the mess I've made of things when all I want is for him to pull me back within the protective wall of his arms. I want to close the distance but I don't. I stand in the doorway and wait.

'You're back,' he says, his hand raking through his hair.

'I'm back,' I repeat. I reach out, my fingers lingering against the smooth skin of his cheek, my gaze never leaving his.

'You said you could never forgive me?'

'I said a lot of things,' my hand curving around his neck but still I keep a distance between us. 'There are also things I never said. Things I regret.'

'What things?' his back stiffening under my touch.

'Things like *thank you*. Without your interference Nigel and I probably wouldn't be here.'

'There's no need to—'

But I stall him with a shake of my head. 'I've also never said I love you, Manus. I love you with all my heart.'

I step back to evade his seeking arms. I have to continue. I have to be completely honest with him even if it means the end - the end of us.

He's confused and I don't blame him. I'd be confused in his position.

'I love you but I come with baggage.'

'You know I love Nigel, don't I boy?' and he's crouching down, trying to control his grin as he's attacked by a relentless tongue.

I watch as man and dog become reacquainted and the flicker inside bursts into a roaring flame, a flame I fail to dampen despite the direction of my thoughts. Will he feel the same way about the news I'm about to impart. Having a dog is one thing but a child? Surely if he'd wanted children he'd have had them by now, my gaze shifting to the top of his head and the faint smattering of grey.

He tilts his head, his eyes seeking mine as he sits Nigel on his bent knee. I heave a sigh, patting Nigel briefly before stooping down and lacing Manus's fingers through mine.

'I know you do, my darling. But Nigel isn't the baggage I'm talking about,' and I place his hand flat over my stomach.

One minute my heart is splintering into a thousand shards as fear takes a grip and the next I'm swept off my feet and cradled to his chest. Our tears mingle. Our thoughts converge as the invisible thread that binds pulls and twists into an unbreakable bond.

Manus backs through the door, kicking it behind him, Nigel yapping at his ankles.

We've come home.

Epilogue

De Telegraaf
Vanessa to stay in Holland

The *Rejksmuseum* are delighted to announce the acquisition of a previously unknown painting by Johannes Vermeer. *Vanessa* is a particularly fine example of the artist's skill in depicting light and shade and with a palette limited to only four colours, including his trademark use of lapis lazuli. The painting is thought to have been executed around 1664 between *A Lady Writing a Letter* and the *Girl with a Pearl Earring*.

The museum is indebted to the estate of Aldert de Wees for their most generous gift.

Marriage announcements
The marriage took place on Saturday, April 7, 2018, at the Nieuwe Kerk, Delft, between Dr Manus van der Hooke and Victoria Marsh, eldest daughter of the late Aldert de Wees.

Birth announcements
Van der Hooke
On 29th October, 2018, to Victoria, *née* Marsh, and Manus, a son, Aldert Manus.

About this book
Tying up the loose ends.

I first saw Johannes Vermeer's painting, *Girl with a Pearl Earring,* as a sixteen-year old and the idea for the book has been bubbling under ever since. Vermeer produced less than fifty paintings, of which thirty-four have survived - sadly none of which are my *Girl in a Blue Dress.* He was born and lived in Delft.

Signature: Vermeer mainly avoided the usual bottom right-hand corner to sign his paintings. In addition, the letter V is often indistinguishable in favour of the letter M because, of course, the letter M contains a hidden letter V within its arms. In *Girl with a Pearl Earring* he signed the painting in the upper left-hand corner with Meer, the letter I standing on top of the M to represent his first name, Johannes.

Guernsey has long been a magnet for artists of all mediums. Victor Hugo, writer of Les Misérables, lived here in exile from 1855 to 1870. His residence, Hauteville House, is a well-known local residence and hence the ideal spot in which to find Victoria.

Pierre-Auguste Renoir, the French Impressionist, spent a month here in 1883 and produced fifteen paintings of the island. In 1988 an exhibition entitled *Renoir in Guernsey*, was held locally and attracted international interest from the artist community. The Victoria Marsh in this book would have been born the following year.

In 1996 Guernsey was the last of the British Isles to legalise abortion.

Finally, daffodils, one of my favourite flowers, always flower early in Guernsey, oftentimes I can spot an ambitious bloom just after Christmas.

If you'd like to know more about Guernsey, and Victor Hugo in particular, talented writer, Anne Allen's latest book 'The inheritance' will be coming out in early 2019 on this particular subject.

To keep up to date with my scribbles you can find me on Twitter (scribblerjb) or my Facebook page (Jenny O'Brien, Guernsey Writer).

ABOUT JENNY O'BRIEN

Jenny O'Brien was born in Ireland and, after a brief sojourn in Wales, now resides in Guernsey.

She's an avid reader and book reviewer for NetGalley in addition to being a RoNA judge.
She writes for both children and adults with a new book coming out every six months or so. She's also an avid collector of cats, broken laptops, dust and happy endings - two of which you'll always find in her books.

Printed in Great Britain
by Amazon